SUMMERVILLE

H.L. SUDLER

AN ARCHER PUBLISHING BOOK
WASHINGTON, D.C.

SUMMERVILLE

Published by Archer Publishing
P.O. Box 21843, Washington, DC 20009

This is a work of fiction. Names, characters, places, and incidents either are the product of the author's imagination or are used fictitiously, and any resemblance to actual persons, living or dead, business establishments, events, or locales is entirely coincidental.

ARCHER PUBLISHING is a registered trademark of Archer Media Networks LLC. The ARCHER PUBLISHING logo is a registered trademark of Archer Media Networks LLC.

Library of Congress Control Number
2013914556

Archer Publishing ISBN
978-09848460-92

PRINTED IN THE UNITED STATES OF AMERICA
10 9 8 7 6 5 4 3 2 1

Follow the author on Twitter @HLSudler
Like ARCHER PUBLISHING on Facebook

For Lee Walker, Carol Fezuk, and Frank Reynolds. None of this would have been possible if not for you and the lovely people of Rehoboth Beach, Delaware. Forgive me in advance for any and all liberties that you know I am apt to take.

Before the autumn of our years, there exists a time when we struggle to reconcile what we are with what we wish to be. This time can be known as summer. After spring gives us life, before winter takes it away.

———————————————————

SUMMERVILLE

BOOKS BY H.L. SUDLER

PATRIARCH: MY EXTRAORDINARY JOURNEY FROM MAN TO GENTLEMAN
SUMMERVILLE

Contents

<u>PROLOGUE</u>
fireworks

Every saint has a past, and every sinner has a future.

Oscar Wilde

I.

He beat her badly.

There was no one present to hear her screams.   No divine intervention to save her.   Nearly everyone in her neighborhood was gathered at the beach, captivated by magical, multi-colored fireworks sailing across a vast, black Miami sky.   She was inside the tiny two-story house in which she'd grown up.   He had crashed through her front door, the chain lock snapping under his weight like a frozen twig.   Just minutes before there had come a knock soft and inviting, unexpected and unassuming.

"Who is it?" she answered skeptically.   She had eased to the door in her bedclothes, slipping from the floor above.   She was a beautiful woman: young, her hair dark and long, her body petite.

There was no response, as if the person who came calling decided it was too late for a visit and had gone away.   She peered out of the living room window but saw no one.   She walked to the kitchen and turned on a small television sitting on the counter.   The knocking came again, sharper this time. Are you up? Was I mistaken? I hear the television. May I visit? *She jumped, startled.*

"Who is it?" she repeated. She opened the front door, but left on the chain.

A man seized her by the throat from the darkness, digging his nails in hard. "Open this door, you fucking BITCH!" he demanded. "Open this fucking door NOW!"

The chain was cast angrily to its limits as she shrieked loudly. "Get out of here! Go away!" The door closed fully then. He had pulled it closed, only to burst through powerfully, the chain lock snapping. He stood in the doorway like an angel of death, panting, seething, enraged. Rushing at her, he flung her to the floor then kicked her as hard as he could. She wailed in pain as he slammed and locked the door.

His shadow covered her like a dark cloud, and she heard a worried voice and the padding of little feet above her. Her heart sank to the pit of her stomach as she looked up to the top of the stairs. Her attacker heard it too, for he stalled above her. He leaped over her and climbed the stairs two at a time.

"NO...!" she screamed, and was on her feet, ignoring her pain, running after him, reaching for his pant leg, his belt, his arm, his shoulder. Just as he reached the boy, just as he shackled his hand around the child's wrist, she landed on his back and dug her nails

into his face. Her weight pulled him backward as she slashed at his eyes. He lost his footing and all three fell: first he, with she and the boy landing on top of him at the bottom of the stairs. Her bones ached as she sat up to see if the boy was okay. Her angel of death resurrected behind her, blood trickling from his forehead, his eyes filled with rage. She shoved the boy toward the pantry and he hid himself far from the door. Her attacker caught her by the arm and viciously flung her into the kitchen, her small body slamming into the wooden table. Her head hit the floor with a thud.

"How you like that, BITCH? How do you like that?" he taunted her.

He headed for the pantry but she rose up, protesting with what little strength she had. Enraged by her persistence, he flung aside the kitchen table and looked down at her. She was exactly as he wished, begging and groveling. He turned her over on her back and ripped open her pajama top, sending buttons flying across the room and exposing her breasts. With the last of her fading strength she fought, but he wrapped his hands around her neck and hammered her head against the floor until all her energy was sapped, until her eyes glazed over and her body fell nearly limp.

His tongue then painted and flicked at her breasts; his rough hands tore at her panties. She had no strength as he climbed on top of her. No way to defend herself, to prevent her son from hearing *her as she was raped and subsequently murdered. There was no one else present to hear her screams. No divine intervention to save her. Nearly everyone in her neighborhood was gathered at the beach, captivated by magical, multi-colored fireworks sailing across a vast, black Miami sky. Her world, which had recently become colorful again after a long and difficult period, began to drain, returning to its awful black and white state.*

After awhile, her world simply faded to black altogether.

<u>BOOK ONE</u>
building a mystery

Alone. Yes, that's the key word, the most awful word in the English tongue. Murder doesn't hold a candle to it and hell is only a poor synonym.

Stephen King

COMING HOME

I love you, Dad.

That was what Jarrett wanted to say to his father before they ended their conversation on the phone an hour ago. The words died on his lips and had been choked down and carted off to that great heap of things he always meant to say to his father. It had not been all one-sided; his father, too, seemed to want to say something more; a thought that had been carted off to his own great heap of things unspoken. This was the way Dallas and Jarrett, father and son, had come to communicate in recent years. Theirs was a relationship filled with unsaid words and unexpressed emotion.

Jarrett Olsen Hemingway was en route from Miami Beach to Rehoboth Beach, from Cedar Manor in Florida to Cedar House in Delaware, two of the four Cedar guest resorts his father owned along the east coast. Jarrett managed the two establishments, enabling him to live in warm weather nearly year round. From October to May he lived in Miami, and from May to September in Rehoboth. The 31 year-old now cruised up I-95 North, many miles away from Rehoboth Beach, less than forty miles outside of a town called Summerville in South Carolina. He had already sent his father off to bed on this clear spring evening and soon Jarrett would grab a quick bite at a nearby diner and check into a motel for the night.

For Jarrett, going home was never without complication. His mind was on his father and their relationship, on how they communicated, on whether he could talk to his father about *anything*. There was a disconnect between he and Dallas, one that had grown over the years to frustrate the younger Hemingway, because he knew there was a reason and yet he failed to see that reason. Was it *she*, then, who was between them, he wondered? Was it his mother who halted them from communicating the way they should? Or was this just the way they were destined to be for the rest of their lives?

Answers to these questions eluded Jarrett as he later lay down onto cool white sheets in the darkness of his motel room and his body succumbed to his fatigue, as his eyes closed against this issue with Dallas. He had no way of knowing that ahead lay a summer unlike any other in his life, one full of tests, revelation and devastation. And he would later wonder, a different man than he was today, how he had managed to survive the ride, or even hold on and bear it at all.

THE FIRST OF MANY SECRETS

Why was there always a pall cast over his son's homecoming? And why did Jarrett's arrival home always seem like an interruption? Was it *she* who held them together, who kept them communicating to some extent? Was it his dead wife, Jarrett's mother, Laura?

Dallas Hemingway had hung up from his son some time ago and had stepped from the warm comfort of his bed's blankets. In the illuminating glow of cascading moonlight, Dallas slipped a robe over his nakedness and eased his way over to the nearest window, his thoughts on his son. The room was dark and quiet, the moon outside full and alone, without stars, standing simple and remote against a black screen of sky. The 51 year-old patriarch, handsome with his salt and pepper hair and neatly trimmed beard and goatee, seemed to scrutinize the night, but was instead studying the ebb and flow of his own emotions, his feelings regarding his son's arrival and how it affected him. He considered the arrangements he would have to make and how long he would have to hold his breath until Jarrett was gone again.

"Was that your son?" his lover asked; he was swaddled in blankets and sheets on the bed.

"Yes," Dallas answered after a long pause. He could not bear to face his lover, to say the words he had to say.

"Is he on his way home?"

"Yes."

The heavy sigh from his lover gave permission to Dallas's inevitable plea. "You know this has to a stop for now."

A long silence passed between them and Dallas prayed there would be no tears or angry words, although he could feel in the atmosphere their predictable precipitation, their volcanic threat.

"Come to bed. Make love to me again," his lover said. Dallas felt a tidal wave of resentment toward his son's impending arrival as he sighed and returned to bed, undoing his robe and letting it slide off of him like a snake's skin. He then stepped out of the moon's light and into the shadows. Dallas, a man who looked ten years younger than his actual age, stood before his lover, feeling appreciated and loved, feeling whole again. He smiled then and eased into the bed next to his lover's warm body, their silhouettes becoming one. And like his son, he too would allow the problems that plagued him to ease away and out of his mind, to be saved for another day. A day that would mark the unleashing of all hell, a turning point for the two appointed for the not-so-distant future.

HOW WE CAME TO BE

It was Olsen Hemingway who set everything into motion by bringing the family name *Hemingway* to Rehoboth Beach, Delaware. The year was 1910 and he was 25 years old. He had traveled mostly by foot or on the back of a horse-drawn carriage from the faraway city of Madison, South Dakota. This was long after the 1872 founding of Rehoboth by the Reverend Robert W. Todd, who initially envisioned this seaside community as a religious retreat for his Methodist Episcopal church. Back then the town was called Cape Henlopen.

In Madison, Olsen's father had been running a destructive course, descending often into a drunken and crazed madness. Olsen's mother had died from prolonged complications of multiple childbirths and her passing had left her husband broken and angry. Two of the older children had mustered enough courage to leave home, setting out for land-of-dreams California, and as if unable to escape an unavoidable bad ending to an already tragic story, both died in a fire following the 1906 Earthquake that leveled the city of San Francisco. Olsen headed east, eventually arriving in Rehoboth Beach. He found work at The Henlopen Hotel as a groundskeeper, and struck up the fancy of a slightly older schoolmarm named Charlotte Tolliver from the neighboring town, Lewes. The two married and later conceived a son named Fredrik.

After the Second World War, at the age of 32, Rehoboth welcomed home a decorated and battle-weary Lt. Fredrik Olsen Hemingway, who eventually took over his father's established fishing business. A year later he married the beautiful schoolmistress Nancy Louise Mayberry, and a year-and-a-half before Fredrik's father Olsen Hemingway would put a gun to his head and pull the trigger, Dallas Hemingway was born.

At the age of 18, Dallas left Rehoboth Beach for college in Philadelphia, where he met and married Laura Lafferty. A year later, she gave birth to a handsome baby boy they named Jarrett Olsen Hemingway. For a time life was easy, but the tranquility the Hemingways had known, the easy existence that was their lives, came to an abrupt end when Jarrett Hemingway left for college. The twenty-year marriage between his parents had arrived at a standstill, and it was at this time, with Jarrett away, that Dallas confessed to his wife that he was gay. Something over which he agonized for months before telling her, something he knew before marrying her.

It was odd how Laura maintained her composure, her dignity, how she seemed to not be surprised by the news. Her only concern was for their son, his reputation, and his reaction to this admission.

Following long, difficult conversations, Dallas and Laura decided not to divorce but only to separate. It was also concluded that Dallas would remain at their home in the Henlopen Acres section of the city, while Laura moved into the family business, the bed and breakfast they called Cedar House, a place she viewed as a fresh start for herself, something she could consider her own domain.

However, it was not long after that a second admission sidelined the family's stability. Jarrett arrived home during summer break defiantly announcing his own homosexuality, a confession that secretly vexed his father. *She can't win, can she?* Dallas imagined the gossips around town lamenting over Laura's plight when the news became known. *A gay husband* and *a gay son*? *She did something heinous in a past life, I'm certain of it. To have so much bad luck, imagine!*

This second revelation took a back seat to a third that came a few years later: breast cancer for Laura, an illness that tragically snowballed into lymphoma. Twice she beat it. The third time she did not. There was not a dry eye in Rehoboth Beach when she died. Who could forget how lively she was, and beautiful? Who could name any other person who was more giving, more generous and polite? Her wide smile, her blonde hair, her beauty queen wave from the garden as you passed? Who could forget Laura? No one. Not as long as Cedar House stood.

WELCOME TO CEDAR HOUSE

The ghost of Laura Hemingway was everywhere at Cedar House. And it was the daunting task of opening the business, of entering it, cleaning it, airing it out and walking it through, that Dallas Hemingway secretly dreaded. It was midday, less than a week before Memorial Day weekend, and Rehoboth Beach began to unfold beneath the magnanimous umbrella of a vivid blue sky. Despite its arresting small town beauty—the fluttering of butterflies, the budding of daisies and geraniums and tulips, the swirl of leaves tickled by a giddy spring wind, the presence of an imperial sun that hung over the massive Atlantic Ocean—it still remained terribly cool. In contrast to inland cities, the arrival of the last weeks in May guaranteed very little warmth here, as if winter's greedy, clutching claws refused to let go.

Dallas was banging out a tune on his steering wheel when he came upon Cedar House, standing tall and knowing like a governess. He sat at the corner of First and Maryland, a block from the boardwalk and the beach, and gazed at Cedar House, initially in rebellion, eventually in fear. This house that was once his wife's home after they'd separated. This house that had in each room a marking of hers: a pen touched, a bed slept in, a photo of her, a beloved plant, a special gift from a guest, even the paint, even the carpeting, even the front lawn's flowerbed. It was her, her, her— smeared on every wall, over every square inch, like Manderley. And now in death she *was* the house, every part of it. It seemed as if Cedar House was built specifically to contain all the mysteries that would soon inhabit its halls in just a matter of days.

*****

Cedar House held down its share of Maryland Avenue, and like many other streets in Rehoboth, with huge houses and equally huge trees standing guard beside them, the street was both quiet and picturesque. Three stories tall, Cedar House was painted butter yellow, except for the trim, the shutters and the doors, which were all in white. The grass outside was a luxuriant green, fenced in by white wooden pickets. A gravel driveway ran along the right side of the house to the back. In the rear was a large lawn, shaded over by the limbs and leaves of two 100 year-old oak trees.

Dallas turned into the driveway and sat in silence a moment, not courageous enough to look up at the house. When he did, the building seemed to tower over him; it seemed larger, darker than it actually was. Intimidating. Cedar House stared back, in the sun genial and warm, but back here, up close, unlit, the property was dark and stoic. Getting out of the car, he unlocked the back door, feeling completely guilty entering her house. Guilty for not being able to give Laura all she deserved as her husband, as a man. Still and quiet, Cedar House unnerved Dallas. The shutters were all closed, cloaking the house in darkness and shadows. The air was still and stifling. Any noise from the other side of these walls was muted, creating strangely both a womb and a tomb.

Dallas slowly made his way through the house. He felt Laura's presence as thick as humidity. Even the furniture covered with white sheets arrested him, provoking the feeling he would hear her voice suddenly or see her pale apparition staring at him from a corner. Dallas quickly drew back the curtains, opened the shutters and windows, and then the front door. He breathed easier with the rays of sunlight and the fresh air moving through the house. He put on music, changed his clothes, started uncovering the furniture. As he progressed, the beauty of Cedar House came to life once again.

*****

Cedar House was a deceptively large property. From the street it seemed as quaint as a doll's house, but inside there were nine bedrooms divided among the second and third floors, each with its own bath. The first floor contained a spacious living room, a cozy library with a fireplace, a dining room, and a kitchen. In the basement was a laundry room and pantry, and in front of the house sat a garden filled with a profusion of Laura's beloved peach, cream, and orange roses. By the time guests arrived, there would be colorful hanging plants on the front and back porches, and wooden summer furniture for lazy afternoon reclining on the rear lawn.

Dallas made his way from one room to another, passing the hours sweeping, mopping, dusting, laying out fresh linens, filling up candy dishes, composing a grocery list, cleaning the vases for fresh cut flowers, removing the dishes and silverware from storage, checking the fire alarms, inspecting the fireplace, laying out towels and wash cloths, polishing the furniture, cleaning the mirrors, washing the curtains and windows, vacuuming the carpets, mowing the lawn. He worked *hard*, conscious of Laura's eyes upon him. When he finally stopped, he was exhausted, both he and the sun ready to quit for the day. Before he left, Dallas gave the house a final once-over. The well-ordered rooms, the cleaned and polished oak floors, and how the hazy sunlight played off of them, gave Dallas a false sense of security. This thing with his son would work itself out. This summer would go smoothly and without complication.

Dallas did not bother to look back at Cedar House as he drove away. His dead wife had already been too much with him today. Besides, he was eager to be with his lover, to see him, hold him, and make love to him. Before his son arrived home and the war between them began.

REHOBOTH BEACH: OPEN FOR BUSINESS

Jarrett arrived in Rehoboth at noon the following day, speeding through a row of familiar signs that gave direction to the Lewes-Cape May ferry, to shore points Slaughter Beach, Bethany Beach, and Dewey Beach. When Jarrett spotted the billboard reading "WELCOME TO REHOBOTH, THE NATION'S SUMMER CAPITAL", Route 1A had converted itself into the slimmer Rehoboth Avenue. There were car dealerships on either side, a bank, a pharmacy, mini-marts, a bookstore, a library, a firehouse—establishments that acted as punctuation for the shops separating them, and which Jarrett knew stayed crowded during the summer season. Businesses offering men's and women's clothing, with t-shirts and jewelry and postcards and beach towels and beach balls. Stores that sold ice cream, pizza, french fries with vinegar, chicken, cotton candy and fudge, that played loud music to attract youth, and sat next to bars and taverns.

Jarrett drove through town before arriving at Cedar House, up Rehoboth Avenue. He took a right onto King Charles Avenue and drove several blocks through a quiet neighborhood filled with large homes surrounded by rose bushes, and huge elm and oak trees. Making a left onto Prospect Street, he headed a block toward the beach. There, he stepped out of his car and walked to the edge of the sand. This was the end of the boardwalk; the section nicknamed Poodle Beach for the hordes of gay men who sunbathed here together during the summer. Jarrett gazed over the ocean as it attacked the beach. It was vast and blue, sparkling and magnificent, with large vessels perched distantly on its horizon. Jarrett smiled, removing his sunglasses and shading his eyes. He looked from the ocean to the beach, and tried to see all the way to the other end of the boardwalk as he used to when his mother brought him here as a boy. Overhead, gulls swooped and circled and dived, and puffy white clouds accented the vivid blue sky. Soon this sand, these waters, would be thick with bodies, and Rehoboth Beach would begin to resemble the most active of beehives.

*****

Jarrett reached Cedar House by one o'clock, plagued by uncertainty. Would he be able to work here again, seeing his mother's face in photographs, recalling her in memories, knowing she would never come back to him? Dallas watched his son from the living room window, and although he had dreaded his arrival and the interruption it would cause to his life, he was happy to see him, the only family he now had left.

"Jarrett Olsen Hemingway," Dallas called stepping out onto the porch.

Jarrett looked up from the trunk of his car where he was pulling out his luggage. The smile on his father's face melted away any reservations he had about returning to Cedar House.

"Hey, Dad!" Jarrett said, walking up to the porch and embracing his father.

"You look well, son."

Jarrett smiled. "You don't look too bad yourself, tough guy. Still hitting the gym, I see."

"How was your trip?" Dallas asked, as the two headed into the house. With each step, Dallas felt the life he had when Jarrett was not here being closed in a box and stored away. He was a father now, not a lover. These two worlds should not ever meet.

"Traffic was actually great this time around," Jarrett answered, but as they stepped inside, he frowned. "Dad, you didn't open the house yourself did you?"

Dallas looked to Jarrett, then down. "Yes."

"Why?" Jarrett asked, but Dallas avoided his son's eyes. In a flash, Dallas thought of his lover, their bodies in his bed, and them fucking hard and exhaustively. He walked away, and Jarrett watched his father head almost remorsefully down the hall.

"Dad, what's the matter?" Jarrett asked.

Dallas did not respond, and all the joy Jarrett felt in this moment at being home with his father drained out of him. All at once he was brought back to a horrid time, to the days just after his mother's death, when it seemed he had lost both parents. His father shut him out and went deep inside himself, when Jarrett needed him most. Watching him now, he could see it was happening all over again. He was barred. No longer a son, but an intruder.

Dallas left Jarrett standing alone, his anger flamed by an unanswerable question: *Why are we always like this?* His father's aloofness bit into Jarrett with the sharpest of teeth, and he closed his eyes to help swallow down his pain. After a while, he followed his father deeper into his beloved mother's house.

It was like walking through all four chambers of her heart.

THINK OF LAURA

The tour of Cedar House went more smoothly than either Jarrett or Dallas expected. Dallas led his son carefully through each room, and when Jarrett lagged behind to gaze at a picture of his mother, to sit in her favorite room, or just to stare at the sunrays beaming through the kitchen window, a scene beautiful and serene, Dallas allowed Jarrett his time, would sit in another room patiently until Jarrett was ready to continue.

The photographs, the rooms, even the smell of the house, brought Jarrett right back to his mother's final days. A parade of people had come through to see her ghostly figure, her translucent skin, the pain engraved in her eyes. They were mesmerized by her unwillingness to go on, yet her refusal to die. Each step had delivered a new image from his memory, as if to say: *Do you remember this? This is where you stood and watched your father's best friend Bradley Thomas cry over your mother's deathbed as if she was his own wife. And this picture here? The one you clutched to your chest on the day she died, the one of her in the garden with her hat and gloves on. Do you remember? You wished for this specific picture to be displayed at her memorial service.* Jarrett did remember.

"The place looks great, Dad," Jarrett muttered. The two stood in the library, the afternoon sun surging and waning throughout the room with the passing of clouds. The house was very still. Dallas did not reply, his gaze was fixed on a row of photographs that sat on the mantle above the fireplace. His eyes were weary and empty.

"Dad?" Jarrett called, starting over to his father.

Dallas asked abruptly, "Will you be staying here at Cedar House for the summer?"

Jarrett halted in his tracks. "Yes."

"Good," Dallas replied, that single word that seemed to say: *Excellent! Let's keep our distance. Let's not get too close.* Without looking at his son, Dallas said, "Why don't you unpack and get some rest. I'm going home to pay bills. I may be back sometime later tonight." Then he left.

Jarrett stood dumbfounded, the slamming door, the ensuing silence, saying something much, much more than words. Like an omen. Like fate.

FATHERS AND SONS, FRIENDS AND LOVERS

"Ladies and Gentlemen, the man of the hour who's late by an hour!" Bradley Thomas cried out as Dallas walked in. The crowd around him erupted into a deafening roar of drunken laughter.

It was cocktail hour at Dorian's, a cozy and dimly lit watering hole on Rehoboth Avenue that was a playground for mature partygoers. The space was filled with conversation and packed tightly with people. There was a thick layer of sexual tension spread over the room, fueled by alcohol, evident in over-friendly hands.

"Oh, shut up, you Keystone Cop!" Dallas yelled back, battling the familiar crowd to get through to his friend. "You're just mad that a fag beat you out of two hundred bucks over the Super Bowl!"

The tavern was once again overcome with laughter.

"You're gonna be late to your own goddamned funeral, you know that right?" Bradley said, standing up from his barstool. He offered his hand out to Dallas. His face was already glowing and his eyes twinkling from an apparent buzz.

"Sorry I'm late," Dallas apologized, taking Bradley's hand and giving him a hug and a kiss on his cheek. With the show over, the crowd returned to their own animated conversations.

"Don't worry about it. Sit, sit..."

Bradley Thomas was the police chief of Rehoboth Beach. He was also Dallas Hemingway's best and oldest friend. Two years Hemingway's senior, with his own dose of salt-and-pepper hair, Bradley stood slightly taller and straighter than Dallas, somehow managing to be respectable and intimidating simultaneously. His face was round, amiable, and far less chiseled than his friend's, although it could be said just as full of deeply rooted sadness. He was less fit than Dallas, and being a wide man, more beefy than muscular. These two had known each other since childhood and had grown up together. Their fathers had been fishing buddies, their mothers bridge partners, and their sons were best friends. And while Bradley Thomas was not gay, he did not give up on his longtime friendship with Dallas when Hemingway's homosexuality became public.

Dallas took a stool next to Bradley as Chip, Dorian's longtime bartender, came over for his order. "What can I do you for, H.? Regular?"

Dallas shook his head. "Too hard, too early. Let me have a black and tan, and another round for Brad, whatever he's having."

Bradley smiled at Chip, who nodded and then was off. The police chief spun on his stool, letting his gaze rest on the crowd. "I'll catch you next go round."

"No worry," Dallas said, before sinking in his stool. He suddenly realized that his spirits grew sour now that he was in Bradley's presence. It came as a surprise, like a small voice in harsh winds carried through the distance to his ears.

"Tired?" Bradley asked.

Dallas chuckled mirthlessly as he rubbed his temples. "Like a whore on Sunday morning. Cedar House will be the death of me yet."

Bradley was silent as he drank in Dallas's comment, feeling his own mood suddenly darken. Within him was borne a sudden, steely contempt, the result of Dallas's use of the words *whore* and *Cedar House*.

"Where's your boy?" Bradley managed after a beat. Inside of him thrashed a storm, between the summer of yesterday and the winter in which he now lived. He breathed in deeply and made a concerted effort to close Pandora's Box.

"At Cedar House," Dallas responded. He spun around on his stool to face the crowd and smiled weakly at the fun being had. In the center of the floor was a little dancing, silly and drunken. The women were wild and uninhibited. The men flirted shamelessly. "He got here just this afternoon."

Dallas and Bradley then turned to face each other, and each saw in the other's eyes their own melancholy. Chip came to the rescue, bearing drinks. "Black and tan, and a lager..."

Dallas threw out a ten. Bradley threw out some tip money.

"So, Dallas, is it true? You're opening up Cedar House?" Chip asked.

Dallas and Bradley traded glances. News got around quickly in Rehoboth.

"Friday'll be our first day."

"Good." Chip nodded. "Just wanted to know where to send people when they pass through."

Dallas raised his beer. "I'll be sure to send them to the best damned bartender in Rehoboth!"

Chip smiled and winked. "That's what I like to hear."

There was a long silence after Chip's departure. Dallas sipped his black and tan and Bradley nursed his lager. The noise and laughter swirled around them. Bradley brought up his son.

"Drescher's been asking after Jarrett. He missed Drescher's show in New York."

"I'll be sure to tell him," Dallas said distantly. He took another sip of his beer, and then gulped down the rest in a blatant move to end this conversation.

Bradley blurted out, "Was it hard for you to open Cedar House?"

Dallas blushed as if struck, his heart pounding against his chest. It was all too much for him today. Jarrett. Laura. Bradley. Even the crowd in this room was getting on his nerves; too loud, too close, too much. It hadn't been like this last night, in bed with his lover. "No," he said. Then: "Yes. This will be the first time Cedar House will open without Laura."

"Let's pray for lots of blue skies," Bradley said, and when Dallas abruptly stood up, he asked, "You're not leaving, are you?"

"I'm dog tired," Dallas groaned. "I'll catch up with you later."

Bradley did not stand, but stuck out his hand as he had done earlier; Dallas squeezed it tight. He looked deeply into his friend's eyes and leaned in close to him, so that they were face to face. For a moment, Dallas remembered a time when all he fantasized about was kissing Bradley. Two teenaged boys, making out in the woods, skinny-dipping in the late night ocean. He had masturbated constantly to that fantasy.

"I did love her," Dallas said. His voice was low and hoarse, meant not to reach Bradley's ears, but his heart. "I do love her—"

"Laura," Bradley said quickly, jealously. Alcohol colored his answer.

"Laura," Dallas repeated lightly, knowingly. There was a ghost of a smile on Dallas's lips, brief sunlight on his face as his and Bradley's eyes committed strange intercourse. Dallas was grateful for the slight buzz from the beer he'd guzzled so quickly. It would give him courage. "I wish she had married *you*. You were so much better for her than me. Handsome. Strong. Dedicated. Becky left you all those years ago, and I never needed a wife to begin with."

"What are you saying?" Bradley whispered, mystified.

"You really loved her, didn't you? I can see it in your eyes."

Bradley sighed. "Don't..."

"I've always known it. Why didn't you make a play for her?"

"Don't!" Bradley warned him.

Dallas retreated but not immediately, as if he should understand something more than he did. Reluctantly, he let the mystery go.

"Take care," Dallas said.

"I'll walk you out," Bradley said. He slapped the bar so Chip would see they were going; they waved goodnight. Outside, evening had come, the air more brisk, an invitation to set a fire at home, to watch the flames dance, to mull over a strange day. Bradley hugged Dallas tightly, then whispered, "I love you."

Dallas rested in his friend's arms, his hand at the back of Bradley's head, buried in his hair as they stood cheek to cheek. The heat from Bradley's body was comforting and erotic. "I love you, too."

Bradley said before walking away, "I know."

Dallas watched Bradley walk down the street to his car, observing the loneliness in his friend's gait, the defeat. Oddly, it mimicked his own.

HAPPY GOLDEN DAYS OF YORE

Bradley Thomas lived on a tiny street in Rehoboth called Munson. His was an attractive yet quaint home, with its basement converted into a photo laboratory for his son Drescher, a professional freelance photographer for newspapers and magazines worldwide, and who, at 33, was handsome, muscular, and as good natured and light-hearted as his father. They were each other's No. 1 priority, and while Drescher could have lived in any city he wished, he preferred to be with his father in Rehoboth.

"Stop hiding and come down the stairs, old man," Drescher called out. He had been working in his laboratory cleaning lenses. "Stop spying and make yourself useful."

"How did you know I was there?" Bradley asked when he reached the bottom. "And did you just call me an 'old man'?"

It was the day after Dallas and Bradley's strange conversation at Dorian's. "That's what you are, aren't you? Besides, I'd be deaf not to hear you come barreling into the house."

Bradley huffed. "Well, I guess I can't argue with that, now can I...smartass?"

A sly grin spread across Drescher's face and Bradley duplicated the smile, then he gave his son a hug.

"Hey, Pop."

"Hey, son. When did you get back?"

Drescher stepped away from Bradley, as if his father would intuit something through their proximity. His hair was blonde, cut short into a crew cut. His eyes were a deep blue. His five-o'clock shadow surrounded two full and pouty lips. When he smiled, as he did often, he revealed straight white teeth. He resumed the cleaning of his lenses. "About an hour ago."

Bradley followed his son around the lab. "So how was Washington?"

"D.C. was good, hard, but good. I think they're going to pick up my 9/11 retrospective."

"That's great, son!" Bradley said enthusiastically.

"I'd like to think so," Drescher returned, beaming proudly.

"Dallas and I met up for drinks last night, and he mentioned Jarrett got in from Miami just yesterday. Now, I know you're sore with him for missing your show in New York, but Jarrett is your best friend. This is that boy's first time at his mother's house since her death. It's going to be hard for him. He'll need you."

Drescher stopped cleaning his lenses and muttered, "I'll go see him."

"Good," Bradley said, slapping his son on the back.

And so it begins, was all Drescher could think.

*****

"So I heard you got back yesterday."

"In the afternoon. You?"

"Today."

Jarrett and Drescher sat in the silence of Cedar House's kitchen, eating Peach Melba pie. It was an annual ritual for them; every spring when Jarrett returned they sat and caught up over heated pie. Twilight was upon them, both figuratively and literally, the two would never be the same again after this summer. And some hint of that was in the air, like the passing scent of roses.

"Been a long time," Jarrett said, pouring them both glasses of water. "I'm really sorry I didn't make it to your show in New York. I heard it was great."

Drescher picked over his pie, not basking in the spirit of this event. "Don't sweat it."

"No, really, I'm sorry. I couldn't get away from Miami–"

"Jarrett, it's cool," Drescher interrupted him.

"My father said he was there."

"Yeah."

"And your dad was there."

"Yeah," he repeated. Then he asked, "How was your trip back?"

"Good," Jarrett answered, shooting a curious look. "What about you? Any love in your life?"

Drescher put down his fork, and then wiped his mouth. "You know me, boys everywhere."

The two were silent for a moment.

"So how does it feel to be back?" Drescher ventured.

Jarrett shrugged. "Some days you're the pigeon. Some days you're the statue."

"Still trying to figure it all out?"

"I miss her, I know that," Jarrett said. "In fact, just before you got here I was about to go up into the attic to look over some of her things."

"You want me to come up with you?"

Jarrett smiled gratefully. "Would you mind?"

Drescher said sullenly, "That's what friends are for."

*****

The attic in Cedar House was cramped, musty, and packed with more items than any one person could go through in a single day. Breezing through boxes and trunks, Jarrett appeared to be looking for one item in particular. All of a sudden he said, "Remember this?" He was holding a Rosemary Clooney album that Laura would play over and over again during the holidays?"

Drescher smiled. "Yeah, I remember that. You should put it on."

Laura's favorite song was Clooney's rendition of "Have Yourself a Merry Little Christmas." Jarrett found what looked like an old orange box with a black handle. As Drescher dusted off the album, Jarrett plugged in the record player. The familiar orchestration filled the room and then Clooney's silky voice. The two sat on the floor next to the player, remembering huge decorated trees with icicles and colored glass balls, holiday parties, lit fireplaces, the Carpenters and Nat "King" Cole, snowstorms in time for Christmas Eve, cookies and ribbon candy and mixed nuts and eggnog, ham *and* turkey, new bikes, and a metal train set Jarrett and Drescher played with for *months*.

"Remember when you and your dad used to come over on Christmas Eve?"

"Yeah," Drescher nodded. "We'd come over, and you and I would play and eat until we passed out. I don't know why we went home, because we'd wind up back at your place as soon as I'd finished opening my presents."

They laughed, but Drescher added somberly, "You know, I miss your mom. I miss everything she ever did for me. Treating me like I was her own son. Including me and my dad in your family's celebrations."

"She always liked you and your dad," Jarrett said. "She felt bad your mother wasn't there for you. I miss her, too."

"I know you do."

"She died two years ago," Jarrett said. "It seems like yesterday but it feels like forever. I think about her all the time." Clooney had stopped singing and the room fell silent. "I miss her. I really, really do," Jarrett whispered, his voice cracking. "And truth be told, I just wanted to sit up here with you and say that. I know you knew what a special woman she was."

Jarrett raised his eyes to Drescher, tears sliding down his face. Drescher held him in the dying sunlight. "She was a good woman."

"Yes, she was," Drescher agreed. "She was a very good woman."

Jarrett cried for a long time while Drescher held him, saying nothing, just rocking him back and forth. These two would never be this close ever again.

GUESS WHO'S COMING TO DINNER?

The eve of Memorial Day weekend pounced on Rehoboth Beach like a hurricane and the entire town excitedly geared up for the start of another season. The merchants all hoping that this year's financial take would outdo the year before. Reservations had already been booked for the coming months with many hotels, motels, inns, and B&Bs showing an encouraging promise of a profitable summer. Cedar House stood just as ready as any other accommodation to receive guests. Jarrett had hung potted plants in the morning, put out some lawn furniture by noon, and made sure to check every room for last minute touch-ups by two o'clock. He was well aware that Cedar House, which had been closed for over a year, needed to look its very best in order to attract future reservations and walk-ins, re-establishing its position within the community.

Jarrett hadn't seen much of his father since his arrival, leaving him with the distinct impression that Dallas was avoiding him. Had he done something wrong? Did he remind his father of something painful? He felt like he was interrupting his father's life simply by being home.

"Where have you been?" Jarrett asked Dallas when he finally showed up at Cedar House.

Dallas had entered carefree, and he was dressed handsomely in black. He pasted a broad, false smile on his face, which irked Jarrett. "Excuse me?" Dallas said.

"It's just that I've been here three days and I don't think I've seen you that number of times since I've gotten back."

A cloud passed over Dallas's face, making it darker, edgier in a flicker of a moment. "I've been busy. And not that I need to explain myself, but I do have other things to do besides Cedar House. Was there an emergency?"

"No."

"Well, given that this is your first time back since your mother's death, I thought you might want to spend some time alone here."

"Yes, but I want to spend time with you, too."

"I can't tonight. Peter Rabin is having a cocktail party at his home and I promised him I'd be there."

Jarrett stood still, choking back words.

"There is something I wish to discuss with *you*, however. You called from Miami to say there would be friends of yours staying here this summer. Who are they?"

Jarrett turned away from his father. There was a window over the kitchen sink, one that looked out into the yard. The sun shone on the luster of the green grass where he used to play as a boy, and in that instant Jarrett could not comprehend the very thin line between happiness and unhappiness. "I thought you had someplace to be."

"A direct answer would be helpful."

Jarrett faced Dallas and instantly saw in his father's eyes that he was deliberately holding him at arm's length. His resentment grew. He said, "Stephanie Newcomer will be staying with us this summer."

"Who is she?"

"She's from New York, socialite's daughter, rich, very pretty, young. She stayed with us down at Cedar Manor in Miami this past winter and I talked her into staying with us here this summer."

Dallas nodded. "That's a start."

"The other will be Ethan Safra. He's a young doctor from a suburb outside of Philadelphia. He's 28, 29."

"How old is the girl?"

"About the same age."

Dallas looked at his watch. "Anyone else?"

Jarrett looked away from his father's eyes before answering. "Jarvis Watson."

"Who is he?" Dallas asked, sensing something.

"Jarvis is a friend of Ethan's. They both come from the same town. He's black, a law student, smart, on the quiet side, a little shy."

"But...?"

"He can't afford us. He comes from an impoverished background."

Dallas was silent a moment. "You want to give him a room for the summer?"

"He's the type of person mom would have welcomed with open arms," Jarrett answered. "She was that type of woman."

Dallas fixed his gaze on his son, and then allowed it to fall. The comment stung.

"Not to worry, I'm not giving away the store," Jarrett said looking back out of the window. "He'll pay what he can and I'll pay the rest. He'll be *my* guest."

"How often will they be here?"

"Stephanie will be here the whole summer. Ethan and Jarvis mostly on weekends."

"And this Ethan, can he pay?"

"Yes."

"What about this girl?"

"Dad, Stephanie could buy Cedar House three times over on a bad day."

A terrible silence followed with Dallas as still as marble. Suddenly, he rapped the countertop with his knuckles and was out the door. "I'll catch you sometime tomorrow." Before Jarrett knew it, Dallas was outside in his car and screeching away, leaving him overcome by a well of pain into which he could not help but to slip and fall.

*****

Dallas was on autopilot as he smiled and shook hands and ate and drank at Peter Rabin's party. There were plenty of others at the gathering, many young faces, many new faces, already claiming Rehoboth as their home for the summer, and yet Dallas contained his conversation mainly to the older crowd, the crowd he knew and with whom he was most comfortable. Much of their talk was limited to their businesses, what they expected out of the season, and horror stories from past years. When polite conversation dwindled he turned to survey the room and saw a group of gay men talking, faces jabbering at faces, mouths moving ferociously, laughs incredibly loud. There were others present, older gays like him, their faces subdued, defeated, as if they suffered from neglect and were eager for companionship.

Dallas thought that it was hell to be this age and gay. That it seemed after 50 or 60, you become invisible in this community. Who wanted to be middle-aged and alone when the advanced years of one's life were already like a punishment? He considered the friends that died one by one, the daily complaint of the body, the ruminating over past regrets. It was then that Dallas thought of his secret love. Because of his son's presence, Dallas was separated from his lover and it was torture. What he wouldn't have done to have his lover here with him now, squeezing every bit of happiness out of this day. But their love had to remain a secret, for the summer at least. In this town, for certain. If one person found out—the way gossip spread around Rehoboth—there would be nothing but hurt and pain. They would not be able to continue on. Not if Jarrett found out; and especially not Bradley.

THE SECRET STORM

The Velvet Lounge was very popular among its mostly gay clientele. Its music was loud, and its main attractions were impressive front and back decks, a massive sunroof, a pool table, a DJ, and the stiffest drinks in town. A small passageway connected it to its sister restaurant, the Lounge Café. Drescher arrived at The Velvet Lounge during happy hour, and once inside he waved to people he knew, friends from Philadelphia and New York, New Jersey, Maryland, Virginia and Washington, D.C. He hit the bar to order a beer and once there, someone sidled up close to him.

"Hey…"

Drescher turned and beside him was a tall, thick, broad-shouldered guy about his age. His hair was short, buzzed, brown, and his eyes were intense and dark as pools of oil. To Drescher, he oddly appeared both handsome and dangerous. "Hey, there," Drescher answered cordially, and was instantly ensnared by his eyes.

"Busy night, my God!"

"I know," Drescher said, taking a swig of his beer. "It's usually not like this until *after* Memorial Day weekend."

Suddenly, as if he had forgotten he said, "My name is David

Youngblood."

"Drescher Thomas."

The two shook hands.

"What do you do?" David asked.

"Photographer," Drescher answered. "And you?"

David waved his hand. "Eyeglasses."

"An optometrist?"

"No, my dad's an optometrist. I sell the eyewear to my dad's customers. My mom manages the store."

"Where?"

"D.C. Why, you need some glasses?"

"No, no. I thought I detected an accent."

David smiled brightly. "South Carolina. We come from a little town there called Summerville. Where you from?"

"Rehoboth born and raised." Drescher drank to that.

A silence hung between them, as they turned their attention to the crowd. David nodded toward someone across the room. "Looks like you got yourself an admirer, boy."

Drescher looked where David was indicating and saw someone staring at him. He was an extremely attractive man who looked out of place in a bar like this, let alone a town like Rehoboth. He was a tall African American, and his eyes were penetrating. There was something in his broad, muscular body, an undeniable sex appeal connected to his masculinity. His eyes were glued to Drescher.

"You know him?" David asked.

Drescher shook his head. He was pretty sure he'd remember someone like him.

"Good looking guy," Youngblood said. "Wouldn't mind my ass getting tapped by that."

Drescher turned to David. "You should go for it."

David shrugged. "I don't know. Maybe we should go over and talk to him together. We could be one fucking hot threesome."

Drescher laughed. "Not my speed, but thanks for thinking of me." Drescher waved to the bartender, and then turned to Youngblood. "David, it was a pleasure meeting you. I'm sure you'll have all the fun you can find in Rehoboth...without me."

David's face reddened, taking Drescher's comment as dismissive and condescending. He reached out and grasped Drescher's arm, jerking him back. "Where ya going, boy? To see *him*?"

Drescher was stunned. "What are you talking about?"

Youngblood took a step closer to Drescher and glanced over his shoulder. "Is that your brutha on the down low? Your nigga on the side?"

Drescher's jaw fell open. "Take your fucking hand off of me right now."

David's glare was defiant, but there was something else in his eyes. Genuine hurt. Jealousy. He released Drescher. "My bad, bro."

Drescher did not move. He was tense, unaware that people around them were now staring. After a moment he backed up and walked away. David almost yelled after him, "Yeah, that's right! Go chase after your big black dick!" Instead, he turned his back on him and took another swig of his now warm beer. He slammed the bottle on the counter and demanded another. After a few minutes, he peered over his shoulder to see Drescher and the handsome African American already talking. His emotions raged like a stormy ocean slamming against black rocks. In his eyes were salty tears, but in his heart bloomed a calculating evil.

*****

"Hi, my name is Drescher Thomas. Do we know each other?"

"You don't remember? My name is Griffin Walsh. We've met before."

Griffin Walsh was even more striking up close, clean cut and with an air of sophistication.

"You had a show in New York. A 9/11 retrospective I thought was magnificent–"

"My God, yes!" Drescher exclaimed. They shook hands. "You were at the reception! You came by to speak to me."

"Plenty of people came by to speak to you. The show was wonderful."

"Thank you. What brings you to Rehoboth? Are you passing through?"

"Not really," Griffin said. When he smiled, his eyes sparkled. "A friend of mine owns a place down here. He's in Brazil for the summer and offered me his place to stay. Considering he'd been telling me about this little town called Rehoboth for years, I decided to take him up on his offer and skip Provincetown this year."

"You should've stuck with Massachusetts," Drescher joked.

"Rehoboth seems pleasant enough."

Drescher's shrugged. "Rehoboth is what Rehoboth is."

"And what is Rehoboth?" Griffin asked.

Drescher paused, and then said with a smile, "My home."

"Well then if it's good enough for you, it's good enough for me."

"That's good to hear. Your friend, does he live here?"

"No. He lives just outside of Philadelphia but has a vacation home here. I live in New York."

"What do you do for a living?"

"Family business. Walsh Publishing."

Drescher paused. "You one of *those* Walshes?"

Griffin shrugged boyishly.

"Well, Griffin Walsh, as a citizen of this proud city, we certainly welcome you to Rehoboth Beach. I hope you have an unforgettable time here."

Across the room David Youngblood watched with interest. Outwardly he seemed calm, but inside he was seething.

THE MYSTERY MAN

Jarrett decided to call it a day. The twilight sky, a purple painted masterpiece, darkened the landscape of Rehoboth Beach, chilling the salted air, calling all out to dinner and nightlife. Hemingway had promised to meet with Drescher at The Velvet Lounge for a drink. Something quick and then he had to be off. With the official start of the season beginning the very next morning, he'd need to get a good night's sleep for what would assuredly be a long day ahead. When he arrived, he was stunned. It seemed as if everyone in town had decided to crowd every square inch of the place. The lights were already dimmed, the music loud, the voices even louder. Jarrett saluted Simon Tu, who worked the door of the club. They swapped hugs and kisses, played catch-up, inevitably joking about the coming of tourists, the necessary evil that kept this community alive.

The Virginia, Maryland, and Washington, D.C. men among the crowd looked wealthy and educated. Most were dressed casually in collared shirts and slacks or khakis. The New Yorkers were comprised of muscle boys in form-fitting shirts, designer jewelry, and crotch hugging pants. The Philadelphia, New Jersey and Delaware men wore sweaters or sweat shirts with jeans and sneakers. Hemingway squeezed his way through the crowd and spotted Drescher talking to someone just out of view. He was smiling wide, and Jarrett could tell that Drescher was attracted to him.

In all the years Jarrett had known him, Drescher seemed able to get any guy he wanted. Drescher's blonde hair and cherry lips, his blue eyes and broad smile and ripped body all made him a catch. He had been Jarrett's first and Jarrett had been his, during their college years. Something neither of their fathers knew. The fact that Drescher was desired by almost everyone who met him destroyed any chance of a relationship the two might have had. Drescher spotted him and waved.

"Hey, there!"

"Hey."

"How long have you been here?"

"Not long. I saw you were talking and I just went ahead and ordered a drink."

"Did you send invitations to all these people?" Drescher joked.

Jarrett cracked a smile. "Since when do we get all these tourists in town the day *before* everyone is supposed to show up? You'd think The Lounge was giving away something for free."

The music changed, increased in bass and volume.

"Who were you talking to over there?" Jarrett yelled over the pumping bass.

"Someone I know from New York who came to the show,"

Drescher said pointing to where he'd been standing. "His name is Griffin Walsh."

A path cleared then and Jarrett saw a man so striking and handsome he could not help but stare. The man looked at him and nodded. Jarrett returned the nod, the sudden attraction between them undeniable. The space was closed again, filled with bodies and faces. Jarrett would later recall this as the exact moment he fell in love with Griffin Walsh.

Nearby, David Youngblood clocked Jarrett's every move.

FIRST ARRIVALS

Stephanie and Warren arrived in Rehoboth Beach the following afternoon. It was mostly Stephanie who had driven from Virginia through Washington, D.C. and Maryland, up I-95 North and into Delaware. Her good-looking boyfriend Warren Cassie had wanted the top to Stephanie's BMW convertible up because of the sun, but she wanted to drive with the top down, and so they did. The whole way he sat mostly in silence, discreetly checking the rearview mirrors as they sped down the expressway toward a fate neither of them could have ever predicted. The two had started their journey in Miami; he with a large black duffel bag and she with several suitcases. They entered Rehoboth through Route 1A and had traveled down Rehoboth Avenue toward the enormous sky and magnificent Atlantic Ocean, which sat just beyond the boardwalk.

"Wow," Stephanie said, impressed by the view. She was a redhead, beautiful and svelte, her smile wide and bright like the sun. Her face was full of wonder, like a child's. "Look at this beautiful little town."

It is, Warren thought. They sat at the light at 2nd Street, the city around them like a movie set, and they were like characters whose arrival was shrouded in mystery. Warren knew, as he knew all things, he *felt*, this place would be critical to his destiny. There would be life-altering events and decisions to be made here, and this town would change their lives forever.

They continued on to Cedar House, passing trees and cars and businesses. Already impressed by Rehoboth's beauty, Warren was struck by the grandeur of Cedar House. It was like something from a postcard. The vivid hanging plants on the porch, the fragrant rose garden in front, its white picket fence and the lush green grass, the sunlight shimmering on the windows were all so arresting. There was a feeling and an aura surrounding the property that gave an almost human presence to the house. Here, too, he intuited his destiny would be played out, that he'd never be the same once he passed through its doors.

When she pulled into the driveway, Stephanie turned off the ignition and they sat in silence: Stephanie looking at Warren and Warren, his eyes hidden behind sunglasses, looking at the house. She sighed. "What's wrong? You've been quiet the last two hours."

Warren shook his head.

"Please don't embarrass me," Stephanie begged.

He turned to her. "The guy who owns this place is gay, his father's gay, and most of the people staying here are gay, and you talk about *me* embarrassing *you*–"

"If you have a problem with this–"

"I don't have a problem with this," Warren said, cutting her off. "There are faggots everywhere in Miami. Trust me, I don't have a problem with this."

Stephanie jammed the keys back into the ignition. "That's it, we're out of here! You will *not* embarrass me!"

"Calm down!" Warren snapped, snatching the keys away from her. Stephanie threw him a scathing look. "It doesn't matter to me what they are."

"Well, it matters to me. Jarrett's my friend. In fact, you can just go. I'm staying."

"I'm not going anywhere."

Stephanie huffed. "Why did you even agree to come here with me?"

When Warren leaned in close to her, Stephanie pulled back. Warren whispered in her ear, *"Porque yo te quiero. La verdad es tu estas muy bonita y quiero hacer el amor contigo todo el dia y la noche."*

He could feel her resolve give way, as it always did when he spoke to her like this. She asked him, "What are you saying?"

He lied. "I said I'm sorry and I want to make you happy."

She placed the palm of her hand softly against his chest. "Please don't be mean to them."

"I won't," Warren whispered against her lips. He kissed her lightly on her cheek, allowing his body heat, his proximity, to arouse her. Two of his fingers caressed her nipple and when he squeezed it, she gasped. *"Estas mojada?"* he asked.

Stephanie looked into his eyes and whispered, "Let's go inside."

The murderer kissed her again, and smiled.

BOOKED UNDER SUSPICION

Before Stephanie and Warren's arrival, Jarrett had risen to a glorious morning, the fog lifting as he stepped onto the porch with his coffee. During the night, he dreamed of Griffin Walsh and had started the day with him on his mind. Jarrett had tried not to seem too interested in Griffin, lest Drescher claim *he* was interested in him or had slept with him back in New York. Regardless, Griffin Walsh was like a knight to Jarrett, he was that handsome and had made that much of an impression on Hemingway.

Had he never had a black lover? Had he never slept with a black man? If he did hook up with Griffin, he knew some of his friends would question him. They would classify his attraction as nothing more than a walk on the wild side, a curiosity satisfied. Jarrett didn't care. There was something about Griffin, his poise, posture, and aura of strength that was unlike any other man he'd ever been attracted to.

"Hey there!" Dallas called out to Jarrett from the front gate.

Seeing his father after their tense interaction the day before caused in Jarrett a giant shift in emotions. His mood plummeted, not knowing what type of disposition his father would be in. Without answering, Jarrett stood up to go inside and shower.

"Hold on there," Dallas yelled, walking up the lane.

Jarrett turned, his father in front of him now. Dallas handed him a simple white bag, rolled closed at the top. "Bakers PLUS," he said.

"You didn't." A small gleam danced through Jarrett's eyes.

"I did."

Inside were piping hot bagels. "Bless your heart," Jarrett said, and they both laughed.

"Jarrett Hemingway's kryptonite," Dallas said as they both sat down on the porch steps.

When they were close like this, like family, it was easy to forgive his father anything. With Dallas laughing, mussing his hair, splitting bagels with him, he felt loved and protected, that he had not lost both parents with the passing of his mother. Jarrett thought that perhaps he had been insensitive, had not taken into consideration that his father may have been hurting over his mother's death and distanced himself from Jarrett because of it. Perhaps if they didn't discuss her death or even talk about her for a while, and just got back into the rhythm of things, it would be easier for him to handle.

"I was thinking we should give a dinner party for the guests tonight," Dallas said. "Something small to celebrate Cedar House re-opening."

"You sure you're up for that?"

"I'm up for it if you are," Dallas said. He looked at Jarrett. "Let's start the summer off right."

Jarrett smiled and said, "I know you're doing this for me. Thank you." He nudged his father with his shoulder.

Dallas ran his hands through Jarrett's thick, dark hair and kissed his son on top of his head. They sat in silence awhile, enjoying the morning, apologies accepted all around.

*****

Jarrett sensed something wrong the minute Stephanie and Warren arrived. Stephanie was as beautiful as he remembered, with her incredible red hair and delicate features, her petite frame, her big trademark smile and radiant personality.

"Give a girl a hug!" she said, her arms opened wide for Jarrett. All three stood on the porch of Cedar House, amid the chirping of birds and sunlight.

"Well, hello there yourself," Jarrett said smiling brightly. As they embraced, his eyes found Warren and stayed on him. He was standing a little off, stoic, his eyes shielded behind sunglasses. "How was the drive from Miami?"

"Longer than I thought! Next time we fly," she said. They laughed. "I'm not one to sit long, and I have absolutely *no* patience at all."

"Understandable. That drive's not for everyone," Jarrett said, his eyes now shifting between Stephanie and Warren. "At least you didn't have to travel alone. It looks like you brought your bodyguard."

Stephanie shot Warren a warning glance. "Jarrett, this is Warren."

Jarrett cautiously put out his hand. Without a word Warren shook it once and let go. Jarrett assisted them with their bags and led them into the foyer. Jarrett and Stephanie chatted on their way inside, but Warren's silence seemed louder than any discussion they were having.

*****

"Dad, this is Stephanie Newcomer and her friend Warren."

"Is it me or did you say she would be alone?"

They were standing in the library, Stephanie and Jarrett near the fireplace, Warren next to a large window that looked out onto Maryland Avenue. Dallas had just returned from running errands. He went to Stephanie, smiled and shook her hand. She was shapely, easy on the eyes, and her wide smile called to mind a young, vibrant Laura. When he turned to Warren, he almost did a double take.

"I'm sorry," Stephanie apologized, walking over to Warren and bringing him over to Jarrett and Dallas. "I brought Warren along at the last minute."

"Does Warren have a last name?" Dallas inquired.

"Cassie. My last name is Cassie." Warren finally spoke,

removing his glasses.

"C-A-S-S-E-Y...?" Dallas asked.

"I-E."

Dallas nodded. "I see."

He found Warren striking, his skin a little like creamed coffee. He was definitely Latino, but thought he may have also been Greek or Italian. His hair was jet black, his lips full and red, his body thick but not overly muscular. There was something in the way he stood and his eyes were the sexiest he'd seen on a man in a long time.

"So you'll both be paying?"

"I'll be paying for the both of us," Stephanie said quickly. "Warren's here as my guest."

Dallas raised an eyebrow and looked at his son.

"How about I show you both to your room?" Jarrett suggested.

"That would be lovely," Stephanie said.

Jarrett told them they'd be on the third floor, that the second was reserved for their infrequent guests, and that he hoped they didn't mind the climb. He then mentioned the dinner party he and Dallas were hosting at Cedar House that evening. When Jarrett looked back and saw his father watching him intently, he understood the message. Watch Warren Cassie closely. Very closely.

DOWN TIME

"What is wrong with you?" Stephanie said to Warren once they were alone. She threw her purse on the bed, and then retreated to the furthest spot in the room away from him.

Their room was cozy and quaint. The bedspread covered in purple violets matched the window treatments and a set of pillows on the loveseat. There was a small television, a radio, an antique desk, a tiny vanity, photographs of the beach in faux vintage frames hanging on dusk-blue walls with white trim, nightstands with attractive but inexpensive lamps, and two chestnut colored bureaus completed the room. This was their home for the summer.

"What did I do *now*?" Warren asked, removing his shirt and shoes.

"I ask you to do one thing, *one thing*! Please don't embarrass me, I said. Please don't. And what's the *first* thing you do?"

"Calm down!"

"You don't *have* to be here!"

In her voice was the threat of tears that struck a chord within him. Her face was flushed and she had her back to him. He went to her.

"Don't touch me," she warned him, and then she muttered, "Why does this always happen to me? Why can't I find the right man?" He turned her around to face him.

"What's the big deal? They're just a bunch of faggots."

Stephanie fixed him with a withering gaze. The tears that threatened finally came, filling her eyes, as she looked on him as something ignorant and vile. "And what are you, a grease-monkey? Worse than a faggot, if you ask me!"

Warren stood away from her, astonished at her rage. She turned away from him. If she had watched him a second longer, she would have seen his vulnerability and hurt, his sudden boyishness.

"You don't know anything," she said, her lips trembling uncontrollably. "He was so kind to me."

Warren frowned. "Who?"

"Jarrett."

He stepped toward her. "Don't tell me you…him…"

"*What?*" She rolled her eyes, and there was something imperious in her gesture that struck him like a pitchfork. "He was around when my parents…"

"When your parents what?"

She shook her head, too emotional to continue. He touched her gently on her shoulder and tilted her chin so her gaze met his. She saw his genuine concern for her and threw her arms around his neck, burying her face in his chest. He staggered a second confused, but then put his arms around her, and knowing what she needed, hugged her tightly for a very long time.

"I want you," she whispered. "Fuck me, now."

She kissed him deeply and forcefully, and he understood what she needed. She wanted to close her eyes and plunge with him, down into the ocean, leaving their problems ashore, like lovers who have abandoned their swimming clothes. She hastily undid his pants, and slipped her hand inside his underwear. Her fingers ran through the soft tuft of hair and caressed him to hardness. He stopped kissing her, examining her like a woman he did not know. His heart pounded in his chest as she placed his hands on the zipper of her jeans; he must undo them now, fast. When he unzipped her, she slipped his large hand inside her silk panties. His hand was warm as he caressed her, slipping his fingers between her thighs as she moaned deep in the back of her throat. Warren squeezed, then entered her. She let out a gasp, her eyes, her hands, running over his bare chest. She took him by his forearm and urged him deeper. He closed the distance between the two of them. She opened her legs.

"Take me," she begged breathlessly. "Take it all."

Warren slid his hand out of her panties, lifted her up and carried her to the bed where he gently undressed her, then himself. They were going down beneath the water's edge, descending rapidly to the heart of their blue underworld. Stephanie and Warren were immediately nude, she spread flat and hungry on the bed. He kneeled over her, examining her soft skin, her slim waist, her legs teasing at a hidden treasure. Her hands ran up his tanned thighs to his erection, thick and poised. Warren kissed her, digging his fingers through her long, red hair. She smelled of perfume, enticing and seductive. Soon, he straightened himself out and was on top of her, his body's weight and heat serving as an erotic charge. She moistened and writhed, her arms pulling him close.

"*Abrase tus piernas, mami. Te quiero ahora, te quiero ahora.*" Warren's nails dragged along her arms, down her sides, her hips, the backs of her legs, creating delectable sensations. Then he was deep inside her. She arched her back, her legs dividing involuntarily for him, her chest thrust upward. Her mouth was open, her eyes closed, her head thrown back. His mouth found her neck, her nipples. She was crying, the pleasure and pain viciously juxtaposed. They were down at the bottom now, the surface world so very far above them. And he *thrust*—leading her into a nearby cave, dark and secluded. And he *thrust*—she moved with him, found his rhythm, swam inside. He gave all and she took all, here on their ocean floor, unaware their secrets, like bubbles of air, were rapidly floating back to the surface above them.

PRIVATE WOES

The afternoon quieted down after Stephanie and Warren's arrival, and outside of two other couples checking in, the day slowed to a crawl. Jarrett decided to run errands, from the drug store on Rehoboth Avenue to the outlet mall on Route 1A to a late afternoon haircut. On a whim, he decided to drop in to the police station to visit Bradley Thomas. It was a small building hidden beneath the huge sky blue water tower emblazoned with the words "REHOBOTH BEACH."

"Sir, there's no loitering here!"

Jarrett turned around in the entrance to see Bradley hurrying out of his office. There was a wide smile plastered on his face, and Jarrett wondered how he could be so much happier to see him than his own father. They embraced long and hard.

"Let me get a look at you!" Bradley said as he spun Jarrett around, embarrassing him, studying him from head to toe. "You look good, kid. Your mother would be proud to see how well you've turned out. Say, got any girlfriends yet?"

Jarrett frowned. "Huh...?"

Bradley burst out laughing. "I'm just *kidding*!" He hugged

Jarrett again, leading him over to sit on one of the waiting room benches. "I'm so happy you stopped by to see me. I've missed you."

Jarrett loved Bradley's eyes. They were filled with a wealth of humor and generosity not found in his father's. Dallas's were always guarded, distant. "I came by to see you for a reason."

"And I assume that reason has nothing to do with my lot of corny jokes."

Jarrett smiled. "Actually, I did come to hear your jokes." A cloud passed over Jarrett's face, then Bradley's. Jarrett looked away.

"Jarrett Hemingway, I have known you since the day you were born. I promised your mother I'd watch after you. What's wrong? And no holding back."

"I came here to ask a favor."

"What's that?"

"I was wondering if we could go fishing like we used to. Before mom died."

Bradley let out a little sound. "You want to talk, do you?"

Jarrett nodded.

"Done deal. I'm gonna call you real soon," Bradley said reassuringly. "That okay?"

Jarrett nodded again.

The police chief leaned in close to Jarrett and whispered, "Your mother loves you so much. She's so damned proud of you, even in heaven."

Jarrett closed his eyes against tears. He was surprised they were so close to the surface. He said, "Thanks for seeing me." He pat Bradley's hand and stood slowly and walked out. He exited like a lone cowboy into the afternoon sun.

*****

Warren flicked on the television, making sure the volume was turned all the way down. Stephanie was in the shower. He sat nude on the edge of the bed, only inches away from the screen. They had been asleep for the past hour, or rather, she had. He had been awake, turned away from her, his eyes wide open, thinking, remembering, keeping still, mentally holding his breath, as he had been doing for some time now.

How much time? How much is left?

CNN had nothing, nor did FOX, NBC, CBS, or ABC; not even the goddamned Weather Channel. And for Warren that was good. He turned off the television. He returned to bed. If he played his cards right, in no time he would be out of Rehoboth Beach without anyone knowing this mask he wore, this role he played, was false. Perhaps even without Stephanie ever knowing that everything he had told her about himself was a lie, starting with his name. When Stephanie stepped out of the bathroom, she found Warren asleep.

He would have to remain still only a little while longer.

HAIL! HAIL!

His name was Ethan Safra and he had a secret. He was a Lebanese-American, whose parents had fled their war-torn country to immigrate into the United States from Beirut back in 1970. Georges and Neena were both doctors and Ethan, their only child, was a medical student. He was tall and well built like his father, dark-featured like his mother. When he rang the bell at Cedar House, he spoke to Dallas as if he expected him to assume Ethan to be an extremist from the Middle East.

"Hi, my name is Ethan Safra," he said defensively, counting the moments until the profiling began.

Dallas thought him just as attractive as Warren, if not more. Ethan was tall, slim and athletic, built like a tennis player, broad shoulders, strong arms and legs. His hair was straight and black with long sideburns, his eyebrows thick, arched, and dramatic. His skin, the color of a toasted almond, was unblemished. His face was rectangular, chiseled, and humorless, his eyes chestnut. When he spoke, his dark red lips revealed his straight, white teeth.

"I'm Dallas Hemingway. We've been expecting you. Please come in."

Ethan entered cautiously. "Is Jarrett here?"

"No," Dallas said, showing Ethan into the living room. "He stepped out for a moment, but he should be back soon. We've already chosen a room for you on the third floor. We have some other guests staying up there as well. We hope you don't mind."

Ethan smiled. "What of my friend Jarvis?" he said. "He's waiting in the car."

For a moment Dallas drew a blank, and then he remembered Jarrett's words. *He comes from an impoverished background.*

"I'm sorry, I'd forgotten. Why don't we go out and escort him in."

It would be the start of an acquaintance Dallas would never forget.

*****

To Jarvis Watson, Rehoboth was one of the most beautiful places he'd ever seen. The sky above was a beautiful blue and through it a small aircraft trailed a fleeting message: "EAT AT FAMOUS GRILL! HOLIDAY WKND BUFFET DINNER SPECIAL $15.95! ALL YOU CAN EAT!" Jarvis sat in Ethan's silver sports car. He dared not move. Since they'd arrived in town about an hour ago, he had not seen one single African American. They'd sat in a restaurant, walked down the streets crowded with holiday visitors, and perused a shop or two, but he'd not seen one single black person. This didn't frighten Jarvis. He was used to traveling in circles where he was the only African American. But here out of familiar territory he became self-conscious of his race, his education and the way he walked and talked, believing the citizens of Rehoboth Beach would be just as mindful.

Jarvis looked nothing like Dallas imagined. For one, he was small and Dallas guessed he weighed no more than 170 pounds soaking wet. His face was intelligent, but plagued with sadness, his posture nearly defeated. He was handsome, but seemed to do everything in his power to suggest otherwise. He shook Dallas's hand with a simple hello and then remained quiet. Dallas, who had expected something quite different, felt embarrassed. Just then Stephanie stepped out onto Cedar House's porch. She wore a billowy white dress, her red hair and exotic jewelry, making her look like a movie star. When Ethan looked at Stephanie, and Stephanie looked at Ethan, it was lust at first sight.

*****

The evening brought clear skies and sparkling stars and a cool breeze off the ocean. It seemed the perfect night for a dinner party. The house shimmered with soft lights and candles. The stereo's suggestive saxophones made for an elegant atmosphere. Stephanie entered the party just as cocktails were served. She had left Warren upstairs, in bed; he'd begged off dinner. Too many gay people he said. At this party, however, Stephanie was in her element, having been born and raised in New York City, the daughter of a banker and a socialite. Stephanie had mixed with the best of the younger crowds across the globe. In London, Naples, Cannes, Newport, Big Bear. The selection of people here was not nearly as high profile, but the party was intimate and the crowd overwhelmingly good looking. There would be no pretensions here, no pressures. She could simply enjoy herself.

Stephanie spotted Dallas laughing with a guest. Across the room, she caught Jarvis Watson nearly hiding in the shadows of a corner. To her left, she spied Ethan talking to Jarrett, and when he saw her, his eyes flashed with a silent charge that sent shockwaves to her heart. Dinner was called, and Stephanie filed into the dining room behind everyone. Intrigued by Ethan's good looks, she was pleased to be seated across from him at the large dining table, already dressed with plates and silverware and small vases filled with fragrant peach-colored roses. When she sat, their eyes locked across the table, and they both knew before the summer was over that they would sleep together; a mystery in and of itself, considering they did not know each other and had not yet been formally introduced.

Dallas took his place at the head of the table, while Jarrett sat opposite him.

"I just wanted to thank all of you for joining my son and me for the re-opening of Cedar House," Dallas said. "This dinner used to be a tradition in my family before my wife passed away. It was a way to get the summer off to a great start, and to wish you all a wonderful season. We hope that you find Rehoboth as magnificent as we do, and invite you to stay with us again whenever you're in town."

When Dallas finished, Stephanie raised her wine glass to him. "Cheers," she said.

Everyone else followed suit.

After sipping his wine, Jarrett offered Dallas a generous smile. To his left, Jarvis sat silent, barely touching his drink. To his right, Stephanie continued to be warmed by Ethan's lustful gaze. At the top of the stairs, Warren watched from the shadows.

One of them would be dead in a matter of weeks.

NOTHING SO BLACK AND WHITE

Jarrett invited Stephanie on a short walking tour of Rehoboth on the evening following the dinner party. Jarvis declined to join them, as did Warren, but Ethan agreed to tag along and the trio ventured up and down Rehoboth and Baltimore Avenues, where a large crowd was out enjoying a beautiful night.

"So how do you two know each other?" Stephanie asked as they walked lazily in the direction of Poodle Beach and toward the end of the boardwalk at Queen Street.

"Jarrett and I attended the same university," Ethan said.

Stephanie's eyes danced over him admirably, recording the way his shirt was shaped by his chest, the way his jeans clung to certain areas, his large, strong hands, his bright smile. If only Ethan had known she could not stop thinking about him after dinner the previous evening.

Jarrett chimed in. "He was Pre-Med and I was Tourism and Hospitality."

"Really?" Stephanie feigned interest. She was not terribly interested in Jarrett's connection to Ethan, only Ethan. "So you're a doctor?"

"Resident." Ethan smiled, feeling her curiosity. "How do *you* know Jarrett?"

"I stayed with him in Miami at his other guest house."

Jarrett asked absentmindedly, "Is that when you met Warren, Steph? While you were staying at Cedar Manor?"

Startled by the sudden introduction of Warren's name, Stephanie nodded then looked away from Ethan. When she looked back at him, he was no longer looking at her.

"Is Warren the guy who stays with you? Is he your boyfriend?" Ethan asked, his voice strained.

"Yes, I met him in Miami," she answered curtly, wanting to leave the subject of Warren.

"Is he your boyfriend?" Ethan repeated.

Neither noticed that Jarrett had stopped walking, that he was looking out at the beach at a tall figure silhouetted by the setting sun, his pants rolled up, the waves washing at his feet.

"Yes," she uttered quietly.

"You've not gone out with him long, have you?" Ethan said, making her smile.

"No," she replied, then stopped walking.

Ethan also stopped, and looked at her with neither pleasure nor dissatisfaction.

"It's him," Jarrett said, pointing out to the beach.

Stephanie and Ethan turned to look. It was Griffin Walsh.

*****

"So what's the deal here? Why didn't you stop to talk to that guy back there?"

Jarrett looked up at Stephanie; they were having coffee at one of the local cafes. Ethan had said he was tired and headed back to Cedar House. "I have my reasons," Jarrett said passively.

"Should I begin pulling teeth or are you going to tell me?"

"There's nothing to tell, really. I only know his name. I've never met him, but I can't stop thinking about him. He's so handsome and stylish, and looks well-educated too."

"Have you ever dated a black guy?" Stephanie asked.

"No. How is it dating Warren? And what *is* he anyway?"

"Warren's Latino and something else. Italian, I think. That's different anyway."

"Different how?" Jarrett asked, feeling this line of questioning was headed into an uncomfortable direction. Something he knew was coming.

Stephanie sighed. "It's just different, I don't know. If you've never had a relationship with a black guy before, there's all this other stuff that makes your life complicated. There's a lot that comes along with it. A lot of," and she said this quietly, emphatically, "*shit*."

Jarrett looked at Stephanie as if he had misjudged her light and fluffy character. As if beneath her beauty lay something surprisingly rotten.

"Don't get me wrong," she said, reading his thoughts. "I'm your friend and I care about you. Let me tell you this story about a girlfriend I have in Atlanta. Her father's a big shot architect with his own firm. He once designed a space for a spa and cosmetics boutique, a chain, Seventh Heaven or something like that it was called. The owners were black, and she, working as her father's assistant, started dating the owner's son. Before long, everyone assumed she was keeping him, and that they were only together because of the sex. The relationship fell apart not because they didn't love each other, which they did, but because of outside pressures. And here's the kicker–"

Jarrett answered for her. "His family had more money."

"Two or three *times* more," Stephanie said pointedly. "She had a B.A., he had a J.D. and an MBA. So go ahead, Jarrett, find this guy, date him, have a relationship, but don't walk into it blindly. Don't think it'll be easy, don't think you're safe, because people will talk and things will change. Mark my words."

Jarrett looked to Stephanie, suddenly a little angry. "This is not 1950…"

"I'm not saying that it is. I'm just saying there are some people out there that are ignorant, that are going to question your choice, your motives."

"Did people question your choice with Warren? You two could not be more different. Or is this piece of advice you're giving me only reserved for people involved with black men?"

"Jarrett, that's not what I'm saying. Don't be like this."

"Never mind. It doesn't matter anyway," he said. His mind was made up. "People can talk. I don't care. People can question, and I won't give a damned. I just want to be happy. And with the year that I've had, with my mother gone, I'm willing to do anything to make that happen. And anyone who doesn't like that can just kiss my ass."

David Youngblood would be the strongest to object.

NIGHT FEVER

Night in Rehoboth is a different beast. The beach is lost, as is the vast, mesmerizing ocean. The night covers them. And while the moon is brilliant in its kingdom of stars, its light cannot cut through the darkness. Once out of the illumination of lit streets, the night is filled with rustling leaves and watchful eyes. Off the major thoroughfare, the town appears docile, still, the streets bare, the houses darkened and quiet, even in the height of the season. Yet one gets the impression that sin in all its myriad form is taking place all around.

Ethan Safra lied; he was not tired at all. He had heard the calling, the urging to sex. It is why he had come to Rehoboth. It was a party town, where one could enjoy all sorts of fun. And he had a need for that out of the presence of his family. Night in Rehoboth was conducive for this sort of behavior, the lowering of inhibitions, and in Ethan's case his need to copulate, to *fuck*. He wanted to sow some seeds. He did not wish to be like his father, having only loved one woman all his life, sex like a holiday, living through pornography, his age, his work, his familiarity with his wife, offering no new excitement, no new perspective. There was the brightness of youth, summer, still within Ethan. He could do what he wanted, be who he wanted, right here, right now in Rehoboth, before he had to give it up, get married, settle down, and have children.

Ethan had ventured into the wilderness of Rehoboth's evening and was now a little turned around. It was late, and he had passed through bars, a restaurant, and shops. He had slowly taken in the nightlife, not wanting to appear too eager or hungry. Within an hour he found himself on the boardwalk. There were children laughing, the shuffling of feet up and down the wood planks. He could hear the ocean rushing onto the sand, its fizz as it receded. He was soon at Prospect Street, the end of the boardwalk. He turned off into the street, and a block or two later was lost. Should he turn left or right? Where was Cedar House again? What street? Where was he now? He had even misplaced the boardwalk in exchange for houses and oaks and shadows and quiet. He stood now on the street turning in circles.

Then he remembered what Jarrett said when he first arrived, that if he got lost, to look up to the skyline and try to find the tall water tower marked "REHOBOTH BEACH". If he used it as a landmark, he'd be able to get himself back to Cedar House. Despite the darkness, he was able to locate it. He continued on the street where he was, toward the tower, a street he later found out was named Bayard Avenue. He walked in silence. As he got closer to the tower, he noticed a figure coming toward him on the opposite side of the street, and he looked over into the shadows. It was a man, in his twenties, tall, dark hair, dark features, thick-bodied. They exchanged glances. Ethan nodded, the guy nodded back. He kept walking.

He had only gotten five feet further when he heard a whistle from behind him. The guy stood in the shadows, under an old, overhanging tree that sat in front of a Catholic church. Ethan stopped, and to him, somehow, time did too. He could not see the guy's face, but could feel a pull. He wanted Ethan to come to him. A fear gripped Ethan, as if he had suddenly been called onstage to perform and he was not quite sure he knew his lines. Ethan looked left and then right, checking to see if anyone was watching. All the lights in the nearby houses were off. It was one in the morning. There was no one here but them, and no one watching. No cars passed. No other persons. The guy turned toward the church and disappeared behind it. After a moment, Ethan followed.

His fear became a thrill, like riding a rollercoaster. This is what he wanted, sex with a man. To lose himself in this cloaked same-sex interaction. The man was leaned up against the wall, at the rear of the church, with both his hands in his pockets. Ethan approached him, passing through shadows, into silvery splashes of moonlight.

"Hey," the guy whispered.

"Hey," Ethan replied.

The guy was handsome, with pupils like midnight. Ethan could tell, although he would be hard-pressed to say how he knew, that he was Jewish. They stood in front of each other, less than a foot apart assessing each other's bodies. He touched Ethan first, rubbing his hands on his chest. They felt warm, heavy. They fell into a kiss that was passionate and hungry. A connection had been made and all else fell away: the town, the world, their histories, consequences. All was forgotten. All that mattered was here and now, their lips engaged, their tongues probing, their hands exploring, their bodies pressed together, and in their animal charge, fiery and electric, there was borne a tenderness, a correlation between power and beauty, force and surrender.

They broke apart suddenly, both gasping for air.

"Let's go back there," he suggested. When Ethan nodded, he led him by the hand into the inky darkness of the cemetery behind the church. "I want you," he said, and there was greed in his eyes. He kissed Ethan again and then pulled off his shirt, revealing a firm, hairy chest. Ethan stroked its smoothness. He whispered in Ethan's ear, "Fuck me…right now, right here."

Ethan watched him strip down to nothing, down to his erection and his desire, so pungent he could smell it in the air. His own desire was fueled by it and he quickly slipped out of his shirt, then his jeans and shoes. When they kissed again, their naked bodies clung, the heat between them binding, urging them on. They became intertwined. Ethan knelt, then pulled him down onto the grass and started to caress his body, taste him, and devour his sex. Ethan took him, and as he did he listened to his partner's moaning, his commands. Their rhythm varied, slow, fast, their breathing ragged. Ethan worked furiously and his partner begged for more, harder, faster.

Then silence, as they lay on the grass embracing, spent. Minutes later, as they dressed, Ethan was gripped by an unexplainable and disabling sorrow, a regret. The two shook hands solemnly, the contract expired. Each was homebound. Ethan Safra would never again interact with David Youngblood. For him, this was good. Others would not be so lucky. For them, it would be disastrous.

SUMMERVILLE

You my boo?

David smiled coyly. Lincoln could be such a tease.

*****

Neighboring Dewey Beach is to Rehoboth Beach what a bratty younger brother is to an older one. It is the designated hot spot for college spring breaks, overpopulated with the wild and rowdy twenty-something crowd. Dewey, like Rehoboth, was full of shops and bars, and all the amenities a visitor might want. It differed only in its tourists, the kids that packed the sidewalks, the motels and bars that were overrun with shirtless young jocks and scantily-clothed and tanned young women. It was at one of these outdoor bars that David Youngblood sat having a beer. He had a summer timeshare with a few of his buddies in Dewey. It had been two weeks since his rendezvous with Ethan. As in Rehoboth, early Saturday afternoon brought out everyone and the bar was crowded and loud with rock music and chatter.

"Dude…!" It was Pat, one of his roommates. Like David's other buddies, Pat served in the military. He was Irish, in his mid-twenties, boyish, with a blonde crew cut. He and David had known each other since high school. "What's going on? You gonna join us or what?"

David turned to a group of soldiers in a corner of the bar. He had known them only a few years, and this was their first summer doing a timeshare together. There was Thom with his stark blue eyes; Edgar, short and portly, but still popular with the girls; Ken, a bodybuilding redhead who was good-looking and knew it; and Blake, small and attractive and soft-spoken. A group of young women hovered around them.

"Ken told them we're in the military and now they're inviting us to a keg party," Pat whispered in David's ear. "We even got you a girl."

David grunted. "What does she look like?"

She was a short and buxom brunette named Cathy Mason. A few minutes later, David stood next to her, beer in hand, as she prattled on about her background. She was a native of Virginia who sold Mary Kay. David nodded in spots, pretending to be interested, but in his head he was miles away.

You my boo?

David smiled coyly. Lincoln could be such a tease.

****

David Youngblood lived in Washington, D.C., working at his parents' business, with college and loathsome Hebrew school behind him. His parents had wanted him—no, *needed* him—at their store, an establishment filled with underpaid and disgruntled workers, with college students who worked summers and took turns fucking each other, with managers who were strung out like the best tweekers on power trips and rages. He wasn't yet a manager, only a helper behind the counter. David's parents needed their only child to be prepared to take over the business one day, but that was the problem.

David seemed to have no attachment to anything, was passionate about nothing, except for his love of alcohol. He turned up late to work every day and stayed late to count the day's take with the managers in the evenings. He lived in an apartment in the Adams Morgan section of the city, in a building owned by his parents; he paid no rent. He drove a Jeep leased through his parents' business; he made no car payments. His credit cards were through the business, paid by the business, and he received his paycheck every week, much to the consternation of the rest of the staff who received theirs every other week.

Yet for all these perks, David seemed alternately depressed and resentful. Many women found him extremely handsome but they never stayed for very long. Friends were few and far between, and conversations with his parents, particularly his father, usually devolved into angry words over old arguments about the responsibilities he was reluctant to take. It was as if he were awaiting something better in his life. A miracle. A godsend. Still

David and his parents remained shackled to each other, their failures—as his parents, as their child—bound them together.

Then one day David encountered Lincoln Williams, and his world, oppressive and draining as August heat, changed. He had been walking through his neighborhood one sunny Saturday in June. He came upon a basketball court where a group of black teenagers were playing. There was a crowd gathered, many hanging on the chain-link fence that enclosed the court area. David took a spot alongside a young girl who was pregnant, and trained his eyes, as all eyes were trained, on the scene's apparent star, Lincoln.

His skin was a reddish brown color that resembled baked clay. He was shirtless and his muscular body was slick with sweat. His soaked shorts clung to him. His features were drawn and angry, his face full of music; the drum of champions, of the hungry and determined. His eyes were inquisitive, and his thick lips were constantly pulled back in a sneer.

"You go 'head, Lincoln! Act like you know, boy!" the girl beside him cried. "Play for *us*! Play for *us*!"

David was drawn by the passion, energy and determination that seemed to emanate from him, like waves of heat. To David, Lincoln was mesmerizing, as sleek and dangerous as a panther. For days, he could not get Lincoln off his mind. Was he like the other black guys he secretly slept with while at college, the ones he found lurking on the Internet? *My job is to hit dat booty so hard you think it will neva close! This thug is on the DL and is waitin' for you, so come correct or don't come at all!* He thought Lincoln might be different. There was an intelligence in his eyes, sharp and analytical that complimented his aggressive energy.

David was sure Lincoln wasn't into guys, was sure there would be nothing between them, but still he hung out at the court, watching him play Saturday after Saturday, until one day in July, when Lincoln took on two friends in a game of roughhouse, he asked David if he wanted to play. David said yes before he knew he had spoken, but soon his insecurities came like a biblical downpour. He was lost, painfully aware of his race, his lack of rhythm, his lack of *something*. He hated himself; he cursed his stiffness, his lack of soul and beat. *Did other white guys feel like this around black men?* He was afraid that every move he made threatened to give him away, would tell them he really didn't know who the hell he was. That unlike them, he wasn't really living life, he was merely phoning it in. Their faces were seasoned with pain and determination and struggle, which made them seem more defined, more real, than he could ever imagine himself to be. As he entered the court only Lincoln offered to shake his hand. "I'm David," he said, nodding at each of them.

"I'm Lincoln," he said. "That over there is Micah and that there is Kevin." Micah grunted and glared; Kevin nodded curtly.

"You want to pair up with one of them?" Lincoln asked David. There was sympathy and pity in his eyes, but also humor. Like a god with a mortal.

Micah objected. "Naw, you picked it, man; you might as well keep it."

Bouncing the ball, Lincoln looked over to David and smiled. "You stick with me, dawg. These thugs don't know nothing about no basketball. They might know something about cricket, but they don't know nothing about no basketball."

Kevin laughed, ready to play. "Nigga, *please!*"

"David, you ever play basketball?" Lincoln asked, bouncing the ball, sizing a shot, walking the court as if he owned it.

"Naw," David said, dancing on his toes. "Football, in college. A rusher."

David wanted desperately for this banter to be an icebreaker, but it wasn't. They played and it was disastrous. All three of them ran circles around David, became impatient and aggravated with him, and none more so than Micah. "Man, back up off me!" or "This ain't godammit-football! Stop hogging the ball and play!" or "Linc, man, what the fuck is he *doing*?"

David hunched over, hating himself. Micah called the game early and left with Kevin before they even played a full twenty minutes.

"I'm sorry," Lincoln said a little distant. "Micah hates white people. Cops shot his cousin four times outside some club in New York. Micah called it a legal lynching."

The two decided to walk together for a while, and that was when David learned of Lincoln's history, that he was the oldest of three, raised by his grandmother. He played college basketball on a scholarship, was hoping for NBA recognition some day. They sat on the stairs outside of David's apartment building and talked for two hours, sharing food, laughing in spots, warming to each other. When Lincoln rose to leave, his handshake was overly long, his hand hot and gripping like the sun. David watched him walk away, and at the corner Lincoln turned and looked at him, communicating without words. In his heart, David felt that summer had finally arrived.

AUTUMN LEAVES

It did not last long between them, summer.

Not until many weeks later, in August's murderous heat wave, would David receive a call from Lincoln. The bass in Lincoln's voice breached the distance between them. It was two in the morning, and David, even in his sleepiness, could tell that Lincoln was at the mercy of his own flesh.

"Dave," he whispered. "It's Lincoln…from the basketball court."

David's slumber evaporated like a fog.

"What are you doing?" Lincoln's question was silky, seductive.

"I was asleep."

Quietly, tenderly: "You want to go for a ride?"

David knew where this was going, and yet he didn't. The prospect of seeing Lincoln again filled him with an intoxicating rush, and yet, Lincoln also evoked in him a relaxed state, a truer David. He came for David and they drove around, the summer night seeming endless. There was music on the stereo, mellow; there was not much conversation between them. They toured the empty, darkened streets of Washington, passing houses and closed businesses with rich, colorful neon signs that cut through the night. They arrived back at David's place more than an hour later.

The air surrounding them had become thick with suggestion. Lincoln's hand laid invitingly close on the armrest between them, their knees touching. David invited Lincoln inside, and once in the darkness of the apartment Lincoln came up behind him, close enough for him to feel the heat coming off his body, to smell his cologne, his earthy scent beneath it. When David felt Lincoln's lips, his tongue, his teeth, at the back of his neck, he melted. The night became a blur, time lost in frantic, erotic movement. David had never known such intensity in a lover, in actions that had less to do with love or passion, but plain raw sex. That first night, Lincoln stripped David naked, bound his wrists, and laid him down on his stomach. David felt Lincoln's entrance as a searing, branding heat, like a mark laid on him. Lincoln whispered in his ear, *You my boo? Do I please you? Make my sound.* And David did, a high-pitched whine of pain and ecstasy, an identifier that said to Lincoln: *this is mine, this belongs to me.*

For a time, David believed that this thing between them would grow into something more, but it didn't. Lincoln never invited David any further into his life. They would sit and watch videos in David's apartment, then sex. They had chicken and beer and watched basketball games; then later, sex. And while Lincoln was always very polite with David, their sessions were one-sided with

Lincoln setting the rules for when he would see David, for how long he would see David, and what he would do to David when they were together.

Regardless, David had hoped against hope that he would be able to find happiness, that through this love he would be liberated, unshackled, allowed to be himself. He believed in Lincoln, even after he found out Lincoln had a girlfriend who was pregnant.

You go 'head, Lincoln! That's right, boy. Play for us! *Play for* us...!

"You still my boo, right?" Lincoln whispered after this revelation. Then sex.

After a time, the affair trickled to its end. Lincoln was a prime candidate for several national basketball teams. There were televised appearances, rumors of drafting, talk of endorsements. David followed him still, at games, on sports shows. He traded in his identity for something he believed would bring him closer to Lincoln. He began listening to hip-hop music, R&B; he wore clothes he thought Lincoln would like to see him in. It was all for nothing. The excitement, the airtime, the love David prayed would save him disappeared into the night. Lincoln was shot in the back by a police officer after playing hoops with his cousin late one night. It was broadcast as an unfortunate incident of mistaken identity. Others would call it a legal lynching.

*****

You my boo? Make my sound.

David could think of nothing else while sitting in the hot and crowded church at Lincoln's funeral. The women wailed and the men were reduced to tears. He was no longer Lincoln Williams, but by the preacher's measure Brother Williams. Micah had spotted David and hatefully stared at him. Lincoln's girlfriend was seated in the front with his grandmother and siblings, all so grief-stricken they could hardly rise to approach the coffin for one final viewing. As the organ played, everyone stood and sang "Go Tell It on the Mountain." David studied the people from Lincoln's life, wondering if they knew that he too had been very much a part of Lincoln's world. And he asked himself if any of them knew about the other side of Lincoln Williams. *They must*, David thought, his eyes resting on a few of Lincoln's friends, young men he somehow knew were gay when their eyes rested on his.

The preacher brought his sermon to a close with a rousing call that demanded to know why there was so much senseless pain in the world and why happiness was sometimes so elusive. That demanded for the people in this church to love their neighbors, their family, and their friends in the time they were given by the Lord. Life was too short and love was not guaranteed. He asked God to provide comfort for all the hearts and lives that Lincoln touched. In David's heart, it was no longer summer. Winter was here.

You my boo? Make my sound.

RING OF FIRE

David had been indifferent to Cathy Mason at the party that night. Still she clung to him, tending to his every need like some dutiful wife. He had tired of her long ago, his senses dulled from an endless stream of alcohol. The party carried on around him like an X-rated circus. There were more men than women here, and soon hands became free, slipping up dresses, inside blouses. Together they watched David's drunken friend Edgar take one of Cathy's girlfriends into a closet, only to emerge twenty minutes later wearing her brassiere on the outside of his t-shirt. Across the room, Ken sat chomping on a cigar, a blonde and a brunette nibbling at each ear. Meanwhile, Thom was sandwiched in a dance between two exotic-looking Latin women who removed his shirt and yanked his pants below his waist. Later, all three disappeared upstairs. He could tell Cathy thought him handsome and intriguing, that she envisioned him as a knight in shining armor compared to the other guys at this party, but David showed barely any interest in her at all.

You my boo?

Cathy examined his face, tried to communicate to him that she was not a princess, a high maintenance whiny bitch. That she was his if he wished, a nice Jewish girl, available and willing to go the extra mile it took to be a girlfriend...or more. Instead, David offered her only clipped responses to her questions.

"You want a beer?" he asked without looking at her. "I'm going to get me another."

"Yeah, sure," Cathy answered quietly. She was teetering on something of an emotional tidal wave, tears banked in her eyes. Did he hate her because she was a little heavy? Was she not interesting or sexy enough for him?

He returned a half-hour later and stood close enough to lead her on, rooted far enough away to leave her guessing. She dared not ask him any other questions, and he said nothing more to her, his mind on Lincoln, on his past, on this burning attraction he had developed for Griffin Walsh. Cathy Mason would later testify as a character witness at David Youngblood's criminal trial. There, the tables would be turned.

THE ISSUE WITH DALLAS

Jarrett had been anticipating his fishing trip with Bradley Thomas for weeks. At first he felt guilty, given he and Dallas had been getting along well in the days immediately following Memorial Day. But it wasn't long before his mention of his mother prohibited any conversation Jarrett wished to broach about anything else. *Was it she that held them together, or was it she that kept them apart?*

Summer had come early to Rehoboth Beach, its official date a little less than a week away. Bradley arrived for Jarrett at an early hour, and by dawn they sat on a fishing boat, Jarrett unsure how to broach his issue with Dallas as they bobbed gently on the water. Bradley started singing, first something from the musical *Oklahoma* (a song about a girl who couldn't say no), and then he mimicked Paul Robeson by singing "Old Man River." Jarrett laughed out loud when Bradley burst into a throaty rendition of "I Feel Pretty" from *West Side Story.* Bradley stopped and raised an eyebrow. "You're laughing. Good, because I don't know anything from *Evita*, even though I saw it with you and your mother–"

"I remember."

"–*and* I saw it with that Madonna you all like."

Jarrett turned with a raised eyebrow. "You watched Madonna in *Evita*?"

Bradley rolled his eyes skyward. "Drescher."

"Ahhh..."

Bradley pointed an imaginary gun at Jarrett and pulled the trigger.

"Thanks for seeing me today."

Bradley gave Jarrett a pat on the leg. "You don't have to thank me. It's my pleasure."

"Honestly, I don't know where to begin."

"Well, in my book the best way to say something that's heavy on your chest is to start with a laugh and we've done that. I meant what I said the last time we saw each other. Your mother is awfully proud of you."

Jarrett's face darkened. "I don't understand him. He acts like she never existed."

"Dallas?" Bradley questioned.

"Yes!"

Bradley frowned.

"It's the way he behaves. Like he couldn't wait to get rid of her!" Jarrett looked at Bradley and saw the truth in his eyes. "You think it's odd, too, don't you?"

Bradley bit his lip and sighed. "I've known your father a long time–"

"Don't *do* that!" Jarrett snapped, the words he struggled to find suddenly in his grasp. "I just want someone to tell me what the hell is going on. Can you do that?"

Bradley cleared his throat. "Son, your father and I grew up in a very different time. A time where expressing your feelings was not necessarily encouraged or seen as a masculine thing to do–"

"*You're* not like that! You have no problems talking, expressing how you feel."

"Son," Bradley chuckled, "I grew up with a mother and five sisters. There was never a quiet moment in that house."

"*I'm* not like that!"

"You are your mother's son. You have all her fire."

Jarrett shook his head, dissatisfied with Bradley's answers. "There's something wrong here. There's something wrong with him!"

"Jarrett, he probably feels guilty. Think about it."

"Guilty for *what*?"

"For letting your mother down. For not being the man," and Bradley paused here for just the briefest of moments, "for not being the man she wanted, needed, intimately. He feels he let her down, and to talk about her is to talk about his failure, or what he thinks is his failure, at being a husband. In some ways simply at being a man. Then she dies after a long, painful illness, and he's left wondering if he brought any goodness into her life. He would have let her go, you know. He would have let her remarry, find happiness, if it were not for you. They were both committed to keeping the family together. To open all that up is to open up a difficult period. There is more than one side to all this."

"He made a choice."

"Yes, he did. And he's probably making a choice not to talk to you about this right now. Maybe he just needs more time. Your mother's loss was awful for all of us, not just you."

Jarrett bit at his lip. "But you do think I'm right, that I have a right to talk about my mother, to miss her?"

Bradley turned Jarrett toward him. "Yes, you have every right to miss your mother."

"And she's proud of me? You know, *he* never tells me that."

"Yes…your mother is proud of you."

Bradley watched Jarrett look out over the water, the sun suddenly brightening the day, interrupting their thoughts, bringing the world closer to them. It seemed odd he was comforting Dallas's son and he wondered if Jarrett had a point, that something was not right with Dallas. That there was a reason he was avoiding the topic of Laura.

Bradley vowed to find out exactly what that was.

GOOD MORNING, HEARTACHE

"Hello, Mother."

"Hello, Stephanie. Is there something I can do for you?"

It had been weeks since Stephanie had spoken with her mother Elizabeth or her father Bertrand. And simply put, the time apart had done nothing for their relationship. There was no mistaking in Liz's chilly salutation that Stephanie still stood as their single biggest failure. Stephanie had not married, nor was she educated beyond boarding school and a few semesters at college. She was not part of her father's business, or even a companion for her mother, someone with whom she could sit with on committees and boards, engaged in charity work, keeping the Newcomers in good profile.

She endured from her parents a heavy burden of disappointment, and a refusal to see or speak with her for any elongated period of time. Stephanie was content to globetrot, constantly on holiday, doing nothing, and in their opinion, being nothing. Acting as a whore for gigolos (mumbled her father), squandering her trust fund (scolded her mother). Fed up with her aimlessness, they made her a deal. Her father gave her all of her trust fund money up front and told her to go. That if she wanted to be nothing, she should be nothing out of his sight. He would explain to all who asked that she was traveling abroad, touring in Naples, in Amsterdam, in Mykonos, somewhere, anywhere but in New York City.

"How are you, Mother?"

"Are you in trouble?"

"I'm fine," Stephanie said. She sat on Cedar House's back patio, the two oak trees shielding her from the early morning sun. Stephanie could picture her mother at the breakfast table, her fair skin, her thin lips, her face intentionally severe, her own red hair pulled back into a neat, tight bun. She would be drinking coffee, her husband the banker already at the office, even on a Saturday.

"Where are you?" Elizabeth asked.

"I'm in Rehoboth Beach."

"*Where?*"

"In Delaware," Stephanie answered. There was a silence. Stephanie knew her mother was thinking of a link to this place, some way to categorize the area.

"Didn't Katie Couric's parents live there for a time? Or her late husband's parents?"

"I…I don't know."

"Why are you there? Last I heard you were in Miami."

"Because I've never been and I was invited."

"By *whom*?" Elizabeth asked doubtfully.

"The Hemingways."

"Of course not connected to the writer's family."

"Of course not, Mother. They own guest houses."

Elizabeth asked rather flatly, "Are you broke?"

"No," Stephanie answered truthfully. She still retained a sizable portion of her trust, investing regularly through her broker, the son of a friend of her father's.

"Then why are you calling?"

The question hurt. It made clear that she and her parents were still on opposite sides of the world in understanding each other. That her parents still did not grasp that she was waiting for something to click, a light to shine on the path she was meant to travel to her own happiness. Until then she would travel the world, praying every day to be struck by inspiration. This thing that would finally clue her in on what she was meant to do with her life, and who she was meant to be.

"I called to ask how you are doing."

"I am fine," Elizabeth replied, as if there could be no other answer.

"How's daddy?"

"He's fine as well. Is there something else?"

Stephanie paused, her emotions hardening into a giant wall of discontent.

"No, Mother, there is nothing else."

"Well, I must be going. Things to get done…as I am sure you have things to do as well."

Another silence.

"Yes, Mother."

Stephanie had never felt so low.

*****

"Let's do it again," Stephanie said from under the sheets.

Warren, who sat on the opposite side of the bed, turned to her and offered an incredulous look. "Steph, I was asleep."

"So what," she said, throwing the sheets off. She had been watching Warren from behind, his nude body like a work of art. His back, the muscles residing there, lead downward, like a path, to his rear, beautiful and slightly paler than the rest of him. She crawled up behind him, wrapping her arms around his neck, resting her chin on his shoulder, pushing her breasts up against his back. After the call to her mother, Stephanie ran upstairs to a sleeping Warren, eager for him to rescue her from a descending depression as only Liz Newcomer could provoke.

"C'mon," she whispered in his ear, toying with his nipples. "You know you want to–"

"Yeah, says you."

"I'll make it worth your while," she sang. She nibbled his ear and let her hand venture below his waist. He began to grow thick in her grasp. "See there. Ready for action."

He smiled. "It's supposed to be like that. I'm Latino."

Stephanie pulled away in disbelief. "You are so full of shit." They both laughed.

She pulled him back on the bed, loving him this way, before he was bathed, rough and unpolished, the musk of his male scent drawing her like a magnet. He looked boyish, his hair mussed, he grinning through cherry red lips, his chest, with its large darkened nipples, looking like the almond colored landscape of a desert. She had a moment, a brief one, where she felt like this simple interlude between them was one of the best moments of her life. There was warmth associated with it, like Christmas morning, which bound them together. She said, "Stay there. Since you're too tired to perform, I'm going to show you my special powers."

He raised an eyebrow; his fingers knotted behind his head, he too enjoying this episode that allowed him to forget for the briefest of moments his dark past. And while he couldn't explain it, at least not then, he felt as if they had *arrived*. As if on some level he and Stephanie had achieved some form of indescribable rapport, the way they communicated, this intimate moment where Stephanie proclaimed *she* was going to please *him*.

Was he falling in love with her, was that it?

When she slid down the bed to his waist, he inhaled sharply, grabbing the spokes of the bed. He closed his eyes and turned his head into his shoulder, feeling her tongue on him exploring. He opened for her, raised his right leg, and moaned his approval. He pulled her away before he climaxed, he quivering, his face turned away. Stephanie watched him as he had watched her on so many occasions. His whole body pulsed and she thought—no, she knew—he was crying. She turned his face and made him look at her. Warren kissed her then, so hard, so fast and so passionately, it frightened her. He turned away again, wiping the tears from his face. He got up and went into the bathroom to shower. When he came out, she was watching television, the bed made, she in a robe. He did not look at her.

"You okay?" she asked quietly.

He nodded, pouring a glass of water.

Yes! Yes! That was it! He was falling in love with her. He felt at home with her. His lost soul was at home with her lost soul. They were two drifters in a small town, feeling their way through life. Trying desperately to forget their past mistakes.

"Let's go out," Stephanie said, hanging on his arm. She flashed him a smile and slapped his bare bottom. "We should go to the beach and get some of those salted cashews they heat up under the lamps–"

"No," Warren said simply. No malice was in his tone, only sorrow.

"Why?" she asked, concerned.

Warren could tell without looking at her that she was offended. They were having such a great time, and here he was, the murderer, about to ruin it. "Just go out yourself. I'm tired. I want to lay down." He thought she would cry, but she didn't.

"Well, I'm getting in the shower," Stephanie said. "We're going out and I'm not taking no for an answer." She marched herself into the bathroom humorously, and for his benefit.

He weakened. *Loco! You cannot love her! You can't!*

He went to his jeans lying across a chair and frantically fished out his wallet. Inside was a picture of a beautiful woman with long, dark hair, and a boy, her son. *Murderer!* He thought, disgusted. *Murderer!* His heart swelled as he slowly replaced the picture in his wallet. He lay back down on the bed, put his large hands over his face, and cried furiously.

LUNCHTIME BLUES

Stephanie was wrong, Warren did not join her for a day at the beach. In fact, he was so reluctant to venture outside Cedar House he nearly ignited an all-or-nothing argument between them. Was it her, or did he almost never leave the room by day? She found herself in Rehoboth's hot sun, at lunchtime, in a wide-brimmed straw hat and sunglasses. She looked beautiful but felt insecure as ever, despite her morning with Warren. The culprit here was her past; one that she had been trying to erase in London, Montreal, Paris, Vienna, L.A., Miami, and now in Rehoboth Beach. She had traveled to more cities, had experienced more scenes, than anyone she knew, and still she had come away from it all with only an abysmal sense of dissatisfaction. When would it all begin, the good part of this story she was living? When would she find her destiny, her purpose? When would she have the control her mother wielded, the drive her father possessed? When would she cease living the same wretched days over and over? And was Warren to be part of her future, or was he like all the others before him? Good sex and then good-bye. Why was she still feeling empty and meaningless? Why—after all this time—did her purpose in life still escape her?

"Stephanie!"

On the way back to Cedar house, she had passed Jarrett and Drescher as they were seated outside a restaurant. Jarrett waved to her, and she, needing a distraction, decided to join them for lunch.

"Hello there," Jarrett said, clearing a space at the table.

She sat, removing her hat and sunglasses. "I hope I'm not crashing."

"No, not at all."

"Who's your handsome friend here?"

"Stephanie, this is my best friend Drescher Thomas. Drescher is a professional photographer. Drescher, this is Stephanie Newcomer, one of our guests at Cedar House this summer. She stayed with us in Miami at Cedar Manor last winter."

Stephanie held out her hand and Drescher cordially shook it.

"So what are you boys up to today?" Stephanie asked, studying the menu out of habit. She was not in the least bit hungry.

"Having lunch, enjoying the day. I went fishing with Drescher's father, so I'm starved."

"You didn't go along?" Stephanie asked Drescher.

"I had other things to do." She detected tension in his answer.

"Besides," Jarrett said equally tense, "we don't necessarily do all the same things."

Drescher pointed to Jarrett. "He's a homebody and I'm a nomad."

"He's a party-boy," Jarrett countered, crossing his arms. "He comes home with stories about how he goes hopping all around the world, hooking up with hot guys."

Drescher reddened, annoyed Jarrett would bring up details of their private conversations in front of someone he did not know. "Don't listen to him," he said defensively to Stephanie.

"For my two cents, I don't believe there's anything wrong with hooking up with hot guys," Stephanie said, coming to Drescher's defense. "More power to you."

Drescher beamed.

"Besides," Stephanie continued, "if I were you, Jarrett, I'd be more concerned about what's going on in your own back yard."

Jarrett turned quickly, following Stephanie's gaze to a corner of the restaurant's patio area that was shaded and nearly out of view. His breath caught in his throat.

Drescher turned to look as well. "I know him."

"I know him, too," said Stephanie. "His name is Griffin Walsh. He's from New York. His family owns a publishing house."

Stephanie and Drescher waved, and Griffin waved back. Then he offered Jarrett a wink and a look that said *We'll meet again soon*. Their lives would never be the same again after that day.

WHATEVER HAPPENED TO JARVIS WATSON?

This was not how he grew up, with the soft colored walls of Cedar House, its fine wood furniture, its handsome library, its charming fireplace, or its bouquets of fresh flowers. Yet, Jarvis Watson always dared to believe a life like this awaited him.

You ain't nothing but a white man in black skin!

To believe the woman who had a hand in raising him, this was out of his reach and wasn't the way blacks really lived. The words she used—*You still a nigga, boy!*—the words she used—*Faggot!*—the words she used—*Nerd!*—all stung him far worse than he cared to admit. What would have happened if his parents had not given him away? What if Nelson Ruiz and Belinda Jackson had opted to struggle and raise him instead of his grandmother, Mildred Watson? She hated that he had big dreams like his parents. She hated that he kept his nose in a book and "talked like he was white". She hated that he was not street smart, was not black enough for her, and she hated his Northern liberal attitude; she was a conservative woman of the South. What if his beginning had been different? Would he have still arrived at the same juncture, feeling at a loss as to where to fit in and how?

As Rehoboth Beach heated up and more tourists invaded the town, the ratio between blacks and non-blacks still remained vastly uneven in Jarvis's estimation. Even in the gay spots around town, he could walk in and suddenly realize he was the only person of color in the room. He faced questions in all the eyes he greeted. *What's he doing here? Does he think he's one of us?* How ironic that even here in the nation's self-proclaimed "gay summer capital" he should feel unwanted, excluded. He imagined this was part of the reason he found solace in books, in Morrison and Wright, in Sheldon and Koontz, in Smiley and Maupin and Jakes and Forster. Even some of the new writers were really very good.

"You should try this book," Dallas said at the threshold of the library.

Jarvis jumped, startled. He had been perusing Cedar House's book collection.

"It's called *Peyton Place.* It's by a woman named Grace Metalious." Dallas walked the book over to him. "It's probably long forgotten by people your age, but I think you'll like it. It's about scandal and secrets in a small New England town."

"Thank you," Jarvis said, timid.

"And if you like that," Dallas continued, "you'll like this book *People Like Us* by Dominick Dunne. I haven't read it, but my late wife loved it."

Jarvis accepted this also with a whisper of thanks, his eyes down.

With each second Dallas spent with him, he could see in Jarvis a likeness of himself at an earlier age, lonely, isolated, eager to fit in and somehow quite unable to do so. He remembered wanting to kill himself. How could he have thought Jarvis would be an issue because of his *impoverished background*?

"I've noticed that you like reading," Dallas said, now curious. "I'm not a big reader myself, but you wanna know what my favorite book is?"

"What's that?"

"*To Kill a Mockingbird.*"

"Harper Lee," Jarvis said, finally raising his eyes to meet Dallas's.

"You've read it?"

"Who *hasn't*?"

Dallas, noticing Jarvis's lively response, risked another question. He had a sudden warmth for him, wanted to know him better. "Who's your favorite author?"

"Baldwin."

Dallas nodded. "Well, I think we may have one or two of his books here in the library. You know, you don't have to read those upstairs. You're more than welcome to stay down here and read them. I can get you a snack or something."

"No," Jarvis said, "but thank you." The light faded from his eyes. "Excuse me."

Dallas allowed Jarvis to pass, feeling he should say something more or reach out to him. Except he didn't know what to say then and he wouldn't know what to say later when their lives took a dramatic turn and time would be short for words or anything else.

WARREN'S BAD DAY

He was undeniably in love with her, but if she knew who he was, what he'd done, if she knew his past, the lies he told, *the blood on his hands*, he would lose her forever. As he saw it, the only thing that kept them together, bought him time, was his ability to physically please her. It certainly wasn't because he was educated or well-traveled or made a shitload of money. His sex and his company was the extent of her interest in him.

For Warren it was different. When he questioned himself about it, the answers petrified him. How deep did his love go? Could he imagine a life with her? But what did he have to offer, a spic, a wop, a grease monkey from Miami's slums? He had no education and no future. Love had come to him with a most beautiful woman and he stood woefully without his house in order. He now realized he was unprepared for her, and for love.

When he thought about why he loved her, it was not her obvious attributes on which he rested, her beauty, her money, her poise and sophistication. It was that Stephanie seemed to instinctively understand his Scorpio nature, perhaps because she was a Virgo, the Virgin Maiden. Stephanie possessed something he'd never had in a woman, the ability to nurture. It challenged him, made him want to be better, made him want to love her, to make love *to* her. She brought light to his life when it was at its most dark. She comforted him when she held him close. It made him believe that she was his and he was hers. Now, he would have to give her up. He could not stay here with her, and she could not come with him. If only he could give her all that was in his heart and that was enough. If only he hadn't screwed up his life.

But he had.

Warren was distracted. He and Stephanie were making love and he couldn't concentrate, not with all these thoughts running wild in his head. He stopped while still on top of her, the two vainly attempting to find a rhythm. It was the day after her lunch with Jarrett and Drescher.

"What's the matter?" she asked breathlessly.

"I'm sorry," he said. He started kissing her again, touching her again, but his hands felt foreign and clumsy. *Get your hands off of her, you fucking murderer!* Warren shot up.

"What is going on with you?" Stephanie demanded, puzzled and annoyed.

Warren lay on his back beside her. He shielded his face with his hands. "I'm sorry," he said again, but he really did not feel like speaking at all.

"Something is wrong," Stephanie said. "I don't know what it is or why you're acting this way, but I want you to tell me right now." And when Warren didn't answer, she snapped. "Damn it, Warren, what is it? You sit in this house all day, you never go out–!"

"I go out–"

"Not with me, you don't!" she said. A certain pain, sharp and accusatory, crept into her voice. "Is it someone else? Have you come to Rehoboth and found some other girl? Is that it?"

Warren sat up suddenly and branded her with a condemning glare. "No!"

She challenged his eyes with own her tear-filled ones, then looked away. "You sure?"

He grabbed her arm and turned her around forcefully. "*Mira!* Don't you *ever* say that again, you hear me? *Ever!*"

"That's the way it *feels!* You act like you don't want me, like I'm not good enough for you! If you don't want me just say so, Warren. Then pack your shit and get the hell out!" She rose, snatching the sheet from the bed. She pounded off to the bathroom. "I don't need this! I get enough of this shit from my parents!"

She slammed the door, shaking the room, and cried beneath the run of the shower. Warren collapsed again onto the bed, exhausted at the mess he created. He *had* to leave Rehoboth Beach, *had* get out of the United States, and in order to do that he needed cash. Certainly more cash than he had on him. He thought about asking

Stephanie for money, but then she'd want to know everything, and after he told her she'd hate him forever. He needed a job, and blending in with the gay crowd in Rehoboth seemed like a strategy. He would cut his hair, maybe grow a goatee, and rework his clothes. After he raised enough cash, he'd blow this town. Blow it quickly before *they* came looking for him. *That body could not stay hidden forever!* Warren knew that trouble would follow him here, and Stephanie could be in danger. She must now be washed clean from his heart, must cease to exist to him. It would be the only way to save them both.

*****

The rain came without much of a warning.

The late June sky, which for most of the day had amounted to nothing more than a gray threat, suddenly became agitated. White waves rushed the shore, sending even die-hard beach lovers packing. The rain that followed—its one...two...three drops increasing to a drenching—evolved quickly into a downpour, leaving tourists scattering for cover. Stephanie, caught on the boardwalk after her spat with Warren, ran under the shield of her purse, but found herself hopelessly lost in the blinding sheets of rain. There were screams all around, laughter, frantic scurrying to find shelter, as she bolted for Rehoboth Avenue to find an eave that wasn't already crowded. Someone grasped her arm, and she jerked around, startled. It was Ethan, yelling at her, pointing, guiding her.

They found shelter at the corner of Rehoboth Avenue and First Street, which had been a railroad depot at the turn of the twentieth century but had now been converted into an indoor-outdoor mall that contained boutiques, restaurants and other assorted shops.

"Are you okay?" Ethan asked. The mall was packed, abuzz with chatter and exclamations, everyone soaked and excited. Stephanie brushed the hair from her face and smiled. "Yeah, I think so! Thanks for saving me!"

Ethan looked out into the storm, but the deluge was so heavy he could not see to the curb. "Thank God I was here shopping. I hardly got wet, but you...you're going to catch a cold."

Stephanie looked down at herself. Her tennis dress was completely drenched, her sandals all but ruined. Ethan took off his shirt, a white, long-sleeved oxford, and put it around her arms.

She laughed shyly, looking up to him. "Thank you very much."

He offered to hold her purse as she stuck her arms through the sleeves, and gathered her hair in back. He watched her buttoning the front of the shirt, her beauty undiluted by the rain. Without invitation, he felt compelled to roll up the sleeves of the shirt, and she stood there, her eyes on his bare chest, on his watchful gaze, protective, methodical, organized.

"Viola!" he said when finished. "Take two aspirin and call me in the morning."

"Thank you, Dr. Safra," she teased.

It was his chance to smile, his face good-natured, his teeth bright. That she could find a man more attractive than Warren took her by surprise, but if she was truly honest with herself, she had been flirting with Ethan since she laid eyes on him. She wondered if perhaps Ethan was a better option for her than Warren. He was so full of mystery and beauty, she had but to close her eyes to see herself married to him, a handsome doctor with a future and a purpose. It seemed so easy to fall in step with him and to detach herself from Warren, a man she liked very much but who had no prospects, no future it seemed, no purpose at all. Ethan could be the one to save her, ground her, to finally give her life meaning and direction. What would her parents say to her handsome find? What would they say then to her triumph?

There was a flash of lightening, a crackle, a short silence, and then a thunderous boom that shook the ground. There were yelps and screams from the crowd around them, and Stephanie found herself in Ethan's arms looking out at the rain and the lightning. She could feel his heart, his body heat, his breath on her. Neither said anything. He held her, she held him. It seemed that her intentions with Warren, with Ethan, were becoming clearer by the moment.

*****

That night, in the city of Miami, something strange floated up on the far end of South Beach. A body bloated and blackened with death. A body that had been missing for weeks and that some had been searching for. A body whose discovery would make front-page news in the days ahead.

AN AFFAIR TO REMEMBER?

"You've seen this movie before, haven't you?" Stephanie asked Ethan as they stood in line at one of Rehoboth's multiplex theaters. Stephanie sipped at an iced cherry soda, while Ethan embraced a bucket of popcorn. He boyishly rolled his eyes skyward, his jaw busy chomping, and Stephanie thought she could have kissed him right there, he was so charming.

They had met again, after their moment in the storm, without coincidence, when Jarrett decided to barbecue on Cedar House's back lawn. Their curiosity about each other spilled over into this day, and Ethan accepted Stephanie's invitation to a movie that evening. He did not ask about Warren or how he would feel about Stephanie going out with him; he did not bring up Warren at all. Nor did he raise the topic of his own sexuality. Stephanie sidestepped issues of her own. Warren had been relegated out of the house of her heart. He did not have Ethan's promise. He did not possess Ethan's ability to exist on any other plane but a sexual one. She could not take Warren home to her parents, to show him off, to show them up. And if truth be told, her curiosity about Ethan's sexuality—being surrounded by gay men, having gay friends, in what assuredly appeared to be a gay-friendly town—was silenced. She had made a find and was prepared to take Ethan as she found him and lead him into her life. He would be her coup, her success. A beautiful husband who was intelligent and charming *and* a doctor, who would prove to her parents, to herself, that she was a winner.

"Three times," he admitted, smiling broadly. Stephanie called it his Cheshire Cat grin.

"Full of nothing but car chases and huge explosions, no doubt."

"It has a love story."

Stephanie tossed her hair and lifted her eyes to meet his. "I can't remember the last time I've seen a summer film, but I'm having such a good time with you I'm sure I'll like it." And now it was his turn to believe that he could kiss her. She was very beautiful.

They piled inside with the crowd, Stephanie watching as Ethan calculated how far back they should sit from the screen, how many seats over toward the center. Here in the theater the two felt a sudden need to share, to whisper, to be closer.

"My mother would be very proud of me right now, sitting here with you, a pretty girl at a movie," Ethan said.

"Oh?" Stephanie handed him the iced soda.

He nodded, and in a bold move laid his cards on the table. "My parents would be happy if I were well on my way to getting married."

Stephanie looked at him. "Really?"

"Really," he returned. He did not look at her, only down.

"You don't want to get married?" She probed.

"I do. I just haven't found the right person."

The word *person* stuck with her. Did he mean "person" a man or "person" a woman? She wondered.

"They want me to settle down soon," Ethan continued. "Find some position in the medical profession, find a wife, produce children." The word *produce* made Stephanie as uncomfortably as the word *person*. He said seriously, "I have a strange feeling they want me to be them, a younger version of them. As if my getting married would bring new life to their relationship."

"Do they have a good marriage?"

"Yes. I just think they're bored. It seems as if they've discovered all they can about each other on their own. They need grandchildren, a daughter-in-law, to help them find out something more about themselves, about each other. Or at least to help them remember."

Stephanie said, "Do you suppose you getting married would help them find out something more about you?"

Ethan turned to Stephanie after a long pause. "Do you?"

The question frightened her, made her actually think about the consequences of an action, and particularly one as large as marriage.

"I suppose so," she said. "I mean, my parents want for me to settle down. I think the reason why is so that they could know I was safe, that there was some stability in my life, that someone was looking out for me. But worse than that," she confessed, "they don't trust me to my life alone. They think I need assistance, guidance."

"Parents always think that. No matter how smart their kid is, or self-sufficient, the parent always think they need help, that they're not truly happy or balanced until they're married."

"But parents always think that no one can take care of their child better than them, even if they are paired," Stephanie added.

Ethan chuckled. Stephanie joined him.

"They do have a point, however." Stephanie said, leaning back into her seat. Ethan did likewise, and they leaned on each other as they ate their popcorn and drank their frosted soda. "It would be really nice to go through life with a partner, one that you could depend on, trust and love. Someone who really knew you and would not forsake you, even if you were imperfect."

Ethan allowed his gaze to fall on Stephanie as she stared at the blank screen. Her eyes were glassed. He put his right arm around her and took one of her hands in his. They sat that way, with him looking at her and her looking inside herself, until the theater darkened and the screen came alive.

The movie began.

ETHAN'S DECEPTION

Where was he going with Stephanie, and what did he really intend to do with her? Ethan pondered this question a few days after their movie date; he was lying out at Poodle Beach. He had known since the age of six about his sexuality. He'd caught his father unexpectedly nude, undressing for a shower after a swim in the backyard pool. To see him completely naked marked for Ethan the first time he had ever seen anyone fully undressed, particularly another male. Although he would not identify his sexual orientation as gay until years later, Ethan knew he was different than other boys. Next-door neighbor Paddy Drake seemed like a god to Ethan with his penetrating blue eyes, and Ethan's most lasting crush was his soccer coach Mr. Lucchesi. The pangs of desire that sharpened as he became older made him realize his attractions were all but engraved in stone. The feelings he experienced constantly reaffirmed his fears that this was not a phase. Feelings that could not be disclosed to his parents. Feelings that would not be tolerated by them. It was shameful to them to be gay. To his buddies also. *Sissy, faggot, homo, girl*, they'd used them all. The words people like him established for themselves, names like gay, lesbian, bisexual, transgender, same-gender lovers, whatever, did not have for Ethan the power to erase the stigma of the other names.

There still was this question before him as he sat gazing out at the Atlantic. What was he doing with Stephanie? Could he give up on all possibilities of a relationship with another male? Could he keep up a continuous deception? Could he marry her and have a family?

"There is nothing so sexy as a good-looking man in a good-looking pair of shorts," she said from behind startling him.

He turned to look at her, and smiled. It was the start of the Fourth of July weekend, and he was wearing a navy blue swimsuit; he raised his sunglasses so that they sat on his head. She sat next to him in her orange and white bathing suit, her eyes hidden by huge designer sunglasses. When he reached over and slipped them off, she smiled.

"I was told you could be found here," Stephanie said.

She's so beautiful. My parents would love her. She wants me, *and I need* her.

Ethan leaned over and kissed Stephanie. She did not resist. He understood the risk he was taking here; he would have to be careful and discreet. Having sex with her would not be an issue. He'd been with other women before, just to get the word out that he liked girls. He would treat her as a queen and give her whatever she wanted. He could do no better than a beautiful socialite who worshiped him.

What she did not know would not hurt her.

THE FUGITIVE

It was done.

Warren stared at himself in the mirror, his hair now cut stylishly. It was short and smart—what he considered very gay—and he prayed that it disassociated him from his past.

That's right, bitch, open up that pussy! Let me in...!

He looked away from the mirror, feeling ill, remembering

her naked

the whole scene. Remembering

the blood

that whole dreadful night.

It was done.

He must get a job, get some money, get out of town. He must now become someone else, with perhaps yet another new name. He looked at the bed and thought of Stephanie. He must be prepared to leave things to which he had become accustomed. He made sure the bedroom door was locked. CNN was on, the sound low. From under the bed, he removed his duffel. From within the bag, he pulled out his travel pouch. From within the pouch, he extracted a gun.

THE DEVIL YOU KNOW

Warren became the latest employee of *Shore Time!,* a novelty shop that sat on Rehoboth's boardwalk near Poodle Beach, and sold everything from oversized beach towels to shot glasses and t-shirts *(Surfers do it in waves!)*. The owner was a gruff, red wigged, chain-smoking woman in her fifties named Anna who knew a good thing when she saw one. Warren, with his collared shirt half-buttoned and his tight jeans was made to entice every teenaged girl that walked through the door. And if he heard it once from Anna, he'd heard it a thousand times. *Smile!*

Warren had to nearly beg for evening shifts. Hours when it seemed less likely for anyone to remember his face, when the store was less worked. *Why don't you just ask Stephanie for the money?* Warren had thought to himself. *Or better, just take it!* But he could never bring himself to do it. If he attempted to take money from her, that would require him to know how much she had and where. Besides, she paid for nearly everything in plastic, and his disappearance with one of her charge cards would lead to an easy tracing. He loved her and she had done enough already. She had unwittingly helped him escape Miami and a death sentence.

Stealing or forcing money from her would be too much, and getting arrested would not only affect him.

"I recognize that look," Warren heard on his break. He had been standing across from the store, at the railing that overlooked the beach and the ocean. The speaker was a man impeccably dressed all in black. His hair was short and blonde, and he was very handsome. Warren could not help but to think he'd seen this man before. "Don't worry," The Voice said. "I don't want your soul, only your body. And I'd be more than happy to pay handsomely for it, if you'd let me."

*****

The Voice chuckled. "You should see the look on your face."

Without a word, Warren turned and walked back into the store. He was not in the mood for jokes or complications or touchy-feely old men. The Voice followed and Warren turned on him when they reached the back.

"What do you want?"

The Voice did not immediately respond. He only stood, his hands braided in front of him. He studied Warren, from his short and curly black hair to his scuffed shoes. He took note that Warren's face was tired, his hands worn, that his clothes were a bit dated. He knew Warren was from the streets and could smell on him hard labor and desperation.

"Look, either you buy something or get out," Warren said, but not too loudly. He feared something, and The Voice knew that too. He heard the whine in Warren's throat and accurately guessed that his back was up against some unseen wall.

"I've already told you what I want," the stranger responded. His voice was low and seductive and easy to swallow. It struck a chord in Warren, unnerving him further. "I will pay you whatever you want. I just want–"

"Get the fuck out!" Warren exploded, pointing. "Turn around and walk the fuck out!"

Warren started to cross The Voice, wanting to get away from him and his penetrating gaze. He stopped cold, his face draining of color. The Voice looked over his shoulder toward the entrance of the store. There stood two Rehoboth Beach policemen talking to the owner. The Voice turned back to Warren, who had fled further into the rear of the store. He followed.

"What do you want?" Warren hissed. He stood like a cornered cat, ready to run, ready to fight.

The Voice took out a wad of money, twenties, and started counting. He held up two hundred dollars.

"You're a cop…" Warren croaked, his eyes glued to the money.

"No, I'm not a cop."

The Voice reached into his jacket and extracted a business card. He placed it in between the fold of the twenties, and held them up to

Warren. "If you want more, there's more to be made. You look like you have more troubles than $200 dollars can handle, so I guess I'll be seeing you soon. My card is in here with my number. Use it when you want to make some real money. Consider the two hundred a gift from me, a good faith offering."

The Voice placed the money in Warren's shirt pocket. There was a last look, one that confirmed to Warren that he'd seen this man before, and that he was sure he'd see again. Before he left, The Voice smiled. It was warm and encouraging, like that of a parent.

SOMETHING WICKED THIS WAY COMES

Drescher called Jarrett with an invitation. "My father seems to think we don't hang out enough, so to shut him up I found this cool party in Henlopen Acres. You game?"

Jarrett hesitated. Lately, being out with Drescher made him uneasy, as if his oldest friend disliked him for some reason. "Can I bring people?"

"Suit yourself. I'll call you at eleven."

*****

By the time Jarrett, Stephanie, and Ethan arrived the party was well under way. The first hour of their visit was a Hollywood blur; the house belonged to a rich hedge fund operator from New York. It was dark, bass-filled and loud with conversation. There were shirtless bartenders and an assortment of "candy" from which to sample (*E, poppers, coke, pot*). The three stuck close together, but Stephanie stayed particularly close to Ethan. Jarrett decided not to ask about what seemed to be developing between them. Drescher eventually joined them, and they stood around, dancing a little, yelling in each other's ears, taking in the scene. Jarrett noted Drescher seemed uncomfortable around him. It was as if he blamed

Jarrett for something. Suddenly Griffin Walsh stood at Jarrett's elbow.

"Good evening," Griffin said. "Am I interrupting?"

"Not at all," said Stephanie, smiling warmly. She held out her hand and introduced herself.

Griffin frowned. "Do we know each other?"

"New York." Stephanie said. "My father sits on some committee with a Walsh."

"Banker," Griffin remembered after a second.

"Yes. They say New York is big, but it's really very small. I've seen your picture in the *Post* and the *Times*. They do you no justice."

Griffin gave her a broad smile and then turned to Drescher and he said, "I think I already know you, Mr. Photographer."

"It's good to see you again," Drescher said, smiling. "How's Rehoboth treating you?"

"So far, so good."

Ethan and Jarrett introduced themselves, and a conversation began about the party, the host, the wildness all around. After a few minutes of small talk, Drescher excused himself. He seemed preoccupied and not so eager to spend time with Jarrett. Ethan faded into the background detecting suspicion in Griffin's eyes. *He knows I'm gay!*

"No relation to the writer, huh?" Griffin asked Hemingway.

"Unfortunately," Jarrett answered. "But it's nice to finally meet you."

"Likewise," Griffin said with a smile.

Griffin offered to get drinks for all of them. As he wove through the crowd, Jarrett marveled with Stephanie at how handsome Griffin was, how captivating. The timing was perfect for David Youngblood to walk up and say hello.

THE FIGHT

"Hi."

"Hello," Jarrett replied, caught a little off-guard. David was suddenly right there next to him, a drink in his hand.

"Quite a guy, isn't he?" The dark pools of his eyes and his thick physique were imposing.

"Who?"

"The black guy who was just here. You know, the tall good-looking one you were all over."

Jarrett frowned. "I'm sorry, I didn't catch your name."

"David." He glared at Jarrett and shook his hand tightly.

"So, do you know Mr. Walsh?" Jarrett asked.

"*Mr. Walsh...*" David scoffed in his southern accent. His tone insinuated something ugly, and Jarrett could not help but to believe it had something to do with the fact that Griffin was black and he was not.

"Wait...you don't know Griffin?"

David narrowed his eyes and he put his face in front of Jarrett's. "No, I don't know *Griffin*," he mocked. "You got to him first."

Jarrett realized David was drunk and was ready to fight him over Walsh. He snatched his hand away from David's grip and stepped back.

"What do you want?" Jarrett asked.

"Just one thing. Get off his dick, fucker."

Everything around Jarrett fell away, the noise, the music, even the party. He saw in David's face a look of pure hate. He also saw that David was enjoying the scene he was causing. It was not enough to have insulted him. He also seemed happy to witness Jarrett's loss for words. "What do you want from me?" To his own ears, Jarrett's voice sounded just above a whisper. His eyes searched vainly for Stephanie, Ethan or Drescher.

David pushed his chest against Jarrett's. Conversations came to a halt as people started to stare. They had become a spectacle. Suddenly, Griffin returned with Stephanie. He seized David by his arm, and yanked him away from Jarrett.

"Hey, you got a problem?" Griffin yelled.

David snatched his arm away and pushed Griffin before he had even seen his face. There was a moment of silence, a quick stillness, then Griffin shoved David into a wall full of glassware. There were screams and the crowd around them scattered. They grappled with each other, David clawing at Griffin, Griffin's forearm up against David's neck. This close to him, touching him, David began to ache for Griffin. He looked so much like Lincoln;

his beautiful face and full lips; his eyes were even the same brown. In that moment, David would have given anything to have taken Griffin's face in his hands and press their lips together, to taste his tongue as he pressed his body against him. *I wish I could kiss you just once and you'd understand what's in my heart.*

"What's your *problem*?" Griffin yelled.

"Get off of me!" David screamed, struggling in vain. He wanted him but he was being shown up, was becoming enraged. He couldn't stop what came out of his mouth next.

"That's right, niggah! Fight for your white piece of ass! *Fight for it!*"

Griffin backed away, an expression of horror on his face. His heart was pounding against his ribs, as a wave of rage burst out of him. Griffin slapped David hard, and Youngblood fell back and landed on the coffee table, slamming into bottles, the table smashing into pieces beneath him. There was a gasp from the crowd. When David tried to stand, he felt glass cut into his skin, drawing blood. Griffin was on him again, grasping him just beneath the armpit, lifting him to his feet. He whirled David around and David could feel Griffin's hands at his back, shoving him toward the door. Griffin yelled at him to get out, that he was going to kick his ass if he ever saw him again,

Was he just showing off now?

as he grabbed him by the collar, by the back of his khakis,

Was he just showing off?

to throw him out, to put him in his place, as the king, as the alpha male.

Uppity nigger!

Outside, David ran from Henlopen Acres through darkened side streets, crying, stopping on a deserted road to sob. He was now back to the part of him that was vulnerable, needy, fragile. He cried out as he extracted glass from the palm of his hand, cried out of embarrassment, because he knew he could never have beaten Griffin. The fact that he needlessly picked this fight, juxtaposed against the fact that he lost it, sent him even deeper into an already severe depression.

He would run home now, all the way to Dewey Beach, distraught, under a thick black sky that was stoic and remote. He would sneak in the back door so none of the guys saw him. He would cry himself to sleep. And when he awoke hours later, still simpering, still vexed with humiliation, he would plot his revenge against Griffin and Jarrett.

GOODNIGHT, MY SWEET

"I hope you don't mind us stopping off here," Griffin said as he and Jarrett entered his home near Poodle Beach. "If we were in New York, there would be a hundred different restaurants still open. But since we're here in Rehoboth Beach and it's almost 2:30 in the morning, I guess we're going to have to make do right here."

Up close Jarrett realized that Griffin was taller than he thought, and his voice more baritone. He had a smart haircut, thick arched eyebrows, and a goatee that encased his infectious smile. His skin, smooth and glowing, had Jarrett curious about what lay under his clothes. Jarrett stood near the doorway taking in the magnificent interior, stylishly decorated in what Jarrett thought of as Spanish decor.

"You can come in, you know," Griffin said, standing at the stereo. Music began to softly filter through the air. "You don't have to stand there guarding the door."

Embarrassed, Jarrett stepped inside and closed the door. "This is a nice house you have. Very well decorated, like something out of a magazine."

"Actually, this isn't my house," Griffin admitted, stepping behind an expansive wet bar. "It's my friend Harlan Bianca's house. He's an architect in Philadelphia."

Jarrett looked toward the stairs. "Is he here?"

"No. He's in South America for the summer. When I told him I'd never even heard of Rehoboth, he convinced me to visit. Said I would have a wonderful time."

"And outside of what happened tonight, are you having a good time?"

"Excluding what happened tonight, I'm loving it. Music okay with you?" Griffin asked softly, his eyes seducing Jarrett.

"Oh, yes," Jarrett answered. "You hear plenty of Pancho Sanchez down in Miami."

"You spend a lot of time in Florida?"

"My family owns a few guest houses up and down the coast, one in Miami Beach and one right here in Rehoboth."

Griffin smiled, "Must be nice to spend time down there. Can I interest you in a nightcap?"

"Oh, no thanks. It's late."

"Just one?" Griffin begged a little. "A little teeny-tiny one."

"Yes," Jarrett acquiesced with a bashful smile. He joined Griffin at the bar.

"Well, you don't strike me as a whiskey type of guy."

"Gosh, no," Jarrett said.

"Gosh, no," Griffin repeated. "How about some wine?"

"Wine's okay. Red, please."

"Merlot? There's a bottle already open."

"Sure."

Minutes later they were seated across from each other, Jarrett on a loveseat and Griffin on an ottoman. They nursed their drinks; the atmosphere was mellow and quiet.

"Thank you for saving me. I don't know what I would have done if you hadn't stepped in. He was crazy."

Griffin shook his head. "No need to thank me," he said. "I'm just glad you're okay."

"I'm fine," Jarrett said. "More than fine." He studied Griffin's face.

"I think that it would be very wise and gentlemanly if I took you home right now," Griffin said, his words slow and thick, as if the humidity or the wine had intoxicated him.

Music softly played in the background; a muted horn, a saxophone, slow samba drifting through the air. To them the world seemed very far away.

"You must make me a promise that we will see each other again," Griffin said.

"We have the whole summer."

"No, I meant right away. Soon, like on a date."

Jarrett's breath caught in his throat. He didn't quite know what to say.

"I think we should leave," Griffin said. "You are a very handsome man. And if I kiss you like I want to kiss you, now, in this house, you won't be leaving."

Jarrett looked up to Griffin, now standing with his keys in hand. Griffin smiled nervously, which to Jarrett seemed strange for someone who appeared to have so much confidence.

"Yes," Jarrett whispered. "We will see each other very soon."

"Good," Griffin said. "I was hoping you'd say that."

GAME OVER

The night had been long and tiring, and when Warren arrived back at Cedar House, he noticed Stephanie was nowhere to be found. In their room, Warren turned on the television. A female reporter with a microphone appeared on the screen. She was on a beach, looking distressed and pointing to something off camera. Warren turned up the volume.

She said: "Dawn, holiday beachgoers down here in South Beach Miami got a very horrible surprise today when a body, very badly decomposed, washed ashore."

Warren's heart nearly stopped. He could barely breath.

"Eyewitnesses say a body appeared on the far end of the beach, perhaps floating in from the ocean. Authorities have since come and collected the body and that area of the beach has been closed off until further notice."

"*Dios Santo...*" Warren muttered, closing his eyes as the reporter continued.

"So far, it has not been determined if the body was that of a man or a woman, the corpse was so badly decomposed. There is some rumor that the body had been, uh, feasted on by the sea life. I apologize to our viewers for such a graphic description, but this is merely speculation at this point."

That's right, bitch, open up that pussy! Let me in...!

Warren turned down the sound, slipped to his hands and knees. He shut his eyes tightly against burning tears. He knew then that whatever he intended to do, he must do now.

<u>BOOK TWO</u>
in the dark of night

I think hell is something you carry around with you. Not somewhere you go.

Neil Gaiman

II.

This is what he walked in on. This is what he saw.

There was a footprint stamped on the front door, visible as he approached from the street. The neighborhood was quiet, deserted. Fireworks boomed in the distance. It was the weekend of Cinco de Mayo, and although the actual day had been on Wednesday, a weeklong celebration had carried it into Sunday night. There was revelry going on all around, parties, food, music, fireworks and a carnival. Crowds were thick down at the beach, and he was grateful to have gotten off from work a little early, to be able to come home and relax.

He heard him from the door: "That's right, bitch, open up that pussy! Let me in."

For Leo Suarez, as he was called then (the fictitious Warren Cassie still hours away from being born), this became the most defining moment of his life. He was gripped by a paralyzing terror, knowing almost instinctively this night would end very badly. He drove his key frantically into the lock and opened the door. The living room was a wreck, and in through to the kitchen he saw Nick Costello, straddling his sister, bare-assed and wagging his dick. "You like that, bitch? You like that? That's the last fucking time you ever say no to me!"

At first Leo could not breathe, seeing his sister on the floor half-naked, unconscious, bleeding. "GET AWAY FROM HER, YOU BASTARD!"

He tackled Nick Costello, driving him into a wall, both bouncing onto the floor with hard, loud thuds. They scrambled. Nick to rise, to get his pants up. Leo to get to Nick, to put his hands around his neck, to undo the horrible mistake of having introduced Costello to his sister. Rapid blows traded between them. Thrown across the room, Leo tripped over his sister and landed against the pantry door. Startling him from behind, the small and frightened voice of Buddy, his 5-year-old nephew. "Tio! Tio!" He spun then, surprised to see Nick on his feet, his trousers done up, desperately looking around for something. Seeing his suit jacket thrown behind the overturned kitchen table, Nick snatched it up and began furiously searching its pockets.

"OH, SHIT!!" Leo cried, scrambling to his feet, leaping over his sister as Nick tried to draw his gun out of the pocket.

Out of the corner of his eye Leo spotted a knife in the sink. He reached for it, but Nick was too late, had drawn his gun too slowly.

Leo pounced on him, batting away Nick's gun as he crashed into him. They tripped over a leg of the overturned table, and Leo bore down on him with the knife, could feel it pierce Costello's heart, could feel it sinking into Nick's body, the bursting of the organ.

Time moved slowly as Leo pushed away from Nick. Costello's face was a mask of horror, the pain overwhelming, his face first filled with surprise and terror, then with dread and acknowledgment of his fate. Leo stood over Nick watching him slip away, watching his shirt soak with blood, watching the color drain from his face. Leo covered his mouth, turned away, his gaze resting on a picture of his dead mother and then to the front door, which was still ajar.

"Jesus, be sweet!"

He ran for the door, closed it enough to peek outside and scan the street. The neighborhood was still deserted. He took a deep breath and almost started crying until he caught sight of the blood on his shirt and his hands. He quickly closed and locked the door, his breathing heavy and erratic. He had to think. He had to fix this.

He ran over to Luna and turned her over, gently wiping the hair from her face. He put his ear to her chest, and was relieved to hear her heart beating, to feel her chest moving up and down with her breath. He called her name, called it again. He rose, wet a dishrag and wiped her face. After a time she revived, and when she was able to sit up, he knew what they must do all three. Run.

Their lives would be worth nothing if they stayed.

STRIPPED

Warren had no idea what possessed him to entertain such an offer, that he would take off his clothes and dance for money. What did he know about dancing naked? He already had two hundred dollars in his hand and had intended to reject the offer outright. But once his brain laid out the hard, cold facts, he began to reconsider. Fact: he was a fugitive murderer with extremely limited resources. Fact: a badly decomposed body had just washed ashore at Miami Beach. Fact: there was only a small window of time before certain people, local authorities included, noticed he was missing and connected his disappearance with the dead body. Fact: Those who would come searching for him—and yes, they would come with blood pounding in their ears—would prove to be far worse than the police. Those individuals would be seeking revenge, to inflict on him severe bodily harm before his imminent execution.

However, his fate was only the tip of the iceberg. There were other matters to consider. Stephanie, for one. He needed to get away before this problem became hers, before those seeking retribution traced him here to Rehoboth Beach and everything was turned upside-down. And if authorities did connect him with Nick

Costello's murder, how long would it be before they began airing on every network possible his composite sketch or his wretched high school yearbook photograph? He needed cash now, and every day that passed brought him a day closer to getting caught. No matter what love he felt for Stephanie, or how much he wanted to be with her, he had to disappear without a trace. Bottom line: he would dance, make his cash, and blow this town, end of story.

But where and for whom would he be dancing? How much money was involved? And, most important, could he do it? Could he actually strip down to nothing and immerse himself into an underworld of eager fingers and hands holding out cash like horse-feed? He had an appointment with The Voice, which came on the eve of the Fourth of July. He was to go to The Voice's home to discuss the particulars. He was told to be on time. He had dressed provocatively in snug jeans and a shirt that showcased his well-defined chest. He was thankful his appointment was in a section of Rehoboth called Henlopen Acres, far off the boardwalk, in a small apartment complex snuggly hidden away from the city.

"I'm very pleased you decided to call me," The Voice said to Warren. The apartment was huge; nearly everything in it was white. The Voice sat at his desk and Warren sat across from him.

"I need the money," Warren said simply.

The Voice nodded. "I appreciate that."

"When do I start?"

The Voice's face became complicated, as if to preamble a long stretch of road with a warning. "I think we need to understand each other a little more clearly before we begin."

Warren looked around the room. "Nice apartment," he said. He had been escorted in by a twenty-something male who looked to Warren to have never done a hard day's work in his life. Pretty, but vapid.

"I own the building."

"Really?"

"Really."

"Do I know you from somewhere?" Warren could not help but ask. It had been nagging him since he first laid eyes on The Voice, his mannerisms, the way he spoke.

"We have never met before," The Voice responded coolly. He said curiously, "Have *you* seen me before?"

"No," Warren replied. "I've never been to Rehoboth."

There was something about this man, in his demeanor, that unnerved Warren. He rarely blinked it seemed, and from moment to moment he could be steely or impersonal. He looked dangerous and cutthroat, and the street clung to him like a harsh fragrance, betraying his refinement, suggesting he may at one time have begged for his supper, had eaten some knuckles, had used cold concrete as a mattress.

"Where are you staying, Warren?"

The Voice was getting too personal and this Warren did not like. He just wanted to do the job, get his money and go. "A place called Cedar House," he said.

The Voice rose in his chair. "Cedar House, you say?"

Warren looked up, intrigued by The Voice's reaction. "Yeah, why?"

The Voice was silent for a very long while, a flurry of activity occurring behind his eyes. He said finally, "How *is* Dallas Hemingway these days?"

Warren reddened. "He's fine. Do you know him?"

The Voice avoided the question. "How long are you there?"

"What does that have to do with this?"

"Well, if you're only in town for this weekend I see no need to continue this conversation."

Warren huffed. "Listen, I don't know what this is about, but I do know that I need money. You want me to do a striptease for some birthday party or some girls' night out thing, fine! But let's just get on with it."

The Voice laughed condescendingly. He had a pen in his hand, which he threw upon the desk. "Let's not be naive here," he said, and Warren fell silent. "If I hired you, you would need to be in this town longer than the next few days, and you would *not* be dancing for women."

Warren's eyes widened in the light of a dawning truth.

"If hired, Mr. Cassie, you would be required to dance in a g-string. However, you could earn considerably more dancing in nothing at all. I take half of all earnings. I keep people longer like that, by making them equal partners—especially when I'm supplying them the clients." Warren blinked and his face darkened. The Voice raised an eyebrow. "Mr. Cassie, what is it that you don't seem to understand here?"

Warren dropped his gaze.

"There is a lounge in the basement of this building which I use for private parties. I employ young men like you to dance. Being that I own the building, there are rooms for…other private activities. Men—and a few women—attend my parties. On a summer weekend, particularly a holiday weekend, the earning potential is absolutely astronomical. Everyone wants to get laid. If you want fast money, you've come to the right place." The Voice leaned back in his chair. "Now, Mr. Cassie, why don't you take off your clothes, and show me why I should hire you."

FROM BAD TO WORSE

Warren bolted from The Voice's apartment. Surely this job would leave him with no shred of dignity, would confirm, like all the rest of the days of his life, that he belonged to a lower species; yesterday a murderer, tomorrow a *chapero*, a boy whore!

Thankfully, Stephanie was not there when he entered their room. He could not have faced her right then. He had started to sense their relationship was over, that she wanted more than he could ever give her. They hardly saw each other any longer, had nothing much to discuss, and had even ceased doing the one thing they were good at. Still, to smell the sheets where she had lain brought him a certain peace, lulling him to sleep under the veil of her perfume. He dreamed they were married, running beneath a flurry of white rose petals, and then a door slammed shut, and suddenly he was awake. He was back at Cedar House, and it was night and the room was dark. Stephanie turned on lamps around the room. He could feel her anger.

"Where have you been?" she questioned harshly.

Warren rose sluggishly. He had no desire to argue with her. "Out."

"You weren't at work, so don't bother to lie."

Warren cast her a cynical look. "I was looking into another job."

"What's her name?" Stephanie demanded, catching him completely off guard. There was an unmistakable fury growing in her voice. "Is that who you've been hanging out with? Is that where you've been?"

"What are you talking about?"

"The woman in the picture that's in your wallet? Are you fucking her?"

"What?"

"Are you fucking her?"

Color drained from Warren's face, and he could do nothing but stare at Stephanie.

"Your wallet was lying on the dresser. I opened it and saw the picture."

Warren's head was spinning. He felt sick. "Stop it."

"What do you take me for, Warren, living off of me, playing gigolo?" She followed him, as he tried to get away from her. "Let me tell you something. There are plenty of people out there who like me for me and not for my money! There are plenty of people, Warren, who want to love me–!"

"STOP!"

She fell silent.

Warren was shaking, his hands balled into fists. What words could he use to tell her how much he loved her, or how much trouble he was in? That she was correct, he had been using her, but not in the way she thought? The woman in the picture was his sister, and that all of this—ALL OF THIS—was because of her? Could he ever tell her about his real past, from childhood poverty to fatherless puberty to down-and-out adulthood? Could he ever tell her his real name, or that out of a fiction came a truth? He would have kissed every inch of the earth for her. Could he ever tell her that he only wanted to hold her, love her, make her happy?

The pressure inside him was unbearable and he burst into tears. To her he seemed like a small boy who'd been traumatized, who'd seen something terrible and can't bring himself to confess it. He came to her suddenly, grabbed and hugged her tightly; she could hear fright in his voice.

"I love you so much, you are so beautiful," he said. He stopped for a moment, held his breath. "I will always love you. *Piensa en mi.*"

He kissed her desperately, with both his hands cupping her face, and then he was gone, out of the room, down the stairs and away from Cedar House. It would be one of the last times she would see him before devastation laid waste to their lives.

A DEATH IN THE FAMILY

It was Mario who was in tears, not Frank. Frank was too studied for that. Brando, Bogart, Pacino. Frank Costello was dressed in a black suit, white shirt, freshly shined shoes, one hand in his right pocket, his hair black, wavy and thick; a white handkerchief peeked from his jacket's upper left pocket. He sighed heavily (his sign of grieving), and looked down on his brother's body with a hard glare *(what a mess!)*. The doctor, white haired, droll, and standing opposite him over the body, raised his eyes to Frank's. Costello turned slightly to his brother, measured. "M, give it a rest!"

Mario shuffled over to join them, wiping his face with the back of his hand. Frank squeezed his brother's shoulder, silencing him. He said: "Understandably, my brother is very upset."

The doctor shifted his gaze to Mario Costello. He had a shaved head, a shaved beard, both the length of a five o'clock shadow. His lips were full, and he was a smoker the doctor could tell. He too wore a black suit, nearly identical to his brother's. The doctor looked back at Frank. "Are we finished here?"

Frank took a breath, threw a last bereaved look at his brother's body, and turned to the doctor. "Yes, I believe we're done here. *Grazie*. Thank you for your time."

The doctor slipped the sheet back over Nick Costello's body and closed the drawer without a word. He turned to a woman sitting quietly in a darkened corner of the room. She was a Latina, beautiful, thirties, noticeably gruff. She was Detective Adriana Esteban. She stood up and walked over to the doctor.

"Thank you, Dr. Lott." She shook his hand firmly. They exited the room together, speaking in hushed voices. Frank and Mario followed slowly, but stopped just short of the door. Frank's eyes found Mario's, and taking his thumbs, he wiped away Mario's tears.

Frank whispered, "We have to find out who's responsible for this."

Mario nodded, pretending he was still crying. They both knew the detective was eyeballing them through the glass partition.

"That bitch," Frank hissed venomously.

"She suspects something."

Frank took Mario by the shoulders, consoling him. "Stay cool," Frank said. "We'll play this nice and easy."

Mario nodded, sighing dramatically for Detective Esteban.

Fuck her, he said to Frank with his eyes.

Fuck her, Frank agreed with his.

*****

Detective Adriana Esteban's office was small. Frank and Mario sat there waiting for her, Mario picking up a Rubik's Cube from her desk and working it purposefully. Frank studied every inch of the room, from the photos on her desk to the piles of paper and files everywhere. There was a bulletin board in front of them with tacked-on notes and newspaper clippings. Mario slammed the toy back on her desk and Frank turned to see it completed.

"You haven't lost your touch. Stay sharp."

Detective Esteban entered the room. "Gentlemen, I'm sorry to keep you waiting." She closed the door and took a seat behind her desk. In her hands was a file, no doubt about Nick. So far it was relatively thin, which meant the police didn't know too much about him just yet.

"Is that Puerto Rico?" Frank asked, wanting to take control of the conversation. He knew this interview was nothing more than a fishing expedition and he needed to distract the detective from the truth. He pointed to a picture behind Esteban, one of her on a beach hugging a woman.

The detective turned around, then back to Frank. She answered humorlessly, "No, that is not Puerto Rico. It's Aruba."

"Oh," Frank said. He nestled into his seat, studying her. "Is that your sister you're hugging?

Detective Esteban turned again to the photograph, then back to Frank. "No," she said dryly. "That is *not* my sister."

"Sorry," Frank said, making a funny face. Mario sniggered.

Adriana Esteban did not smile. They knew she was a dyke.

"Let's get to work." The detective opened the file before her. "I need to inform you that the cause of your brother's death has been established." Mario glanced at Frank, Frank glanced back. "He did not drown, he was stabbed. Once through the heart."

Frank's face clouded, changed dramatically. This *was* news to him. "Wait a minute," he said, "are you saying to me–?"

"Your brother was murdered."

Frank looked to Mario again, genuinely alarmed. Mario picked up on Frank's concern; there was something wrong here.

"By the incision, we can tell what type of instrument was used. We have ruled out switchblades, glass, shanks, or any other sharp objects. The wound itself is about two inches in width, clean, which leads us to believe that he was fatally wounded with perhaps a large kitchen knife."

Frank and Mario again traded glances.

"The use of a kitchen knife brings us many conclusions. One, your brother knew his attacker. People just don't carry kitchen knives on the street. And two, he did not die where his body was found. He may have died elsewhere, indoors, and then relocated."

Frank nodded slowly, his mind racing.

"Now," Detective Esteban said, pen poised in hand, "I need for the two of you to tell me about your brother."

The Costellos looked at each other. Frank spoke dully, "What do you want to know?"

"Let's get the obvious out of the way. Do you have any idea who may have done this?"

"No," Frank said, looking away from the detective. He was still thinking, trying to put something together in his mind.

"Are you sure about that?" Esteban asked skeptically.

Speak carefully! Frank said, "I don't know who did this to my brother."

"Your brother have any girlfriends? Girlfriends with boyfriends? Did he get around a lot?"

Mario spoke this time; Esteban turned to him. "My brother had 'em all over."

"Girlfriends?"

"Yeah. All over Miami."

Frank stung Mario with a glare. *Speak carefully!*

"Do you have their names?"

Mario shrugged, his pace slower now. "I can think of a few."

Esteban sat silent, her eyes never leaving Mario's. There was more to this story than these two were letting on. "Any of them you suspect?"

"No," they each answered.

Predictable, she thought. "Where was your brother employed?"

"He worked with us," said Frank.

"At Costello's..."

"Yes."

"Anyone there he might have pissed off, had words with?"

"Our employees are very happy people," Frank said confidently. "They're very loyal to us. They would *never* do anything to hurt The Family."

Detective Esteban raised an eyebrow: *The Family*? She laid down her pen and smiled. "So you mean to tell me your brother winds up in the ocean for weeks with a two-inch gash in his heart, and everyone in Miami just loved him?"

Frank decided he hated this bitch. "That's exactly what we're saying."

"I'll want to interview your employees, family members, and these girlfriends you mentioned."

"Be our guest," Frank said. *We'll be ready.*

MIAMI VICE

Frank and Mario Costello stood outside of the police station. Two hours had passed from the start of their interview with Detective Esteban, and the sun had nearly set.

When did you notice your brother was missing?

Frank: After a couple of weeks. He likes women; sometimes he goes off on his own for a while. You know how it is.

And you had no contact with him?

No.

Do you have any idea who he was with?

No.

When you noticed your brother was missing, why didn't you call the police?

Mario: We did.

Not right away.

Frank: We tried to find him ourselves.

Was he scheduled to be away from the business for this length of time?

No. But Nick does what he wants.

And your brother didn't contact you within that time at all?

No.

"She doesn't believe us," Frank said plainly. His hands were in his pockets, his jacket buttoned, as he scanned the parking lot. *So you mean to tell me your brother winds up in the ocean for weeks with a two-inch gash in his heart and everyone in Miami just loved him?* Frank motioned Mario toward the car.

Explaining away Nick's disappearance was going to be difficult, Frank knew. After all, how could he tell her that he thought Nicky had been hit, that a deal had gone down wrong, that he and Mario had stayed quiet for a reason. They only called the police when they were forced to, when it would begin to look suspicious that they hadn't. It had not even occurred to them that Luna Suarez might have something to do with their brother's death until this afternoon, when the detective informed them that the murder weapon was a kitchen knife.

"But Luna left town last year for the west coast somewhere. If she had something to do with Nicky being killed..."

"It means she must've come back to Miami."

"But why? For what? It doesn't make sense."

Frank shook his head. "I don't know."

Mario said, "Frank, anybody could've done this."

Frank unlocked the car doors. He nodded for Mario to get in. Once the doors were shut, he turned to his brother. "*If* Luna is involved, she did not kill Nicky." Mario's eyes narrowed. "A single stab wound to the heart. Think about it. She couldn't do that herself."

"You think somebody else did it for her?"

"A man."

It came to Mario. "Leo."

"Leo."

"That doesn't make any sense either! She left town because Nick beat the shit out of her. Why would she come back?"

Frank checked the rearview mirror. "Don't know."

"Leo! That cock-sucking sonofabitch! *Jesus!*"

"Maybe she wanted what we all want," Frank said, thoughtfully. "To be home again. She took her chances and Nicky found out."

Mario scrutinized his brother. "You're not sad he's gone are you?"

Frank looked away from his brother. "Are you?"

"Makes things a lot easier for you," Mario sidestepped the question. "You move to the front of the line, being the oldest."

Frank looked at Mario. Mario grinned slyly.

"Then there's the simple matter of Luna."

Frank shook his head. "You're on fucking thin ice," he warned.

"You proposition her, Nicky propositions her. She chooses Nicky over you. He treats her bad, she runs away. Just imagine if she'd chosen you, how different things would have been. Beautiful wife. Lots of kids. Big family. *Respect.*"

Frank leaned forward in his seat, suddenly agitated.

Mario leaned over. "No more 'Pretty-boy Frank' living in Nicky's shadow. He's all man now, especially with his brother out of the picture, rotten bastard..."

Frank started the car. "How's your sister-in-law's pussy tasting these days, M?"

Mario drew in a sharp breath.

"We have to find Leo and Luna," Frank said. He did not look at Mario. "If they're involved, I want to know first before that bitch detective gets wind. I want to handle this myself. As you say, with Nicky dead *I'm* at the front of the line."

"Esteban's going to find out Nicky was involved with Luna."

"But we have the lead on this," Frank said. "If it's true, if those two are involved"—and he stopped a moment to think of the implications—"I want to deal with them. No cops. Just us."

"What about the business?" Mario asked.

"We have to be very careful, no shipments for a while. At least until I say it's safe. And tell those niggers and spics you deal with to stay away from the stores, no drop-ins." He turned out of the parking lot, and on to the road. "We need to bury Nicky, too. Grieve appropriately in public."

Mario eyeballed his brother suspiciously. He knew Frank was thinking of Luna, of getting her for himself. "Whatever you say, Frank. Whatever you say."

DALLAS TAKES A POWDER

Over the last week, Dallas had been in a jovial mood, bouncing throughout Cedar House laughing and smiling and full of uncharacteristic cheer. It was this sudden swing in his father's demeanor, from staid Dallas to spirited Dallas that confused Jarrett. Jarrett had heeded Bradley Thomas's words since their fishing trip: *Maybe he just needs more time. Your mother's loss was awful for all of us, not just you.* But then Dallas surprised him with his new behavior.

"Hold that thought," Dallas said when Jarrett asked to speak to him in Cedar House's library. The phone was ringing off the hook with last minute reservations for the Fourth of July.

Jarrett stood in the library, fuming. All of his pent-up emotion, all of his unresolved feelings about his mother, had darkened his usually upbeat mood. He felt this darkness brought him closer to his true voice. *You are your mother's son. You have all her fire.* After Dallas finished his call, a guest asked him for directions to Poodle Beach. On the heels of that, Stephanie returned to Cedar House from a manicure and made a chatty couple with an affable Dallas. Thirty minutes later, Dallas and Jarrett were finally alone, and Jarrett, whose mood had receded from bitter to melancholy, was at a loss. Watching his father converse so openly and easily with guests hurt him deeply. Jarrett could not remember Dallas ever being that free with him. He wondered if he had given his father cause not to be open with him or worse, if Dallas had moved on beyond his wife's death, had started the second phase of his life, leaving Jarrett and Laura as ghosts of his past.

"You wanted to speak to me," Dallas said, smiling broadly. He was very happy about something. "Oh, and before you begin, I have something to tell you."

Jarrett's rage balled itself into one cooled piece of metal. "What's that?"

"I won't be here on the Fourth of July."

Jarrett inhaled sharply. "This is our busiest weekend!"

Dallas's face drained of humor and Jarrett could see his defenses go up.

"Where are you going?" Jarrett stammered.

"Just away overnight. I'll be back the next day."

"Is everything okay?"

"Never better," Dallas replied.

Their eyes were locked now, and there was a struggle for information. Then it came to Jarrett, who was shocked he had not arrived at this before. His father *had* moved on to the second phase of his life. There was a lover somewhere waiting for him. *This* explained his on-again, off-again moods and the far-off looks that crept into his eyes when they were in the middle of a conversation.

"You're seeing someone, aren't you?" Jarrett pried.

"No," Dallas responded. Nothing in his face, in his eyes, gave him away. "I'm not going into witness protection, Jarrett. I'll be back."

"Where are you going?"

When he said, "To a party," Jarrett knew he was lying.

He nodded that he understood, wanting so desperately to love his father, for them to be close and open, and yet Dallas's actions ensured that would never happen.

"I have to get back to work," Dallas said. He posted a winning smile and headed out into the late afternoon's golden sun before Jarrett could say anything further. They never got around to discussing Laura at all.

INDEPENDENCE DAY

Fourth of July weekend led scores of visitors to Rehoboth Beach, with nearly every available lodging booked. Rooms were overcrowded, with many sleeping on floors, or two or three to a bed. Rehoboth baked under the holiday sun, and tourists plodded around the city shirtless, in shorts, in bikinis and sarongs, in sunglasses and wide-brimmed hats. There seemed not a crack or crevice uninhabited by sunlight and the sand was hot to the touch, glimmering like fine glass, the ocean sitting like a prize, beautifully blue, misting and refreshing and endless. Night proved equally busy with fireworks over the sea, and orchestras and bands playing oldies on Rehoboth Avenue. Restaurants had a difficult time seating the hordes that descended for dinner, and bars and clubs were packed to capacity. The sky in Rehoboth, as always, was black and dotted with stars. Off in the distant ocean, one could spot a cruise ship passing, or a barge, or the red lights of a buoy, like the illumination of a remote city.

When switched into high gear like this, the overall feeling in Rehoboth was one of a perpetual party, as if the volume to the entire city had been amplified. Drinking started early, and there never seemed to be a shortage of outdoor parties or barbecues. Families stayed busy at miniature golf courses and arcades and movie theaters and pizza parlors. Singles could be found engaged in midday sexual adventures, sneaking time away from friends for a secret rendezvous.

Dallas Hemingway braved holiday traffic along I-495S going down to Washington, D.C. He could never tell Jarrett where he was really going. Jarrett would never understand that Dallas had waited a lifetime for a love like this. His son had no idea what it was like to grow up in another time, the 60s and 70s in small town Rehoboth Beach, to be closeted in a town that seemed to require a deeper voice, a straighter stance, a firmer handshake. He did not know what it was like to exist in a time before you could see gays on television and magazine covers. Or what being gay was like before the Internet or cell phones. Dallas had grown up in an era so different from today that the daily headlines always surprised him. It seemed that the only thing that didn't change was the hatred. People were still being murdered for being gay: a boy in a cornfield, lesbians by the side of the road. Jarrett had no idea what it was like to live *before* the Stonewall riots in New York 1969, no idea of the freedom his generation possessed or of the cost to those who'd come before him. That even for years after the start of the gay liberation movement, things still seemed largely touch and go.

The love Dallas now kept and swore to protect was hard won. He had hung on to see this day, to find romance. He had loved Laura for supporting him and giving him a son. But here and now, this love he possessed brought him to life; he was finally understood in every way he needed to be understood. As a man, as a lover, as a friend. If only it didn't come at such a high price. If only it didn't come at the risk of destroying everything else he cared about.

In Washington, he pulled up in front of a downtown bed and breakfast. He was given a key and went up to the room with his weekend bag. When he opened open the door, Drescher Thomas ran up to Dallas and kissed him hello.

THE SECRET LIFE OF DALLAS HEMINGWAY

Every time Dallas saw Drescher he was reminded of his father Bradley—of a time when the two friends were much younger, camping, skinny-dipping, double-dating. Dallas pulled away from Dresher, feeling guilty. *You are sleeping with your son's best friend, your best friend's only son. You have your happiness, but at what cost?*

"How are you?" Dallas asked, and Drescher threw himself into Dallas's arms, hugging him tightly. Dallas knew Drescher had missed him terribly and was in love with him as no one had ever been in love with him.

"I missed you," he said into Dallas's shoulder. "I missed you so much."

"I know," Dallas soothed. "It's been too long since we've been together."

Drescher pulled away and looked into Dallas's eyes, as if to confirm his feelings for him. No matter what his age, Dallas was still the most attractive man he knew. Nothing could make him stop loving him, not the twenty-year age difference, not even the fact that he was his father's best friend.

"Look at this room," Dallas said. There was music playing, and their Victorian-styled suite was decorated with lit candles. "You're amazing."

"You didn't think I could do this sort of thing?" Drescher teased.

"I know," Dallas said smiling, "that you are capable of many wonderful things."

Drescher held Dallas's eyes. "You know my heart belongs only to you."

"I never question that."

Drescher shoved his hands into the pockets of his jeans.

"What is it?"

"Your son is under the impression I'm sleeping with half the country. I've told him as much."

"So he has no idea?"

"None," Drescher said solemnly. "But the truth is that sometimes I just want to stop hiding."

"You know we can't do that."

"I know." He turned to Dallas. "If anyone found out, they would inevitably ask the one question neither of us wants to answer."

"How long has this been going on?"

"Two years sounds harmless," Drescher said. "Since your wife's death sounds much more incriminating. And how long had we been flirting before that?"

Drescher pointed to the table. "Eat something." Instead, Dallas stood peering out of the window onto DuPont Circle. Drescher stood next to him. "Can I make you a drink? Some wine?"

"I can't stay," Dallas said, the words coming out fast. "At least not the whole weekend. I have to get back to Cedar House."

Drescher shook his head in disbelief. "But you said...you promised..."

"Drescher, listen to me. I'm sorry."

Drescher reddened. "It's Jarrett, isn't it?"

"Listen," Dallas said, "it's my decision. I shouldn't have left him at Cedar House alone on a holiday weekend."

"*Dallas!* I've waited weeks for this! For three lousy days in the middle of fucking summer! I love you! I love *you*...more than just about anybody in this world." He paused and took a deep breath. "I don't think this is working anymore. I'm tired of hiding. We have to tell them!"

"Drescher, no!"

"Yes!"

"NO! We would be a scandal. The town would never stop talking. Your *father*!"

Drescher went to the bed to lie down. He stared at the ceiling.

Dallas went and lay beside him. "We still have tonight and tomorrow. What we're doing...we know it's risky, that no one would understand. And I don't want any more scandals. I just want for us to be happy while we can."

Dallas tried to read Drescher's face, but his eyes were angry and distant. Dallas leaned down and whispered in his ear. "Don't leave me," he said. "If I am sure of anything in this world, it is that you and I belong together. I don't know what I would do without you."

Drescher was silent at first, but Dallas could feel hot tears from Drescher's eyes on his cheek. "I don't think you know how much I love you," Drescher whispered, and Dallas rose up a little to study his face. He said, "If I didn't before, I know now for sure."

Dallas held Drescher's face in his hands. "Look at me," he said, but Drescher avoided his eyes. "Drescher, look at me."

Drescher wiped his face and pushed his eyes on his lover.

"I know that you are handsome. I know that you are beautiful. I know that you can have anyone you want. That you don't need a middle-aged man like me making demands on you. But I cherish you above just about anything in this world. And you've given me a new life, happiness I've never had before. So I'm asking you for a little more patience, a little more understanding. Summer will soon be over, and once Jarrett is gone we can spend as many days and nights as you want together. I'll follow you to the ends of the earth to make that dream come true."

Drescher wanted to say something, but words just wouldn't come. Tears flowed from his eyes as he turned over on his side, pulling Dallas by his arms to hug him from behind. Eventually he said, "Okay, Dallas. Okay." The revelation of their romance was pushed off to another day, another time; one that would ignite their lives like a house on fire.

THE HAUNTING

Stephanie spent her Independence Day watching the waves come in at Poodle Beach. Children were screaming and splashing in the water. There was a surfer out on the ocean amazing the crowd. A handsome lifeguard in Ray-Bans bobbed his head to the music on his radio. All around Stephanie was a crowd thick with mostly gay men sunbathing, picnicking under brightly colored umbrellas. Yet with such a beautiful day before her she could not recall ever feeling so lonely in her life, feeling of the world, but not in it. Her relationship with her parents, her breakup with Warren, her thing with Ethan, altogether amounted to nothing more than steps on a treadmill, movement that took her nowhere. It was amazing that all the beauty before her could not cure her of the apathy that had infected her life. How many wonderful sites did she have to see, how many fabulous parties did she have to attend, how many handsome men did she have to sleep with to keep her self-confidence from dissolving into nothing?

Even now she was running on reserves, holding her breath for the page to turn on this chapter. Maybe she was defeated. Maybe her parents were right. Her rebellion had carried her nowhere. Maybe it was time to call it a day, return home to New York, and accept that she had failed. But why did she feel that would be a slow death? Why did the prospect of giving up, giving in, feel like an utter betrayal of her destiny? If only she could identify it. If only she had a hint. Maybe then she would not always be so disappointed. Maybe then she wouldn't always feel like such a failure.

"Mind if I join you?"

It was Ethan. Without a word, Stephanie reached for her straw hat and put it on. Ethan sat beside her, wearing his sunglasses she loved so much. "They told me you'd be here," he said, but Stephanie continued her silence. He looked out at the ocean.

"You're mad because I left you at the party the other night without saying anything. Listen, I'm sorry. I just got weirded out with the whole–"

"You're gay, aren't you?" Stephanie said, and at that Ethan was silent. She shook her head in embarrassment. "I should've known."

Ethan shivered, as if by a sudden chill. He had been creating stories all his life about his sexuality, and it actually felt good to be in a position to unburden himself—at least in part. "I'm bisexual," he lied. It was effortless, rolling off his tongue like so many lies before.

Stephanie removed her straw hat and threw it to the sand. "Bisexual, huh?"

"…Yes…"

"You come to Rehoboth, you come to Poodle Beach with all these men here. I've never heard you talk once about a girlfriend or any other woman. You're friends with Jarrett and that Jarvis person, and I'm supposed to believe you're just *bisexual*?"

Ethan stood up angrily.

"Don't run away like a little boy," Stephanie said. Ethan stopped, his hands on his hips; he was faced away from her. "You know, you may think I'm some stupid socialite's daughter, but I do read. There are lots of magazines that talk about guys like you, hiding in the closet, doing disgusting things on the side. Tell me, do you ever think of anyone but yourselves?"

Ethan turned to her, anger reddening his face.

"My track record with men is such a joke," Stephanie continued. "My father, Warren, you, others. What *was* all that between us, Ethan? Kissing, leading me on?" Ethan was mum. "You disappeared from the party the other night because you were afraid someone would recognize you. And you didn't come to this beach to find me, did you? You came to pick up one of these guys and you saw me here. I'll bet you even have a condom in your pocket in case you got lucky."

Ethan's eyes filled with tears. He stared at her a long time. Reaching into his pocket, he threw down a condom. When she turned from him, disgusted, he said, "Did you think you were the only one with problems? Is that what you think?"

Ethan seized her arm and yanked Stephanie up to him, snatching the sunglasses from her eyes. She slapped him hard across the face, and he took her by both arms, shaking her. "What do you think you know about me?" He tossed her aside dismissively.

Stephanie turned and stomped away.

"That's right, just run!" he yelled. "That's what you do best!"

She spun around to face him. "At least I'm not a lying *faggot,* playing stupid mind-games with women!"

Ethan choked as the words bit into him. "What the hell do you know? You're just some rich girl with her head up her ass, who doesn't understand *anything* about the world she lives in! I love my parents and I don't want to embarrass them with this! This would kill them! They only want me to be happy, and to get married, and to have kids, and give them a family." He was in her face now, only an inch away, with his fists balled and shaking. "What would you know about family? *Nothing!* What would you know about how I live my life? *Nothing!* You're straight, and you think the world's problems begin and end with problems like yours! You sit in the movie theater crying—*poor me, poor Stephanie!*—and you have no idea what I go through every day!"

Stephanie gestured pompously, saying, "My hairdresser doesn't have to hide."

He recoiled in horror. She knew that would hurt him.

"What you do, Ethan, is a choice!" When he still did not respond, she said, "Go ahead and say it. I can see it in your eyes. Call me a bitch. You men like doing that."

Ethan shook his head. "I don't know you at all."

He turned and headed back to the blanket, scooping up his sunglasses, unaware she was running up behind him, unaware that people on the beach nearby were staring.

"Here!" she screamed, picking up the condom and throwing it in his face. "Don't forget this!"

His breakdown surprised her with the look in his eyes. He placed his hands over his face, colored scarlet. Stephanie was unsympathetic at first, disbelieving he was crying when she was the one who had been hurting initially. When she saw his chest heave up and down, the tears falling through his fingers, she went to him and peeled back his hands.

"My God," she said at the pain on his face. "I'm sorry."

He dropped his head in shame and she embraced him as he sobbed.

"I need you," he whispered desperately. "I *need* you."

She whispered back in his ear, "I know. I need you, too."

THE START OF SOMETHING WONDERFUL

"Welcome," said Griffin, waving in Jarrett. Hemingway had been invited over for early evening cocktails at Walsh's place.

"I brought you something."

"Handsome *and* generous," Griffin said as Jarrett handed him a plant with bright red flowers. "Did you know Monet had these at his garden in Giverny? They're Peruvian, called Nasturtium. They contain lots of Vitamin C and you can eat them in salad. I once helped edit a book called *My Favorite Things*."

"By Mrs. Greenhouse, the gardener?"

"Correct," Griffin said smiling.

"There's a lot I don't know about you."

"It's why I invited you over," Griffin teased, "so that we could get better acquainted. Why don't you come into the dining room?"

Jarrett held back for a moment, feeling a bit out of his league. Beyond being tall and handsome and having a great personality, it was obvious that Griffin was educated, cultured and rich. Jarrett felt country compared to Griffin's sophistication. And while Jarrett knew it shouldn't matter that Griffin was black, somehow it did. Did he personally know any African-Americans that could fit into this category? He thought not as he followed him into the dining room, a setting filled with dark wood furniture and an opened pair of French doors that led to the patio. They sat across from each other enjoying wine, fruit and cheeses.

"So tell me, did your housekeeper set this up or is this all you?" Jarrett asked.

Griffin sat intensely watching him, his arms folded on the table. "All me," he said, "although she's helped me out quite a bit since I've been here. There's a gardener too, who takes care of the lawn and plants and things around here."

Jarrett looked around and shook his head.

"What?"

"Nothing," Jarrett said, stifling a smile.

"As you can see, Harlan spares no expense." Griffin drank some of his wine, and started in on the cheese portion of the platter. "So tell me all about you and Rehoboth."

Jarrett sat back in his chair. "Where should I begin?"

"Your dad. What's he like?"

Jarrett huffed comically. "How about we start somewhere else?"

"You two not close?"

Jarrett shrugged. "We have our issues."

"Okay…" Griffin said, pouring more wine. "How about your mother?"

"Dead. Two years ago of breast cancer."

Griffin stiffened. "I'm sorry. I had no idea."

"Chill," Jarrett said, and regretted it almost immediately. The word seemed out of place in this conversation, and he had no idea why he even said it. "Drescher and I are childhood friends, but you already know that."

Griffin nodded. "What about Rehoboth? Why have I never heard of this place? Seems to be one of Delaware's best kept secrets."

Jarrett explained Rehoboth's history, about the long line of Hemingways who'd lived there. "Rehoboth has a year-round population of about 1,500 that swells to about 25,000 throughout the summer, from Memorial Day to Labor Day."

"Why are there hardly any people of color in Rehoboth?"

Jarrett avoided his eyes. "I couldn't honestly tell you. I know that one percent of Rehoboth's population is black, say, compared to other parts of Delaware. I know that Lewes's population is around 14 percent; Seaford's is around 22. Ninety-eight percent of Rehoboth is white. Why the interest in Delaware demographics?"

"Well, when you're from New York City and you come to a place like Rehoboth Beach—"

"You realize you're not in Kansas anymore."

"Or maybe," Griffin said smiling, "you realize that you are."

They both laughed.

"You just carry all this information around in your head?" Griffin asked.

"When you're a business owner in Sussex County, yes."

"Touché."

Jarrett said, "So what about you, Mr. Walsh? It seems you know all about me, but I don't know anything much about you." Jarrett leaned across the table. "Except that you're handsome."

"Thank you."

"And charming."

"Thank you, again," Griffin said.

"And I'm very attracted to you. You must know that."

Griffin was silent.

"Is there a problem with that?"

"You've never dated a black man before, have you?"

Jarrett studied Griffin. "Is that what we're doing? Dating?"

Griffin's eyes were penetrating. "It seems I've gotten a little ahead of myself," he said, stung.

"I think we're on the same page, don't you? Talk to me."

"I'm 35 years old, born in New York City. My mother's side of the family is from New Orleans. My father's is from California. Part of the family moved to New York in the forties, after World War II and has been there ever since. I have two brothers and one sister. Douglas and Sawyer, and Blair."

"Are you the oldest?"

"No, that's Doug."

"Any pictures?"

Griffin smiled and showed Jarrett a photo on his phone.

"Your father's white," Jarrett said, confused.

"Yes, my father's white," Griffin said, soberly. "My mother is black."

Jarrett sat back in his chair. "You are full of surprises."

Griffin threw him a puzzled look. "I wasn't aware that children of mixed marriages were still surprises."

Jarrett reddened. "I'm sorry, that's not what I meant. It's just that…" But he could not think of anything adequate to say and fell silent.

"Do you feel differently about me?"

In some way Jarrett did and was afraid to admit it. He felt self-conscious and in uncharted territory, afraid to say something un-PC.

"My mother's family, the Marcelleses, own three huge plantations down in Louisiana, and made their money in sugar cane. My dad's family published pulp magazines in the early 1900s, and almost went out of business during the Depression. Walsh really made its money after World War II producing textbooks. We broke into fiction and specialty books in the sixties and magazines and children's books in the eighties. Now we're into electronic publishing."

"Makes my life look pretty lame," Jarrett said, only half-joking.

"Not at all."

Jarrett managed a smile. "What's your sign?"

"Leo," Griffin grinned. "What's yours?"

"Sagittarius."

"Good, anything but Cancer." They both laughed.

Jarrett felt safer after this exchange, and dared to ask, "Where do you live in New York?"

"Off Central Park, upper East Side. Have you ever been to New York?"

"A couple of times," Jarrett said. "But it was night."

"So you've never actually seen New York? Central Park, Chelsea, Harlem, Rock Center, Yankee Stadium, the Village, none of it?"

"I've seen Times Square."

"A blind man could see Times Square!" Griffin joked. "New York is the greatest city in the world. It's apparent we have to right some wrongs here. I offer you, my good fellow, a thorough tour of the Big Apple."

Jarrett rapped the table. "Sold!"

There came a silence where Griffin felt compelled to make a confession. "You must know how I feel about *you*."

"And how is that?" Jarrett asked shyly.

Griffin turned serious. "I've wanted to kiss you since you walked through the front door." He moved closer to Jarrett, leaning in to kiss him. It turned long, passionate, and then tender. "I guess it's official, now."

"We're dating…"

"We can be anything you want us to be," Griffin said.

"Let's be friends awhile longer," Jarrett said. "Let's do this right."

Griffin smiled warmly, agreeing.

BLACK AS THE NIGHT

David Youngblood was a Scorpio and 25 years old and had only been to New York a few times himself, but none of that mattered now as he thought back to the night of the party. He was more than angry; he was humiliated. He could not stop thinking about the fight with Griffin Walsh. Within him grew an animosity toward the publisher that sat alongside his undeniable attraction, coexisting as strange bedfellows. When he closed his eyes he could see Griffin's brown skin, his thick lips, his naked body. He could imagine Griffin in bed, sex with him rhythmic and angry and exhausting. He wanted to explore Griffin, touch him, taste him, talk to him. But David also hated Griffin for what he had done to him, for how he had humiliated and embarrassed him.

"Fucking nigger!" David said aloud, surprising himself. He was alone in his apartment in Washington, naked on his bed. The room was still and quiet, the sun gone from the sky. He burst out in tears, miserable. *You're obsessed,* he thought.

"No!" he said, crying. "I just love him."

You just want to be loved.

"Yes…" David swung his feet to the floor, twisted his jaw,

glared through the night. "I'm going to get you back, you fucking uppity nigger," he hissed. Tears tracked down his face, tasting salty in the corners of his mouth. "I swear to fucking God I'm going to get you back."

TRUTH OR DARE

"You're back," The Voice said from his desk, not even bothering to look up.

"Yes," Warren answered humbled, ashamed he was at the mercy of The Voice. He had been escorted in by a neatly dressed blonde named Carl, who disappeared silently into the background after he announced him. "Thanks for seeing me," he whispered.

The Voice said nothing, jotting down notes, punching numbers into a calculator. He said after a while, "I am a very busy man with other interests outside of Rehoboth Beach. I suggest you use that knowledge to get to your point, quickly."

"I've thought about your job offer."

"That's not a point, that's a statement. Try again."

"I'll do anything," Warren managed, skirting tears. If The Voice wanted him broken, he had him now. "I need money."

"Don't we all," The Voice said.

"Did you hear me, I said I'd do anything!"

"Yes, I heard you!" The Voice threw down his pen and leaned back in his chair. He knew he had Warren exactly where he wanted him. "Tell me something, are you intending to run off again like a little girl?"

Warren yelled, "*I'm* not the one who's gay!"

The Voice appeared amused. "Put on your thinking cap so that I might educate you in the laws of business. Everything around here is bought and paid for with hard-earned cash. There is nothing free here. There are no free rides. There are no free lunches. If you are not willing to put up, then shut-up and get out!"

"I *said* anything!" Warren repeated.

"*Anything*? What is anything, Warren? I agreed to see you because I thought you had something interesting to say, tough guy like yourself! You're wasting my fucking time! Get out!"

"Anything, *please!*"

"Anything but what, Warren? Are you going to dance for me or put out?"

"Anything but that!"

The Voice pushed back into his chair, laughing nastily. "And I thought pussies only came in panties…"

Warren was beaten down. He had nowhere else to turn, nowhere else to go.

"What is it with your generation? Do you all think that if you ask nicely, maybe cry a couple of tears, that you'll get everything you want?" The Voice shook his head angrily. "Do you know where I started, how I wound up with all of this? It wasn't by sitting on my ass, I'll tell you that!" He watched Warren turn away, looking desperate, with tears rolling down his cheeks. "And it wasn't by looking pitiful, either!"

The Voice sighed long and deeply before he spoke. "I started poor, a bastard child my mother didn't want." He got up and walked around his desk. "My father was a married traveling salesman, that's how he wound up in my mother's bed once a month, every month. She loved him, named me after him. When my father died in a house fire, the last thing she needed was to find was her half-Jewish, half-Irish faggot son taking it up the ass from the neighborhood bully, but she did. She kicked me out. I had no home, no money, no food, no family." The Voice came up to Warren and hissed in his face, "I ate other people's garbage, slept under bridges with rats! *I was fourteen!*"

He turned away from Warren, disgusted, looking out of the patio's glass doors to the beauty of Rehoboth Beach spread out before him. "With five dollars I bought a one-way ticket to New York City and never looked back. Somehow I wound up trading sex for money. A famous actor, you know him, was visiting, liked me, sampled my services, and took me home to California to be his houseboy. After several months an offer was made to do certain types of films. I did several of them until I realized there was more to be made *behind* the camera. Later, after I made some money, I bought a limo service, a cabaret house, a disco, a few lounges. When I returned to New York, I opened clubs, bought real estate. I survived never knowing what protected me, if it was God or just my *will* to survive. But here I am, still surviving."

The Voice trailed off, fell silent. He seemed not to remember Warren was in the room.

Warren said softly, "Are you going to help me?"

The Voice jolted back to the present and looked at Warren. "…get out…"

"Please, help me…"

"GO!"

Warren ran out of the apartment.

The Voice sat down heavily in his desk chair after he had gone. *Why did you tell him that story? Why did you tell him about yourself?* He covered his mouth, his heart thumping. He looked at the door, thinking of Warren, thinking of himself, thinking of Warren, thinking of himself.

SAY UNCLE!

Frank and Mario Costello had assessed the situation carefully and were now ready to proceed with their plan. The brothers knew it would only be a matter of time before Adriana Esteban found out Nicky had been seeing Luna Suarez, and would deduce that her brother Leo was ultimately responsible for his death, that Luna had secretly returned to Miami, and that Nick had been ambushed and murdered. They had already broken into the Suarez house and confirmed it abandoned. To thwart Esteban's efforts, Frank had Mario call on childhood friend turned cop Joe Taborelli. The two met in the storeroom of Wild Palms, an Italian bistro owned by Taborelli's brother-in-law.

"Let's get this right, you want me to *stall* the investigation?"

Mario nodded.

A burly Taborelli shook his head. "I don't know if I can do that. I'm not on the case."

"Use whatever influence you have with the chief of detectives."

"That's just it, I don't know that I have that kind of influence. I can't just tell the chief of detectives to slow down a murder investigation."

"Are you two close?"

"Yeah, in a professional sort of way. But still…"

"Try."

"M, really."

Mario's face darkened. Tapping the table, he thought hard. "I know what you must do. Come closer." When he finished, Taborelli nodded.

"I know somebody who fits that bill."

"Get right on it," Mario urged.

"You know who killed Nicky, don't you?"

Mario smirked, placing a box with a red ribbon on the table. "Something for the missus."

Taborelli took the box. "Candy?"

"Second layer," Mario said. "Check it before you head home."

They stood.

"*Grazie molto, il mio amico.*"

Taborelli waved the box. "*Grazie per la "carmella."*"

They hugged.

"Keep me posted."

Taborelli exited the front, Costello the back.

*****

Tyree Jackson was deep inside Germaine Smith when they came for him. The lovers were in a rhythm, his slick black skin sliding between her thick brown legs. He grunted his orgasm forcefully into the pillow beside her, and there was only a moment of peace, of heavy breathing and panting, before the police came crashing into the tiny studio apartment, guns drawn.

"Freeze!" Joe Taborelli yelled. "Don't you fucking move!"

But Tyree jumped up from the bed, was on his feet, disoriented. He was cornered, separated from Germaine. She cowered against a wall, covering herself with her hands, whimpering beneath the shadowy threat of Taborelli's partner. They had closed the door behind them and there was nowhere for her to flee. Taborelli holstered his gun and walked over to a very nervous Tyree, who stood with his hands raised, his eyes darting everywhere. He was short and muscular, his erection wilting by the second.

"Hey, Ty..." Taborelli said amiably.

"Whatchu want, man?" Tyree asked.

Taborelli punched him in the stomach hard, and Tyree fell to his knees, his head spinning, the wind knocked out of him. Germaine shrieked.

"Shut that bitch up!" Taborelli yelled to his partner, who immediately seized her by the throat. Her eyes bulged as she struggled to breathe.

Taborelli examined Tyree's clothing near the bed, dug into his jeans. "Lookee what we have here." Taborelli opened his hand. "Crack cocaine, wad of cash, two nickel bags. Possession with intent to sell, easily. You should never deal to an undercover cop, Ty. Bad business."

Tyree decided to run. After all, they wanted him, not Germaine. He made a dash for the bathroom where he could lock the door, grab a towel, and climb out the window. Taborelli was on him instantly, pushing him from behind. Tyree tripped and was sent head first into the bathtub. He lay bleeding a moment, before Taborelli lifted him, dragged him further into the bathroom, out of sight.

"Work with me, Ty," he said pushing the young man up against a wall. "Because you don't want it like I can give it to you."

Jackson's eyes banked with tears. "What do you want?"

"I need for you to cooperate with me," Taborelli said. "Or you see that curling iron over there? I'm going to turn it on and it's going to find its way inside your girl's still wet cunt. She'll never recover; you understand me? Or maybe we'll start with it up your ass."

Tyree was trembling, his face full of fear and hatred. Taborelli threw him to the floor, then stepped on the back of his neck. He pulled out his gun. "Now I want you to run out of this building, as hard and as fast as you can. And I don't want you to stop, even if I ask you nice."

*****

Two hours later, Adriana Esteban received a call in her office.

"I've got your killer."

"Who is this?"

"Joe Taborelli," he said, sounding out of breath. "He was dealing to one of our undercover narcs, and when the narc looked like he was going to stiff him for the cash, he bragged to him about putting some guy in the ocean with a knife in his heart. Does that fit for Costello?"

Adriana was silent. It was the last thing she was expecting to hear. "…yeah…"

"Anyways, we had to track the son of a bitch across four fucking roofs. I got a banged up knee and a broken fucking wrist out of it."

"Where are you now?" she asked, grabbing a pen.

"At St. Barnabas Memorial."

"Where's the perp?"

"He's here, too, but you'd better hurry," Taborelli said. "He took a spill off one of the roofs. They don't expect him to last through the hour."

******

"Where is he?" Esteban asked, arriving at the hospital. Traffic delayed her.

Taborelli nodded to a nearby room. "In there."

Esteban peered through a small window at Tyree Jackson. He was connected to a host of machines, surrounded by a pack of doctors, and looking as if he had done more than fall from a roof. He looked as if he hit every catwalk on the way down.

"How far did he fall?"

"Four stories," Taborelli said. "Trust me, he ain't got long."

"I'd better get in there and see him."

"No need, he can't talk."

Esteban glanced over her shoulder. "Maybe I can get a few words out of him. A confession maybe, or a nod."

"You don't understand, he can't *talk*. He chomped off his tongue on the fall down."

*****

Esteban stood over Tyree Jackson, with more than six doctors gathered around. They had allowed her in to conduct the briefest interview she would ever have in her career.

All I need is a nod, she told them. *I want to know for sure that I have the right guy.*

Tyree Jackson painfully opened his eyes as she called his name. He was heavily drugged, his eyes unfocused, oblivious to his broken ribs, the breaks in his arms and legs, the throbbing of his body as a whole.

She managed softly, "My name is Detective Adriana Esteban. I need to ask you a question."

Tyree's eyes shifted to Taborelli in the back of the room staring at him, and the evening came back to him in a bright, white-hot recognition. "Sorry, Ty," Taborelli had said to him earlier after he had pushed Jackson four stories onto a neighboring roof below.

When he reached Jackson, Taborelli lifted Tyree's head, reached inside his mouth and pulled out his tongue. He placed it between Tyree's teeth, and in one hard, swift move, kneed Tyree's jaw shut.

Tyree Jackson flatlined in front of Adriana Esteban. He was dead before he had a chance to deny that he had killed Nick Costello. Or had even known him at all.

WARREN COMES CLEAN

Warren was determined The Voice would hear him out. "I need a job," he said with conviction.

The Voice removed his glasses and looked up from the papers on his desk. "Are you here to waste my fucking time yet again?"

"You've already done this *Wizard of Oz* thing! I'm serious! I need work! I'll do whatever you want!"

The Voice leaned forward. "Bullshit on your own time, not on mine. Carl, get him out!"

Carl materialized from the shadows, taking his arm. Warren pushed him away hard. He turned to The Voice. "You can't do this! Please don't do this! Why did you even agree to see me?"

"Get him out of here, Carl!"

"I have something to tell you," Warren said urgently. He turned to Carl, who was now just behind him, then again to The Voice. "Send him away. I need to talk to you, PLEASE!"

The Voice looked up, Warren nearly on top of him. The Voice motioned Carl away.

"You have two seconds to say something impressive."

"I killed a man," Warren blurted out.

The Voice looked hard at Warren. He now had his full attention.

"It's true," Warren said, exhausted. "I killed a man."

*****

"Slow down, you're going to make yourself sick," The Voice warned, but Warren kept eating. The Voice had ordered in Chinese and told Warren to choose what he wanted from the menu.

"I'm sorry," he mumbled guiltily.

"Don't worry about it," The Voice said. "Just don't make yourself sick."

"I haven't eaten much in the last three days. The money you gave me and some money I stole, I'm saving. I try not to spend anything."

The Voice held on to that for a moment. He handed him a bottle of milk of magnesia. "I'm confident you're going to need that."

Warren held up the bottle and smiled. *"Gracias."*

There was a guest suite in the apartment. He brought Warren here for privacy. "What exactly is your ethnicity?"

"My father is Italian. My mother, *Cubana*."

The Voice took a seat on a sofa across from Warren. "They alive?"

"My mother died of cancer five years ago. My father ran out long before that."

"Were you their only child?"

"No. It was me and my twin sister Luna."

The Voice raised an eyebrow. "Luna…"

"Yeah, but me and my mother always called her Sass."

The Voice smiled and it was the first time Warren saw him do so without malice. "Why Sass?"

"That girl was always in the middle of trouble. When we were in school I was always in a fight because of her. My mother would have killed me if she didn't come home in one piece."

"So it's Luna and Warren Cassie."

"No," Warren corrected. He paused out of embarrassment. "It's Luna and Leonardo Suarez. My real name is Leonardo, but people call me Leo. My middle name is Warren."

"And Cassie?"

"My mother's name was Cassandra Suarez."

The Voice grunted his acknowledgement. "So how are you here in Rehoboth?"

Warren looked down. "Like I said, I killed a man."

"By accident?"

"*Si.*"

"You prefer speaking in Spanish?"

Warren shrugged. "You speak Spanish?"

"*Un poquito.* Between Los Angeles and New York, you pick up a few things."

They both smiled.

"Tell me what happened. Who was this man you killed?"

"My sister's ex-boyfriend raped her and I walked in on it," Warren said, losing his appetite at the memory. "It was all my fault," he said, pushing the food away.

"How is that your fault?"

"I was tired," Warren said. "I was 20 years old and tired. My mother, my sister and me, we all lived in the house I grew up in. My mother was sick with cancer and I quit school to go to work. My sister only worked part time. We had no insurance and my mother didn't have long to live. I resented everything. My friends were all out partying, having a good time, and here I was working double shifts, taking care of the bills, and the house, and my mother, and my sister." Warren breathed deep, glad to talk to someone.

"At the end, I just wanted my mother's death to be quick. I didn't want her to suffer anymore. More than that, *I* didn't want to suffer anymore. She stayed alive for two more years, and then she was gone. Some time before that, this guy comes by the garage where I'm working. His name was Nick Costello. He and his brothers Frank and Mario owned car washes around the city. After my mother died, I figured this would be a great way to get Luna out of the house. I could finally live a little myself. So I looked the guy up, set up a date, and the next thing I know Luna's pregnant. Turns out Nicky and his brothers are nothing but thugs, running drugs through the car washes. They approached me to be in on it and I said no. Too dangerous."

"I don't take it that these Costello brothers were big time if they're dealing drugs out of car washes."

"Second rate all the way. Frank is the front man, because he's a smooth pretty-boy. Mario is the brain because he actually is very smart. Nick was the muscle. They all thought they were out of *The Godfather* or something. Wore suits every day. Threw around money. Fucked everything on two legs. Luna confronts Nick about the drugs and there's this big blow up. She picks up their son and leaves Miami."

"How did he wind up with your sister again?"

"She came back home," Warren said. "Somehow Nick found out and broke into our house and tried to kill her."

"And then you killed him."

"He was still in the house when I got home from work, on top of her. We got into a fight; he pulled a gun. I grabbed a knife. The next thing I know, it's in his chest and he's dead."

The Voice stood. "Where is your sister now?"

"We have a cousin in San Jose. I'm sure if Frank and Mario haven't figured out that I killed their brother, they will soon. They'll come looking for us I'm sure. It's why I need your help."

The Voice looked at Warren.

"Tell you what. I will help you, but only if you work for your money. Business is business. You make your decision and get back to me. Good luck, *amigo*."

BROTHER TO BROTHER

"Sorry I'm staring," Griffin said, amused. "It's just that I haven't seen a great deal of African-Americans down here."

Jarvis smiled. "I know what you mean."

Dallas was late for his shift at Cedar House, and Griffin struck up a conversation with Jarvis in the library as he waited for Jarrett to tie up some loose ends upstairs before their dinner date.

"I had no idea Jarrett had a new friend."

"He didn't tell you about me?" Griffin asked, assessing Jarvis. "I'm a publisher for Walsh."

"You're kidding," Jarvis said brightening. "You're one of *those* Walshes?"

Griffin nodded. "What do you do?"

"Law student. Another year and I'll be done."

"You enjoying Rehoboth?" Griffin asked.

"Jury's still out on that," Jarvis said. "I'm something of a homebody, anyway."

"You don't go out, a good-looking guy like yourself?"

"Trust me, I'm not on anybody's list."

"I find that hard to believe," Griffin said. When Jarvis did not reply, Griffin walked over to him. "I know it's none of my business, but please tell me you're not hanging out in this house because you're afraid of something."

Jarvis didn't answer.

"Don't do that," Griffin whispered. "Don't let the fact that you're one of a few of us here stop you from enjoying the town or your summer."

"I'm not," Jarvis said. "I'm sure others go through this. You look around and there you are in the middle of a room the only one, or one of a few…"

"Very homogenized, I know." Griffin held out his hand to Jarvis as they heard Jarrett running down the stairs. "You keep living. Don't let anyone ever stop you from doing that. It's foolish, and it's pointless."

The two shook hands, and then Griffin pulled him for a hug that he instinctively knew Jarvis needed. Griffin went to Jarrett. "Ready?"

"In a minute."

Griffin turned to Jarvis. "We'll see each other again."

"I'm sure."

"He's fantastic," Jarrett said to Jarvis, stopping at the door as Griffin walked to the car.

Jarvis followed Jarrett to the porch. "Having fun?"

Jarrett nodded. "Makes me wonder what I did to deserve him."

Jarvis smirked. "Getting looks yet?"

"A few," Jarrett shrugged, "but you've got to learn to ignore it. Listen, I gotta run. Tell my dad I couldn't wait. We have reservations."

"Will do," Jarvis said, watching Jarrett pile into Griffin's car. When they sped away, he turned back to the house and was surprised to see Dallas at the screen door, his face burning with something that looked like jealousy. He had entered the house through the back door.

"No need to deliver the message, Jarvis," Dallas said. "I heard it all."

THE SNAKE PIT

It was night when David and his housemates all packed into his Jeep for a trip into Rehoboth. Pat, Edgar, Thom, Ken, Blake and David had been sitting around drinking beers, watching baseball, feeling antsy and restless. A conversation started about Rehoboth, which prompted this excursion.

"There," David said. He parked the vehicle, a block from Poodle Beach and sat back so they all could see.

Coming off the boardwalk were two men in their thirties, holding hands. One was blonde in a sweatshirt and shorts, the other brown haired and in jeans and a long sleeved t-shirt.

"I can't believe this!" Blake said, leaning forward to see. "Do they all do that, I mean right out in the open?"

"You asking *me*?" David sniped. "*You're* the one who wanted to come down here."

"Damned, look at them now!" Pat said, pointing.

The two men had stopped to kiss below a streetlamp.

"That is so fucking off the wall," Thom said, his stark blue eyes searing with hatred. "How fucking pathetic is that?" As the two neared, Thom rolled down the window. "Good evening, ladies. Either of you interested in sucking a great big juicy cock?"

"Thom!" Pat yelled from the back. Blake sank out of sight. "Oh, shit!"

The couple stopped and glared at the men in the jeep.

Thom made kissing noises, and when the two didn't move he said, "You girls got something to say?" He jumped out of the jeep and approached the men.

"Thom!" Pat called but to no avail. David sat quietly, looking straight ahead.

"You bumping pussies tonight, ladies?" Thom sneered.

"Leave us alone!" barked the blonde.

"Who the fuck are you talking to, faggot?" Thom said, and then he spat in their direction.

The blonde's partner turned for a moment and whirled back, pushing Thom against David's jeep. Blake, Pat, Ken, and Edgar all jumped out of the vehicle. When they got to Thom, the blonde had him by the throat.

"Get off him!" Pat ordered, but the couple seemed disinterested in giving up this fight.

David did not move; he simply sat and watched. When Pat grabbed the blonde, the couple retreated back to the boardwalk, chased by Pat and Ken, yelling to them: *Faggots! Pussies!* Thom was leaning heavily against the hood of the jeep.

Pat returned. "They're going to get the police! Blake! Edgar! C'mon, we gotta go!"

They piled back into the vehicle, and David started the jeep, turned it around, and began to head back to Dewey Beach. Thom sat seething with rage beside him. While everyone else sat cursing the two men, David sat quietly, checking the rear-view mirror for a police car. That's when he saw Griffin and Jarrett on the patio of Griffin's home eating ice cream. At first he was shocked, a mad rush of adrenaline pumping through his veins. He put his foot on the gas and sped by them, watching as he drove past, as he remembered the party, the fight, his embarrassment. He felt a rage bubble up from the pit of his stomach, so strong it nearly choked him.

David checked the mirror again, his fists wrapped white-knuckled on the steering wheel. They were gone from sight now, dots vanished into the night. At an intersection, he saw a wall full of graffiti and something came to him. By the time he returned home, he knew exactly what revenge to take against Griffin Walsh and Jarrett Hemingway.

In David's book, it would be exactly what they deserved.

THOSE WHO TRESPASS AGAINST US

Frank and Mario Costello caught Ed Baker alone for a private interrogation. Baker was a 63-year-old Vietnam veteran, a chain smoker who was white haired and frail. He had owned Baker's Garage since returning home from the war in the mid-seventies and until recently Leo had been one of his favorite employees. Baker's car was parked out back, and as he closed the shop for the night the brothers emerged from the shadows to seize and drag him back into the office of the garage.

"What do you want?" Baker yelled.

Mario anchored him by his shoulders into a chair, as Frank leaned down into his face. "I don't want to hurt you, old man, but I will. Where is Leo?"

Baker had never liked any of the Costello brothers. To him they were thugs, phonies who knew nothing about respect or hard work. He rolled his eyes at Frank's insolence. Frank slapped Ed Baker hard, leaving a handprint on his face.

"We don't have time for this," Mario said to Frank. He took Baker by the wrist and yanked him from the chair, throwing him down to his knees on the hard cement floor. Mario grabbed a drill from a nearby worktable, plugged it in and squeezed the trigger. The tool whirred to life. Mario splayed Baker's hand against a wall, and placed the point of the drill at its center. "Now, I'm going to ask you the same question, soldier boy. If you don't answer *me*, you're going to be using your Medicare card for more than just Viagra."

Baker was terrified now, his body shaking uncontrollably.

"Where the fuck is Leo Suarez?" Frank screamed.

Baker panted nervously, sheet white.

Mario squeezed the trigger and at first, Ed Baker felt nothing but the white-hot sting of the drill, heard the high-pitched whine. Then he felt the metal cut into his skin, the drill digging into the bones of his hand. His blood, warm and plentiful, rushed down his wrist. He screeched. The drill stopped.

Mario turned to him. "Talk!"

"*Please…!*" Baker tried to free himself.

"Talk, dammit–!"

"I don't know where he is!"

Mario pulled the trigger again, fully this time. It was loud and furious.

"*Leave me alone!*" Baker begged.

Mario leaned the drill into Baker's wound and the old man almost passed out from the pain.

"*Stop! Stop!*"

Mario clasped Baker's throat. "The next time we do this, it's going to be through your fucking eyeball!"

Baker broke down. "He stole money! He left a note!"

Mario tossed Baker aside. "*He stole money?* That doesn't tell me shit!"

"I don't *know* where is!" Baker was crumpled on the floor, nursing his hand.

Frank and Mario Costello forced Ed Baker to give them the note Leo left. Neither liked what it said.

FLAMINGO ROAD

Mario Costello had a theory. It was obvious Nick had found out Luna was in town and had come to the Suarez house. Leo must have been there and during a fight, Leo stabbed him. Nick would have driven there himself. Leo drove as well. Four bodies, two cars. If Leo wanted to protect his sister and her son, he would have told her to get out right away, pack a bag, take his car and go. He would know the police could never have protected his family from the Costello brothers. That left Leo and Nick together. Leo would want to dispose of Nick's body and get rid of his car. He would not have wanted to be connected with the vehicle, to have it traced to another state, leaving a clue of where he was or might be going. This could only mean one thing.

"Where are we headed?" Frank asked.

"To The Flamingo."

"For what?" Frank was indignant.

"Leo had Nick's car, I'm sure. Probably dumped it somewhere to be stripped and took the license plate off so it couldn't be identified, which means he left town by foot. Only a moron would have taken the bus or the train. That's the first place police would go if they found out he was connected to Nicky's murder."

"What about a car from Baker's? He could just as easily have taken one of those."

Mario shook his head. "Uh-uh. Traceable. They keep lists. Owners. License plates."

Frank was confused. "So what does The Flamingo have to do with this?"

Mario turned to his brother, resenting the fact that Frank was pretty but stupid.

"He certainly didn't fly commercial first-class. I think he hitched. The Flamingo is the last stop out of town before you hit the highway. It's a diner but it's also a meat-rack pick-up joint. A place where you can go to hook up. Certainly a place I'd go if I were in a rush out of town and looking for somebody to spot me a ride."

"With Luna?"

"No, he wouldn't be with her. He doesn't want her to be found even if he is."

Inside The Flamingo, they approached the counter with a photo of Leo they'd taken from the Suarez house. The waitresses had taken immediate notice of Frank when he entered, and they gathered round as he showed them the picture.

"Excuse me," he said. "I was wondering if you ladies could help me out a little."

"No, I don't think I've seen him," a buxom bottle blonde said, sidling up to him. "He's cute, but not as cute as you," she finished, giving Frank an inviting smile. While Frank was enjoying the attention, Mario noticed a petite brunette frowning at the photo. Mario gave Frank a nod that told him what to do.

"You recognize him?" Frank asked, sliding the picture against the counter so his hand rested against hers.

"Couple of months ago, maybe," she said, and then looked behind Frank at the owner Jules Petros, who had noticed Frank, Mario and the girls.

"What's going on here?" Petros asked. He was a burly man with dark hair.

"I was asking these lovely ladies if they've seen my friend." Frank held up the picture to Jules. "Have you?" Jules glanced at the photo, and Frank saw a look of recognition blow through his eyes.

"Never seen him," Jules lied.

"You sure?" Frank asked, giving him a long look.

"You a cop or a bookie, which?"

"I'm just looking for a friend, is all."

"And you got your answer. You see that clock on the wall? You're taking up my girls' time and I got a business to run. Buy a drink or get out."

Frank lost his pretense. "Look, pal, I don't like your attitude."

Jules looked at Frank's pretty face and dismissed him. He pointed his middle finger. "Look, *pal*, you don't have to like my attitude in *my* joint, especially when you're the one asking questions. Now either you order something or get out. You're taking up space." He turned to his waitresses. "As for you *ladies*"—he did rabbit ears here—"it's time for you to get back to work."

He clapped his hands and they dispersed like pigeons.

*****

Jules Petros left The Flamingo that night by the back door. It was late, but as owner he always made sure to personally count the final take. It had been a long day; so much so he had already forgotten about his earlier meeting with Frank and Mario.

"Hey, *pal*!" he heard as he walked to his car.

The parking lot was full of cars but empty of people, and Jules turned to see Frank approaching out of the darkness. He walked up to Jules and slapped his face so hard, Jules' neck crackled. Petros recovered slowly, one hand clinging to his car, the other on his cheek.

"What the fuck?" Jules flared, but Frank aimed a gun at his face.

"When I ask you a question, I expect an honest answer!"

Jules carried a gun, but knew he wouldn't be fast enough to retrieve it. "What do you want?"

"I asked you a question. I want the right answer this time."

"Jesus Christ! I told you I don't fucking know anything!"

Frank shook his head and lowered his gun. "I asked you nicely, twice. Now I ask you not so nicely."

Jules heard movement from behind him. Mario swung a tire iron against his lower back, and Jules stiffened as if struck by lightening. His face reddened, his eyes bulging, and he slammed down to his knees, and then his face. His bladder released.

They callously turned him over. Frank put his gun in Jules's mouth while Mario held the photo of Leo before his eyes. Frank said, "Now, I'll ask you again. Have you seen my friend?"

Jules could not speak, could not move the air in his throat. His heart was thumping in his chest.

Frank pulled back the hammer of the gun, the echo resonating in Jules's mouth. Jules moaned, trying to speak. Frank extracted the gun, but rested the barrel at his right eye.

Petros whispered through the pain, "Was here…with girl."

Frank looked at Mario, then back to Jules. "Long black hair?"

The pain at the base of Jules's spine was excruciating. "No…red hair…gold car…NY plates…BMW. She came in complaining…oil…leaking oil. Was at Baker's…they did it wrong…he helped her…they left together."

Frank looked at Mario. A smile erupted across his face. "Baker's," he said.

Mario nodded. "Traceable. They keep lists."

THE AWFUL TRUTH

Someone thought Adriana Esteban was stupid. Someone believed she was a fool. During her career, there had been moments of self-doubt for the detective. In her line of work, it seemed an occupational hazard. Everything was a question with no neat answer. For the last few days she'd felt that something was not quite right about the Nick Costello murder, that things simply did not add up. Adriana knew that she was strong, perceptive and intelligent. And although she would be loath to admit it in public, it was plain to her that she sometimes struggled to remember those important qualities about herself. When she was uncertain, she forced herself to breath, to rely on her faith, to remember that she was loved by *Jesus Cristo*, by her mother and father, by a good and beautiful woman at home. Her Sonya. None of *them* wanted to see her fail.

She was in her car, eyes closed, meditating, concentrating hard. She filled her lungs with so much air it hurt, and then let it all go, her insecurities and her troubling thoughts. Now she was Detective Adriana Esteban, clearheaded and sharp. A proud Latina. She would figure out the puzzle of this case. First, she had something to do, an appointment to keep. She opened her eyes.

The scene before her was grim and unnerving. She had received an important call from her informant. This was his territory. He had instructed her to come quickly; he had something to show her. She sat now at the mouth of one of Miami's roughest *barrios*. She was flanked by boarded up properties on either side of this street, dilapidated structures, cavities of blackness in this night. At the opposite end of this cul-de-sac stood darkened houses, crooked like teeth against a purple sky. The street itself was strangely empty, but Adriana knew better. This run-down, garbage-strewn development was home to runaway gangbangers, prostitutes, teen squatters, callboys, and pushers. Now it was deserted, as if out of an old western. Everyone knew she was coming. Ramon had put out the word.

Adriana stepped from her car. No gun, no wire, no radio, no back up. That was the deal. She hooked her thumbs behind the lapels of her jacket. She peeled them open to reveal that she was clean and hid nothing. She had taken years to build trust with Ramon. She would not ruin it now. The street was devoid of much lighting, only three of the seven street lamps were lit. This once up and coming neighborhood, a casualty of 80's drug trafficking and 90's desertion, now resembled a large back alley. She walked down the street. There came back to her no echo of her steps, and she knew, from the shadows, unseen eyes watched her. Ramon's Roaches, as he called them. Many of them armed, some of them underage, none of them visible.

"*Mira!*" called a voice after she had come more than halfway, then two snaps. Adriana saw a hand to her right, out of the shadows of a doorway, waving her over. "*Entre aqui! Rapido!*"

She moved cautiously to the cracked curb, down the disheveled lane, to the front door of a house spoiled with the stench of piss and garbage and ejaculate. Her heart pounded and her mouth dried. She thought that perhaps she had made the wrong decision, and that she should have insisted on coming with someone. She stepped into the house. It was too late to retreat.

"Stop there," she heard. She was a foot or two inside the doorway, and there was a voice, Ramon's, soft but commanding, seductive and comforting.

"Ramon." She did not turn to face him.

"*Hola,*" he said through the darkness, from behind her.

"*Hola, chico.*"

Two Roaches came out of nowhere, startling her, one white, one black. They frisked her efficiently, coldly, never making eye contact. They were clothed in bandanas, baseball caps, large jerseys and jeans.

"She cool," reported one, his young face hard and angry. The two were dismissed.

"*Como estas, mi hermana?*" Ramon said affectionately, as if to family.

He called Adriana his sister for many reasons. They had known each other for as long as she had been a detective, when he was fifteen and had suffered his first arrest. A numbers runner at that time. Later for hustling, petty theft, pushing, assault. He knew she was *lesbiana* and she knew he kept a number of guys as part-time lovers. She remembered him as a young *cubano* in Little Havana's streets earning respect. Now, six years later, he did not allow her to look at him. His beautiful brown face, his thick and desired body, were now memories of a former self. His blood was poison to him now. His days were numbered.

"*Bien, y usted?*" Adriana asked.

"Not good," Ramon replied. She knew he spoke of his health.

"You called for me…"

"*Si*. There is something you need to see. Go forward."

Adriana frowned. "*Adonde?*"

"*A la puerta…*"

Ahead, there was a doorway in the darkness. "Where am I going?" she asked.

"Down," Ramon said. He was just behind her now, still shadowed.

She turned slightly and whispered, "What's down here, Ramon?"

"You will see," he answered.

They descended into the belly of the house. It was bare, cleaner than the floor above. Old, unused plumbing and boilers occupied one corner, in another a mattress, a chair, a table, and a lamp. It was obvious to Adriana what went on in this room. On the bed was a body, covered with a white sheet.

"My Roaches found her. She was dropped off at the corner. Car door opened, somebody threw her out. They kept rolling."

"What type of car?"

"Maybe a Cadillac."

"Was she–?"

"No. She was alive, but barely. She didn't have on no clothes. She looked like she had been attacked. And she was high."

"How high?"

"Sky high. Enough to kill her."

Adriana turned to Ramon. She could only see his silhouette. He stood tall still, his hands shoved into his puffed jacket, his baseball cap askew.

"What do you mean enough to kill her?"

Ramon nodded toward the body. "Look. You'll see everything."

Adriana hesitated, turned, and then went to the body. She lifted the sheet.

"*Dios mio.*" The detective was shocked. The woman w800 an addict, or had been. Her mouth was caked, lips cracked. Her face was ashen and had two black eyes.

"I know her..." Adriana said, as if in a dream.

"Germaine Smith," Ramon said.

"Tyree Jackson's girlfriend. She disappeared after he died. Her sister is looking for her."

"When she fell out the car," Ramon continued, "she scratching her arms so bad we had to tie her down. Smack. Lots of it. She was already going cold."

Adriana pulled back the sheet to reveal Germaine's arms. Both were white with needle tracks, scratched and scabbed. Esteban closed her eyes, furious.

"I think she was...you know...attacked. She was bleeding when we found her."

Adriana opened her eyes, frowned at that. She pulled down the sheet further. The insides of Germaine's thighs were bruised. She had been raped many times. Adriana replaced the sheet. She sighed wearily, and with effort she faced Ramon. Pieces of a large puzzle, larger than she had realized, fell into place.

"We tried to save her," he said, "but you can only do so much when they're that far gone."

Esteban was seething. "She was murdered..."

Ramon paused, then: "*Si...*"

Adriana pointed behind her. "This girl—woman!—was *murdered*!" Tears came to her from below, a furnace raging now in the pit of her chest. "Murdered!"

Ramon surprised Adriana Esteban then. He stepped from the shadows into the light. His face was skeletal, the skin pulled tight against his skull. His eyes, red and glassy, were sunken inside his head. He was ashen and thin. Yet, his eyes were defiant, challenged any comment on his condition.

"Someone killed her, because she knew too much. What everybody knows but is too afraid to say. And I'm too weak now to say it out loud, in the street."

"What, *papa?*"

"Tyree sold, but he ain't kill nobody. He was afraid of *me*, me as I am now. And he was on the other side of town!" Ramon paused, then said, "The both of them, they was murdered."

CUANDO NADIE ME VE

The Voice poured Warren a glass of red wine. They were eating again at his apartment. This time Warren ate slowly, taking stock of the things he ate and drank, of his surroundings.

The Voice put down his fork, wiped his mouth. "Look, I realize you came to tell me your decision. If it is not what I want, just say it. This life isn't for everyone."

Warren's eyes were distant, his mind riding some train of thought.

"I got all these things I thought you would like," The Voice said. "There's chicken, vegetables, salad, beef, rice, bread and butter, dessert, wine. Soda, if you want that."

"I'm not a kid," Warren mumbled.

The Voice leaned back in his chair.

"Are you happy with all this, *senor*?" Warren asked, indicating the room, the apartment, the pretty boys at his beck and call. "Was it worth selling your soul?"

The Voice frowned. "I think you need to explain yourself."

"What's there to explain? You have everything and I have nothing."

"And you think I sold my soul for it?"

Warren shrugged.

"Yes, I sold my soul. To God, to the Devil, to anybody that would have it. To stay *alive*. You have choices to make in this life, and sometimes you pick from what's in front of you on the table."

"You could have gotten a regular job."

"I guess I could have," The Voice chuckled. "But I didn't, because I wanted more. And to get more you have to get your hands dirty. You pay for your happiness, up front or on the back end. That's just the way life works."

"And have you paid for yours?" Warren asked dryly.

"You're damned right I've paid for mine." The Voice leaned across the table, his eyes boring into Warren. "With my ass. Up front, *every* time."

"Now you expect me to pay for mine," Warren said. "Isn't that what this dinner is all about? To break me into the business so you can get your cut, whatever that is?"

The Voice threw Warren a look of contempt. "Do you know why I have you here? It is to make you *see*, because you're so incredibly blind. It is to make you stop your pathetic whining. It is to take that pitiful look off your face. To teach you how to be resourceful, to make something out of nothing, even after you've fucked up and you think you have no other options. It is to make you realize you *have* options. It is to teach you how to stay alive at any cost, to be strong, and to realize that whatever happens, whatever decisions you make in order to keep your head above water, it is between you and your God. It is for your sister and your nephew that I do this. It's for *you*, despite you. It's because—"

The Voice stopped himself, stood and walked away from Warren.

"It's because I see myself in you, cliché as it sounds. Trouble behind me, trouble in front of me, wishing I had someone to tell me what to do. I do this because I like you, Warren. I see you as this little boy sometimes when you're here, a kid who needs understanding and guidance, a firm hand and protection. You need someone to tell you, to show you, how life really is. And how to beat the odds anyway."

The Voice sighed and sat back down in his chair. He did not look at Warren, as they sat in silence for a very long time, each lost in his own thoughts. After nearly thirty minutes, Warren stood quietly, methodically, and removed his shirt. Then his jeans and shoes. Then his underwear. The Voice looked up at him, startled.

"You wanted my answer. Here it is."

CUANDO NADIE ME VE, PART II

"Is this what you wanted?" Warren said. "To make me like you?"

The Voice turned away. "I just want you to learn how to take your lumps."

"I know how to take lumps! I been doing it all my fucking life!"

"You're here on my doorstep, so you're obviously not doing it well enough!"

"*Fuck you!* I'm standing here naked, ain't I?" Warren walked around the table until he stood in front of The Voice. "My body's good enough to sell, isn't it!" It wasn't a question; they both knew the answer.

"Put your clothes on," The Voice said agitated, feeling the conversation slipping away from him. If only Warren knew the responsibility he felt for him. So many boys came through his employ, scared, in trouble, wanting his help. Then comes Warren, a diamond in the rough and so different from all of them. Yes, he had killed someone, but he was not here to live the easy life of a vapid trophy boy or an escort. Warren was here to save his family, to save himself, except he really didn't know it yet. It was clear to The

Voice that he and Warren were now playing the tug of war of father and son. The son does not see the lessons his father has to teach him. To the father, it could not be more frustrating. He himself has been in this position, sees both sides of the coin. To the father it is a necessary love and a tough one.

Warren shook his head, clearly upset. *"Que quieres?* I'm showing you why you should hire me. Here it is. *Mi verga, mi nalga.* You want to sell it? Here it is!"

"Stop it!"

"You're a pervert!"

The Voice stood. The words hurt. "You're afraid! You're afraid to take the risks needed in order to survive! At the rate you're going, you'll be dead by the end of summer! You need to change! You need to realize with life comes hard choices and hard decisions to back them up! You NEED to CHANGE!"

"To be like you?"

"No, to be like *you*!" The Voice yelled, turning on him angrily. "A better version of you! Stronger! You have a choice!"

"I don't have a choice! I *never* have a choice!" Warren backed up against a wall. He was losing his composure. "Nothing belongs to me!"

"What will happen when you leave here, Warren? When you leave this house and run off to God knows where? What will happen to your sister, your nephew, when you have to face another hard crisis and I'm not around to bail you out?"

Warren started to cry. "Just give me some money, *PLEASE!*"

The Voice turned away, hating to see him suffer like this. He started to give him money, a thousand dollars, and yell at him to get lost. He said, "No, Warren. No…"

Warren was becoming hysterical. "You just want to fuck me, that's all!"

"That's enough!" The Voice barked. He slapped Warren hard, once then again. He pushed him against a wall. "Stop it right now!"

Warren covered his face, shaking so badly he was barely able to speak. "I'm a mechanic and a dropout and a murderer! And you want to take the last thing that I have! I *have* nothing else! I have no pride! I fucked up my life! My mother is ashamed!" The Voice went to him, took him in his arms. Warren cried into his shoulder. The Voice saw a throw blanket and wrapped it around Warren, then sat him on a nearby sofa.

The Voice stroked his hair gently. "Being a man is a lot harder than people think it is."

Warren continued to cry and did not stop until he had wept out every ounce of frustration. The two sat in silence for a long while. Finally, Warren looked over at The Voice and said quietly, "You're right. This is my choice. And my choice is that I'm going to work for you." Warren was nearly hoarse as he wiped the tears from his eyes and face. "I need to change. I need to protect my family. I need to earn who I am."

DETECTIVE WORK

"What you're looking for is in here," Ed Baker said. "But I'd be careful. Rats."

Mario tossed him easily into the room. "That's why *you're* going to do it for us."

The Costello brothers had returned to Baker's, requesting his log of jobs dating back to January. He was nervous but compliant and led them to a small room filled with metal file cabinets and cardboard boxes.

"What are you looking for?" Baker asked.

Mario frowned. "That's an easy way to lose some teeth." He went over to Baker and gave his injured hand a healthy squeeze. "How's that hand of yours?" Baker buckled and dropped to his knees. "You just don't get it do you? *No* questions."

Frank yelled, "I got it!"

Mario went to him. Frank pointed.

"That's here in town," Mario said. "Bring it."

Mario returned to Ed Baker, who was still on his knees nursing his hand. He raised his chin. "No questions, pops. And no loose lips." His eyes scrutinized the room. "This place could burn to the ground tomorrow and you'd have nothing. I'd light the match myself."

Baker looked away, terrified for Leo. After they'd gone, someone touched his shoulder. It was Adriana Esteban. She had been hiding in the very back of the room.

"You did the right thing calling me," she said. "They won't hurt you again. I won't let them."

*****

Frank located a number on the ledger sheet, dialed it on his cell. He hung up a moment later.

"What did they say?" asked Mario.

"Some place called Cedar Manor, in South Beach," Frank answered.

*****

Frank called back to Cedar Manor; Mario drove, listening.

"Hello," said a kindly voice, female.

"Hi, I'm calling from Baker's Garage and I was wondering if I might speak to Stephanie Newcomer. She came in to see us about an oil job a little while back. She was a little concerned about leaking oil and I wanted to follow up."

"I remember that," the woman exclaimed. "Some time ago, if I remember correctly."

"I know, I know. We've been really busy here at the shop and I just ran across her number on my desk. Thought I'd give her a call anyway to check in."

"And you said your name was?"

"Uh, Martin..." Frank said. "Martin Summers."

"Well, Mr. Summers, Stephanie's no longer here with us–"

"Really? Did she leave?" Frank said feigning surprise. Mario looked at him and rolled his eyes. Frank gave him the finger. "Then I guess she must've been okay."

"Oh, yes. She left here without a problem at all, I'd say."

"Great! I guess she was headed back to New York then."

"No, she's staying at one of our other locations."

"*Oh...?*" Frank said sweetly, and Mario sucked his teeth and chuckled. Frank pointed at him angrily, signaling him to be quiet.

"She's at our Rehoboth Beach location, Cedar House. Would you like the number there?"

"Well, if she got off okay, I don't see the need really," Frank said. "But then again on second thought, maybe I should give her a call just to follow up." He snapped his fingers, motioning for Mario to hand him a pen. When he finally ended the call, he turned to his brother with a big grin on his face.

"Good news?" Mario asked.

"Good news, indeed."

Adriana Esteban was not far behind.

GIRL, INTERRUPTED

Adriana Esteban did not like it one bit. They really did think she was stupid. That she was a fool. *Muy estupido, Adriana! Muy estupido!* she thought. Because of her, two innocent people were dead and one was maimed. Because of her a number of lives could be at stake. She had been suspicious of the Costello brothers since their initial interview. She sensed they had been hiding something, their stories not making sense. Yet, all her questioning of girlfriends, family members, and acquaintances led to dead ends with no one saying anything substantial. It was because everyone seemed so tight-lipped, so intent on *not* talking to her, that Esteban was convinced there was something to know. Uncovering it, however, was a different story. Nick's driving record was clean and surveillance of the businesses came back fruitless. Costello's employees were indeed loyal to the family. They said nothing and were extremely mistrustful of her. The only trouble Nick Costello had with the law seemed to be an extended string of assault charges starting in his youth. Three battery charges in barroom brawls, two assault charges in his teen years, a domestic dispute with his brother Frank, property damage to a car, two reckless endangerment charges, aggravated assault in a supermarket, and an assault charge in a gym. Things that actually made Adriana's job harder, not easier. It was not a stretch to believe that Tyree Jackson, or anyone, had murdered Nick Costello. But it was Ramon showing her Germaine Smith's body that put everything into perspective.

Esteban's first misstep was that she had been dismissive of claims by Tyree's family that he would never have killed anyone, that he was just another black man being made into an example by a racist police force. Adriana saw it as the natural attempts to salvage some part of Tyree's character. When questioned on Tyree pushing drugs to neighborhood teens, the entire family fell silent. There were no clean hands where he was concerned. Her second misstep was ignoring the tearful sobs of Charlitta Smith that her sister Germaine would never have run away or be involved in a murder. When a reporter asked if Germaine had profited from Tyree's sale of drugs, the family's lawyer called the questioning inappropriate, but still the damage was done. Finding Germaine with heroin pumping through her veins would have made perfect sense. And whoever set it all up knew it. Looking at her body and hearing Ramon's words, Adriana knew then that this had all been part of an elaborate cover-up sponsored by the Costello brothers to conceal the real identity of their brother's murderer. *He was dealing to one of our undercover narcs. It was a long drop. He chomped off his tongue on the fall down.* At least four officers had corroborated that report.

Adriana knew she could not trust anyone in the department. The corruption went too deep. Solving this case rested squarely on her shoulders. She could not let anyone under the Costello's influence know that she was on to them. With Tyree's death, the matter of Nick Costello's murder had been closed. She behaved as such, busying herself with other cases. Secretly, she dug to discover the link between the Costellos and their brother's murderer, and why they wished to keep this a secret. Was his death due to some illegal activity, or was it something more pedestrian? After all, the murder weapon was a kitchen knife. She got her answer from Ed Baker, and then all the pieces fit perfectly. His initial contact was anonymous, and came a week after her meeting with Ramon. He told her about Frank and Mario, about the disappearance of Leo and Luna Suarez, the note Leo left, the money he took. He didn't know where the twins were, but was certain the brothers were after them, particularly Leo.

Working with this new information, Adriana sought to outwit the brothers. She asked Ramon for a favor: *Who buries your people, papa?* and he told her: *Joseba Puente buries all my people.* Adriana photographed Germaine Smith. *We need to take her there. No one can know she's dead, and no one can tamper with her. She's evidence.*

Adriana hid out at Baker's, knowing the brothers would return. He was the closest thing they had to a lead on Suarez. Now, she was tailing them through Miami traffic after their visit to Ed Baker. She deduced the twins were probably not together, that Leo would have wanted to get Luna to safety, that by their visit to Baker, the brothers believed someone helped them escape. All she had to do now was follow the brothers at a safe distance and they would lead her to at least Leo Suarez. Once all three were in custody, she would find out Luna's whereabouts and get the whole story from there.

Esteban frowned when the Costello brothers turned off of FL-968 W to FL-968 E, and then from Miami Avenue to I-95N going out of town. The traffic was now much heavier. She tried to remain inconspicuous, even when the brothers made a sudden turn onto the I-95 HOV LN N exit. When Adriana tried to follow she was cut off by a large yellow Hummer. She leaned on the horn. The driver honked back angrily, a divider between her and the brothers. She ran to the Hummer and slammed her badge against the window. The driver's eyes widened. He tried to find a way out of the traffic jam, and when he couldn't, he raised his hands.

"Sorry," he mouthed.

"SHIT!" Adriana Esteban yelled, looking around frantically.

The Costello brothers were nowhere in sight.

BOOK THREE
the unspeakable

The supreme irony of life is that hardly anyone gets out of it alive.

Robert Heinlein

III.

Leo knew the Costello brothers had once blinded a man by pouring bleach into his eyes. He knew they had once punished another man for withholding drug money by burning his testicles with a lighter. But who could blame him for allowing Luna to return here? Miami was the only home she knew, and he the only close family she had outside of her son. He was her protector, or so he thought. Looking down on Nick Costello's body, he knew now that he had been wrong to think the matter between his sister and Costello had blown over. That thinking he could move on with his life and leave her alone was the biggest mistake he had ever made.

He had shoved Luna upstairs with Buddy and told them not to come down until they were all packed and ready to leave. He had things to take care of before they left. There was the knife in Nick Costello's heart, which he needed to remove in order to get the body wrapped in sheets and out of the house. He pulled, and the knife made a sickening sound. Blood squirt on his face, and marked his hands and shirt and pants. He took the blade and wrapped it in a towel, then Nick in several sheets. Afterwards, he wiped down the walls and floors, and straightened the furniture. He ran upstairs screaming at his sister, telling her to hurry, but she was catatonic and Buddy was crying. The only way he got her to move, after being beaten, after being raped, was to throw her into a cold shower and slap her face repeatedly.

She seemed to come around, to realize the urgency of the matter. Even with Nick dead, damage could still be done. Mario was very handy with fire and explosives, and he or his brother Frank would love to have a piece of Luna. He put them in his car, threw their bags into the trunk, gave her all the money he had, and told her to head back to San Jose to stay with their cousin. Luna cried. Buddy cried. He cried too, hugging them both. Then he screamed at them to get the hell out of town.

He would leave town as well, would need money to get him far away and then all three into Mexico. He searched Costello's jacket and found one hundred dollars. How he got the body into Costello's car without being seen was a miracle. Hoisting it out of his yard, through the shadows of the back alley, he managed to speed the car away and to Baker's Garage. He wrote a note to Ed and took the $150 petty cash kept on the premises. He then drove Nick to a marina and in the wee hours of the morning he dumped his naked body in the inky waters. He sought out Miami's worst neighborhood and removed the car's plates, leaving the vehicle running and the radio blasting. He walked away, knowing The Roaches were powerful in this part of town and would claim it.

Hours later he reached The Flamingo, just on the outskirts of town. Complaining to anyone who would listen about a shoddy repair and her car leaking oil was Stephanie Newcomer. She was getting an early start to a place in Delaware he'd never heard of. Catching her eye, he offered to fix her car. Figured she could help him get out of town. He struggled to be charming, to stop his hands from shaking and from looking over his shoulder every two minutes. He took off his shirt as he worked on her car. He made up a story about moving on and looking for work elsewhere as a mechanic. She brought him coffee in the parking lot and he accepted it. He stood very close to her so that there was little doubt in her mind that she was attracted to him. An hour later, they were on their way to a town called Rehoboth Beach, and in no time at all it seemed he was beside her in bed in a motel in Savannah. Despite being exhausted, he couldn't sleep, his mind drifting back to Luna, the fight, the knife, the body. How its discovery petrified him, the torture the Costello's would inflict on him, his death. He knew the Costello brothers would come for him, and when they did they would make his death painful and the final moments of anyone and everyone around him painful as well.

JUST A GIGOLO

The Voice's underground club was extraordinarily busy with the August crowd. The bartenders hustled to make drinks, while his boys hung on the arms of customers. The noise was deafening. The Voice spent an hour on the floor, offering salutations, shaking hands, checking in with the hostess, the door staff, and his escorts. Everyone was drunk and smiling when the lights dimmed for the first dance. Randy was first, followed by Butch, Caleb, and Skylar. In the back, Warren swallowed a white pill followed by a hard drink that dramatically lowered his inhibitions. Still, he was nervous. He could not believe he was going to dance naked in front of a bunch of gay men, picking up cash from tables, from the floor, from eager, hungry hands. How did he get here? He chased his mother from his mind, cast his sister and his nephew out of his thoughts. Even Stephanie. Still, he could not help thinking of their disappointment and his shame if they knew what he was doing.

Warren watched the dancers on stage to get a feel for what they did, but they all seemed wooden and desperate, vulgarly thrusting their pelvises, crawling on their hands and knees like dogs. He had given lots of consideration to what he would do here tonight. He knew he needed to score big, to amass a minor fortune within the next two days. He approached the DJ with his own music, and when the lights went down he stepped out into the shadows, heard the roll of Latin drums, fast and rhythmic. It was in those beats that he found his pulse, lost himself, danced hard. As the lights came up on him slowly, he discovered something happening, gliding all about the room, twisting, turning, clapping, snapping. He began to feel some part of him dying as he became angry and determined to win this game. He could *see* in the music, could *feel* in his dance, the light at the end of the tunnel. The faces he passed, the hands he touched, brought him to a jarring revelation. He was in the moment he'd been afraid of, and here he was making easy work of it. He danced harder, added flair, blew off steam, moved on to another person. He didn't grovel like the other dancers for the money. Whatever was in arms reach he took, allowed others to give him. When it was over, the crowd screamed in approval.

Warren changed and then worked the floor to pick up extra cash. He felt as if he had taken a big test and it was not as hard as he imagined. Still, he was embarrassed to walk around in a G-string. His hair was slicked back and he wore some designer cologne The Voice had given him. The club itself was a set of dark rooms, stylishly decorated in shades of red, and filled with lounge chairs and bars and wall sized black and white photographs of beautiful naked men. Warren stood observing the older good-looking professionals, whom he could tell were wealthy by their clothes and how they spoke to each other and threw their money around. He headed toward them, reminding himself to smile, attempting to forget he was half-naked, but someone touched him. It was all he could do not to scream, as he felt their fingernails and hands against his skin. He tensed, getting angry, but he tried to calm down, to breathe. Someone else touched his ass, cupped his genitals, kissed his chest, his nipples, and his back. He felt dirty and cheap.

"Hey, fellas," Warren heard. The crowd around opened up to The Voice. He leaned in. "I'm glad you guys are having a good time, but everything you're doing costs money. Let me show you how it's done." The Voice pulled out a hundred dollar bill, showed it around, then folded it in half. Watching Warren carefully, The Voice pulled back the rim of Warren's underwear and placed the bill inside. Then he approached Warren and hugged him. He whispered in his ear, "You don't have to do this, okay? You passed the test, you won the game."

"It's fine," Warren said. "I'm okay. Thanks for coming over."

At the end of the night Warren had a huge wad of cash in his pocket. He was very thankful the time was near when he'd leave Rehoboth Beach, never to return again.

MR. LONELYHEART

Warren stood outside Cedar House, looking at all the windows to see who was home. The house seemed still and watching him through the night. Warren stopped off at the kitchen and poured himself some orange juice. He had never been more thirsty, tired or surprised at himself. He could never have imagined that he would be here in this place, with these people, doing the things he had done. It felt like he was a different man. He noticed Jarvis in the doorway watching him. He had seen Watson around Cedar House, but they had never spoken to each other.

"I just came in to get something to drink," Jarvis said, nervously.

Up close, Warren got the impression that Jarvis was afraid of almost everything. That he had not yet figured out his strengths and weaknesses. Warren considered the men he met tonight, how they presented themselves, how they walked, talked, and shook hands. And he wondered what they thought when they looked at him. Did they see strength, confidence?

"My name is Jarvis."

He replied, "Warren."

Jarvis headed for the refrigerator and Warren pulled a glass out of the cabinet and handed it to him. "Thanks!" Jarvis said as he left the room.

Warren wearily climbed the steps to his room, having no idea his life would become unavoidably intertwined with Jarvis's. He collected his clothes and belongings. On the bed, he discovered a note from Stephanie. It said she'd be out late, but they needed to talk. Warren knew what this meant. It was the beginning of the end, and the end of life as he had come to know it.

*****

All the books Jarvis wanted to read, he'd read, even the ones Dallas recommended to him. And like one of those aimless soap opera characters who mill about the house wringing their hands, Jarvis Watson paced the grounds of Cedar House. The following day was gorgeous, and he imagined how he must give the impression to other Cedar House guests that he was pathetic. *Who's the black guy who hangs around all the time? He never says anything, never goes out.* He could not blame them for their suspicious looks. His demeanor was always serious and quiet, humorless and brooding.

Jarvis enjoyed being separate, distanced, content to be an observer. Yet he was clearly aware that he was both prisoner and captor by his own hand. For as much as he longed to be out in Rehoboth watching boys, basking in the sun and enjoying the social summer whirl, he also found solace in the safe haven of his books. This contradiction appeared even to him to be disease. The books he so loved also kept him from the world of which he longed to be a part. If only he were like the characters in his books, strong, smart, witty. He thought it would be easier to be a part of the world if he had something special to offer. He was but one ordinary Jarvis Watson, a law student—the bookish kind, not a shark. He thought that in order to be important you'd have to have something important to say, do important things, and live an important life.

I haven't lived. I have nothing important to say, Jarvis thought.

You still a nigga, boy!

He thought of a pencil drawing he'd seen years ago, with a little black boy playing with a bird as he sat on a curb. The caption read, *I know I'm important because God don't make no junk!* Jarvis thought, *What a crock of shit! What the fuck am I? A man who likes to read. Big deal!*

Depressed, he headed for the library. His antidote was always found between the covers of a book. *If only I had a voice. If only I had something important to say.* Sitting in the confines of his room, Jarvis Watson turned the page and began reading. Fate turned the page on his life as well.

STEPHANIE REDEFINED

Stephanie wore a light black sweater for her walk on the beach with Ethan. The night was cool and they walked closely together, each knowing a final decision had to be made about their lives. Could she as a straight woman deal with the issue of Ethan's sexuality? They stopped to sit on the sand.

"You cold?" Ethan asked. He put his arm around her.

"I'm fine," Stephanie said, looking at his face, wanting to see a future together. She wanted a big wedding, a successful marriage, beautiful children, lavish homes, and knew there was no way Warren could fulfill her wishes or even understand her lifestyle. He could not provide for her, even in the least bit, and if money were of no issue—which of course it wasn't really—what impression would he, a minority mechanic, make on her parents? However, to have everything she wanted, could she accept Ethan's secret and share in this secret with him? Could her love transform him, make him love only her, if she were a good wife, if she pleased him sexually?

"Do you care about me?" she asked him.

"I was attracted to you the first time I saw you, in your pretty white dress. Every time I'm with you, I want to make love to you."

Stephanie looked out to the ocean. "Do you really want to make love to me, Ethan?"

"Yes!" he said taking her face in his hands. "We belong together. Don't you feel the same?"

"Are you saying you want more?"

"I would certainly marry you if you'd let me, and make you the happiest woman in the world. We'd have beautiful children and a wonderful life. I'd make sure of it." Ethan's promise echoed her own thoughts.

Stephanie flicked back her hair, letting the wind play with it, his words like rain after a drought. She looked out to the water, smelling the salt in the air. She really loved Rehoboth, the boardwalk, the beach, the people, the town and the peace of mind it provided.

"You know how much I want you," Ethan said. "I want to make love to you right now."

She turned to Ethan, pushing Warren and the special way he made her feel out of her mind. "Will you love me forever, Ethan?" she asked. "I need that. I desperately need to be loved."

"I need that, too," he replied, and she leaned over and kissed him, telling him she wanted to make love. He knew then that his secret was safe and that he had won.

*****

Stephanie lay beside Ethan in the bed as he slept. Her sexual afterglow was less pleasurable with Ethan than it was with Warren. This observation served as a key in a lock, opening up her feelings about Warren, how she would miss him, how he instinctively understood her and her needs. There was always something valiant in his eyes when they made love. He was generous and attentive, her satisfaction always first and foremost in his mind. He'd penetrate her slowly at first, his thrusts measured then wild. He'd whisper sweet nothings in her ear, then vulgarities that stimulated her. She always forgot herself when he made love to her with his beautiful body.

Ethan was more concerned with the mechanics of sex. It was not lovemaking as much as it was the construction of something by an unseen blueprint. There were more positions with Ethan, and their sex was painful, laborious, and exhausting. Stephanie had faked an orgasm so they could stop. Ethan didn't have one either.

They had checked into a motel on the outskirts of Rehoboth. Sexual energy was in the room, yet getting this effort off the ground took time. Both agreed to undress themselves (something Warren always did for Stephanie). Ethan stood naked before her, his body one of the most gorgeous she had ever seen. His organ was thick, bulbous, and erect. He appeared taller out of clothes, defined, his legs and thighs muscular, making her want him immediately. He guided her to a wall, kissed her lips, her neck, tasted her breasts, and did all the things that had been done by Warren. He drove his hand inside her panties, penetrating her too hard, too fast, and without rhythm. He carried her to the bed and ravished her, initiating two hours of hard work, thrusting without consideration, his mouth too vigorous, his hands slapping too hard, his execution too eager as he took her through a range of positions: first on her back, then on her stomach, standing, on her knees, sitting, sideways, on top, on bottom, all of it rushed, without a plan, overwhelmingly raw, and seemingly without a point beyond orgasm.

When it was over, silence fell on them like a dark cloud, and he asked her before dozing off, "Did I please you?" She nodded dutifully, believing their sex life would get better, that things would be great in the end. They'd have a wonderful life.

But with all that, he didn't orgasm.

She reached over him to turn off the lamp, plunging them both into darkness. With a great amount of effort she finally wandered off into sleep, and subsequently into dreamland.

HELL COMES TOMORROW

Tomorrow was to be their final day in Rehoboth, and Stephanie and Ethan toured the city one last time. It was noon and already they had passed through Henlopen Acres, North Shores, Poodle Beach, Silver Lake, down beautiful King Charles Avenue, up raucous Rehoboth Avenue to the outlets, and back again, stopping off at the boardwalk. The two had been exploring since very early morning, eating breakfast, taking photographs in various neighborhoods, remembering places they would probably never see again.

"You're thinking about Warren, aren't you?" Ethan asked.

They were holding hands, trudging barefoot through the sand.

"I haven't seen him in days," Stephanie said, avoiding answering the question. The thought of leaving Warren filled her with apprehension. "If I don't see him before morning, I'll leave him a note."

Ethan did as he was cued to do, and enveloped Stephanie in his strong arms.

"My parents are going to love you," he said. "When you first meet them, you're going to have to bring them a gift. They like gifts, and it would be the proper thing to do."

"My family will be different," Stephanie said, heading for the water. She wanted to feel its coolness against her feet. Ethan followed. "My father is very staid and my mother kind of distant, but once they see that you're a doctor and that you've saved me from a life of debauchery, they will crown you King Arthur!"

Ethan laughed. "I like that!"

Stephanie said, "A family."

Ethan repeated, "A family."

Stephanie stumbled.

"You okay?" Ethan asked.

"Just a little tired and dizzy."

"We've been out since the crack of dawn. Let's get you hydrated and some lunch."

They walked arm in arm toward the boardwalk.

Safe, Stephanie thought of Ethan. *Safe*, he thought of her. And for a short time they were both happy.

*****

At Cedar House Jarvis received a call from Ethan.

"Hey, we need to talk. I'm going to leave Rehoboth sooner than expected." Ethan was excited and Jarvis could tell it had something to do with Stephanie. "You around day after tomorrow?"

"Sure," Jarvis replied.

Both were wrong.

THE WAR AT HOME

"What's the matter?" Griffin asked Jarrett as they drove to a movie.

"Nothing," Jarrett answered, even though he was thinking, *Do I really want to go there? Do I really want to get into the subject of my father and spoil a perfectly good day?*

"It's your father isn't it?" Griffin guessed. "He's the only thing we don't discuss. I know it's none of my business, but let me know if there's anything I can do to make it better."

Jarrett really did want to make sense of what was going on with Dallas, but he hesitated to discuss it. He worried that the negative energy between him and his father would somehow affect his relationship with Griffin. "Don't worry about it," he said as they exited the car.

The relentless August sun beat down on them as they stood in line. Griffin turned to Jarrett and whispered, "I love you."

"I love you, too," Jarrett whispered back, feeling this was the first time he had said those words and really meant it since his mother's death. Jarrett's cell rang. It was Dallas.

"We need to talk," the senior Hemingway demanded.

"What is it?" Jarrett replied in kind.

"It's about your hours. You've been off the last couple of days and I really could use some help here. When are you returning to work?"

Jarrett sighed exhausted and irritated, his mood doing a nosedive at the sound of his father's voice. *Why are we like this? Why are we always at each other's throats?*

"I have two days off a week, you know that. I took them together this time, similar to your July Fourth weekend."

"When are you returning to work?" Dallas repeated.

"Do you have the schedule in front of you?" Jarrett snapped. "You should try looking at *that* instead of bothering me!"

He and Griffin advanced in line; Walsh was staring at him.

"What about Jarvis?"

"What about Jarvis?"

"He's here, in this house–"

"AND?"

"He's been in this house every weekend for weeks now, just sitting around! Someone needs to take him out to see the city, spend some time with him."

"Why don't you take him out yourself, Dallas? Or is that too hands-on for you?"

"What's *that* supposed to mean?"

Jarrett hung up on Dallas and immediately dialed Drescher.

"Hey, I need you to do me a favor."

"Well, hello to you, too," Drescher said. He was going over negatives in his lab.

"Do you know the African-American guy staying at Cedar House? Jarvis Watson."

"Not at all."

"I need for you to do me this favor. Could you please take him out to a party, to see the town? He's afraid to go out because he doesn't know Rehoboth."

"Why can't you do it? It's your business."

Jarrett looked to Griffin. Walsh had turned away from him, buying their tickets. Jarrett whispered into his phone, "I'm busy right now, and tomorrow evening I work."

Drescher sighed. "Well, I can't do it tonight; I'm busy myself."

"It doesn't have to be tonight. Tomorrow's fine," Jarrett said. "Please, please, please, do this for me. I'll make it up to you."

"Fine," Drescher agreed. "Any particular time?"

"No. But call or stop by tomorrow morning. I'm sure he'll be receptive to going out and seeing the town. Take him to a house party or something."

Jarrett hung up, sealing Jarvis Watson's fate. In the theater, Griffin sat silent. Jarrett turned to him. "What's wrong?"

"I would never think in a million years to talk to my father the way you talk to yours."

DIVISION STREET

"I'm sorry," Griffin apologized when they returned to his house that evening. The ride home had been quiet. "It's not my place to judge you."

Jarrett took a seat on the patio sofa. "I'm never like that, really. It's just that he pisses me off so much…and so *often!*"

"I can't say that I understand your relationship with your father. I only know you sounded harsh…and frankly, disrespectful."

"You're angry with me."

Griffin sat beside Jarrett. "Not angry. I just don't understand your relationship. Maybe it's because I have such a great relationship with my own father."

"Am I going to lose you?"

"That's not what I'm saying." Griffin sighed. "We're still friends. I still love you. I think you're quite possibly the most wonderful thing to come my way in a long, long time. It's your uniqueness, that hidden fire inside of you, that attracts me."

"Griffin, I'm still the same person as when we met."

Walsh scratched his head. "What was all that about with your father, Jarrett?"

Jarrett shrugged. "You have no idea what it's like to not have a relationship with your father. He keeps pushing me away, like he hates me, like I'm interfering. A father should be like a best friend. I've always wished for what Drescher has with his dad."

"And you've tried talking to him–?"

"I've tried talking to him a thousand times, and it never does any good!"

"What is it you want to say to him?" Griffin asked.

Jarrett looked up to the sky. It was clear and starry. "Everything…"

Griffin gently touched Jarrett's shoulder. "Maybe one day your father will also realize what a wonderful man he has for a son."

"Don't hold your breath for that," Jarrett said, with a bitter laugh. "Let's talk about something else."

Griffin paused, considered. "I have a surprise for you. The day after tomorrow is my birthday, and I was thinking an escape to New York was in order. It'll surely clear your mind."

"A trip would be wonderful. When would we leave?"

"The next time you have some days off."

The more Griffin looked at Jarrett, the more he wanted him. He pressed his lips against Hemingway's ear and whispered, "Let's not wait any longer."

Jarrett whispered back. "Do you really want me, bad boy temper and all?"

Griffin smiled. "For keeps. Definitely for keeps."

They climbed the stairs together holding hands, and then showered in a lush steam. Their fingers explored each other's bodies, their tongues tasted each other's skin. They found their way to bed and immediately fell into a passion that was blinding, that they had been meaning to express for one another. They struck up a pace, slow and fast and rhythmic, their bodies melding and moving as one. They belonged to each other now. No man, no person would ever separate them.

David Youngblood sat outside their window watching and calculating.

THE WAR AT HOME, PART II

"You decided to show up," Dallas said, sweeping the front lane at Cedar House.

It was the next day, a day the Hemingways would remember for the rest of their lives. Jarrett stood behind Dallas, watching him sweep violently, as if it illustrated his disapproval. It was clear he wished to continue yesterday's ugly conversation. Jarrett's words to Griffin the night before resurfaced and stoked the flame of discontent within him. *A father should be like a best friend.*

Jarrett was measured. "I came early to give you a break, and so we could talk."

"How magnanimous of you." Dallas made busy work of very few leaves.

"Will you please look at me," Jarrett said.

"We have nothing to say to each other. Go and come back at whatever time you're supposed to be here."

Griffin's words came back to Jarrett: *I can't say I understand your relationship with your father. I only know it sounded harsh...and frankly, disrespectful.* Jarrett tried to remain calm. "You're angry about yesterday. I'm sorry. I didn't mean to explode like that–"

"I'm angry about a lot of things!" Dallas snapped. He turned to Jarrett and stared at him, his eyes resting on his son's lips. They had been kissed, and kissed hard. This raised a fury in Dallas, for all he could think of was Drescher, of the love he missed and the secret he kept.

Jarrett watched this transformation in his father, the overwhelming disgust creep into Dallas's eyes. Suddenly he was the enemy. Dallas walked away toward the porch, and Jarrett could not help but to compare his father to his mother. Laura, who loved him so much. Laura, who fought so hard to protect him all through his life. She would never have treated him this way. Out of Jarrett's mouth came a voice he'd never heard before. "YOU STOP IT RIGHT THERE!"

Dallas slammed the screen door and turned back to his son.

Jarrett yelled, "This has got to stop! Whatever is going on with you has got to stop now!" Dallas did not respond. "Why are we like this? What is wrong with us?"

"Who do you think you're talking to?" Dallas yelled back.

"I'm talking to you!" Jarrett answered, stomping across the lawn to Dallas, feeling powerful and angry. "I'm talking to my *father*!"

"Calm yourself down!" Dallas spat at his son, stomping down the stairs toward him. They stopped just shy of each other, breathing heavily.

"No, I will *not* calm down! Not until you tell me what the hell is going on!"

There again was that look of disgust from Dallas, like a flash of lightning. He marched past Jarrett and across the lawn toward the street, leaving Jarrett fuming in frustration. He chased his father and shoved him from behind.

"Don't you walk away from me! Don't you fucking walk away!" He spun Dallas around, snatching at him.

"Back up!" Dallas warned. "I can't deal with you right now, I really can't!"

Jarrett thought about his mother then, how she died. "Are you sick, are you ill?"

Dallas offered him nothing, only continued to the street. Jarrett followed.

"That's right, just walk away. You can't hold a fucking conversation with your son like a normal father. You can't tell me what's wrong. You can't tell me what I've done or what you think I've done to you. You just walk away. Well you know what, Dallas? I'm fucking sick of it and I'm sick of you!"

"Enough!" Dallas barked. "There are people all up and down this street watching us!"

"FUCK THEM!"

There was that look again from Dallas, so resentful that Jarrett stepped back, confused and angry. "You see me suffering and it doesn't crack you one bit, does it?"

A crowd had formed on the porch at Cedar House and all along the sidewalk.

"You know what, Dallas? You're no real father. You're a fucking coward, is what you are. And I don't know why you hate me, but I can't stand being here with you anymore. I can't take living like this. YOU SEEM TO HATE ME AND YET I'M THE ONLY FUCKING PERSON WHO GIVES A *DAMN* ABOUT YOU!"

Jarrett went to Dallas. "I swear to God there are days when I wish that Bradley Thomas was my father! He's more man, more *giving*, than you could be in ten of your fucking miserable lifetimes! To hell with you—"

Dallas struck him so hard and so fast that Jarrett was thrown up against Cedar House's white picket fence. Everyone gasped. Jarrett saw his father's fist streaked with blood, and he touched his face pulling back a similar color. He stood, dizzy, and stumbled. He said with a wink, "Thanks for sharing, dad."

Jarrett Hemingway jumped Cedar House's white picket fence, marking it with his blood. He tripped onto the sidewalk, on his hands and knees. He stood and ran, and Dallas watched him disappear from sight.

"Jarrett," he called, but his voice came out small and distant and lost on the still summer air. He looked down at his bloody hand as though it belonged to a stranger. He wiped it clean on a white handkerchief and stuffed it into his back pocket. He didn't have the courage to look anyone in the eye as he trudged up the stairs and into Cedar House, trying his best to resume business as usual.

THE LAST OF THE NORMAL HOURS

Drescher Thomas found Jarvis Watson quite handsome. He could not fathom why he was single or chose to be reclusive, because once engaged in conversation he blossomed, became animated, smiling and blushing constantly. He was well-spoken, well read and intelligent, and seemed the most easy-going person Drescher had met in a long time.

"So what's planned for today?" Jarvis asked, full of enthusiasm. They were seated outside at one of the bistros on Baltimore Avenue.

"I was thinking we could plan for tonight and that would pave the way for today."

"What do you suggest?"

"How about experiencing Rehoboth's nightlife? Dinner, club hopping, cocktails around town, and a late night house party."

Jarvis grinned, excitedly. "Sounds great!"

"We're going to get you some new clothes and a haircut. I want to show you off and introduce you to as many people as I can in one day."

"Am I as desperate looking as all that?"

"Just the opposite. I think you're handsome and intelligent. We just need to get rid of all that lawyer bookishness." He raised his camera to chest level. "Mind if I take a picture of you, a black and white? I guarantee you'll like it."

Jarvis shrugged, feeling shy. "If you want…"

Drescher shot the picture. Later, he would look at this print and see the melancholy in Jarvis's eyes. He would wonder why he hadn't delved deeper into his life. But that was later. They lunched and then trekked off to shop for clothes and colognes and whatever else struck their fancy. They did afternoon iced coffee and dessert, Drescher introducing Jarvis around to nearly every person he knew. He took photos of Jarvis, promising him copies, watching him blossom under his attention. At the end of the day they left each other, promising to meet up later in the evening. Promising, in the face of a dark fate ahead, to live like there was no tomorrow.

A SPOT OF PLEASURE ON THIS OTHERWISE DISASTROUS DAY

"No peeking and I mean it!" Griffin Walsh said to Jarrett Hemingway.

Jarrett was blindfolded as they drove from Griffin's place to Lewes, the neighboring town. Jarrett had been instructed to pack a bag and be ready to leave the house by noon.

"You have your bathing suit?" Griffin asked nervously.

"For the hundredth time, yes!"

Jarrett had run to Griffin's following the episode with Dallas, surprising even himself that he was able to get there in his delirious state. He explained everything to Walsh, at first incomprehensibly, then calmly and coldly, his voice full of disdain. Griffin held him, kissed him, and forced him to nap, which was a good thing because he slept a full hour and was more relaxed when he woke. By the time he'd risen a late breakfast had been made, and then this surprise excursion.

Griffin had not offered his opinion on the matter. He listened patiently, thinking of his own father, recalling a time when he was a child playing with his brothers and sister in the house they owned in

Westport, Connecticut. His father would enter, his attaché in one hand, his suit jacket in the other, his necktie undone, he a little more disheveled than when he'd left that morning. Griffin, Douglas, Blair and Sawyer would run to their father, who'd kneel down and scoop them up in his arms for a hug. He'd then tickle and play with them until dinnertime, after which he'd tuck them all into bed. Griffin knew his father was important and had another life. But here he was making time for them after a busy day that involved grown-ups shaking hands, suits and desks and ringing telephones, buildings with marble and statues and paintings and guys who drove the elevators. He loved him for his dedication and loyalty to his work, but even more for showing his family how important they were to him.

"We're here!" Griffin announced. Griffin led Jarrett out of the car by the hand. He removed his blindfold, and standing before Jarrett was a sea captain, smiling and tipping his hat.

"Mr. Hemingway, welcome aboard *Sugar Cane*."

When Jarrett looked up at the large, white vessel, he was speechless.

*****

"*Sugar Cane*?"

"This is my brother Doug's boat. We're going to pick up my friends in Cape May and sail into the Atlantic. We'll be in Manhattan by tonight, and then we'll celebrate my birthday in style."

Jarrett was amazed as they stood on the deck of *Sugar Cane*. In all the years he had lived in Rehoboth, he'd never been on a private vessel this large. He was reminded then of all the things he had yet to do in his life, all the things he had yet to see. He thought, *When did I lose my sense of adventure, my lust for living?* He had spent the last ten years of his life wrapped up managing the Cedar properties. Being here on this yacht, on an impromptu adventure, prodded him to reevaluate his life, to meet new people, to adopt a new perspective. Could he brave an existence outside of the Cedar properties and Rehoboth and Dallas Hemingway? Jarrett decided to turn off his cell. He wanted to give it a try, to put some distance between he and Dallas. But most importantly, he wanted to try and navigate these new waters on his own.

RAGE AGAINST THE MACHINE

While Griffin spoke with the captain of *Sugar Cane*, Jarrett ventured to the front deck. On a bench was a miniature mirror ball connected to a key chain. Jarrett lifted the keys and saw himself in a hundred tiny reflections. He heard Griffin come up behind him.

"I can't believe you did this. Thank you so much."

"I'm glad you like," Griffin said, proudly. "I'd do anything to make you happy."

Jarrett looked into Griffin's eyes. "I believe you."

As *Sugar Cane* pulled out to sea, Jarrett and Griffin were given a tour by the captain. The yacht was huge, and Jarrett asked many questions, finding out Douglas had owned the boat for four years, that there had been an impressive roster of guests who'd sailed on it, including royalty, titans of industry, and celebrities, and that Douglas's last wedding anniversary party had been held on the boat. Griffin's friends boarded when they docked at Cape May, among them Griffin's sister Blair. The afternoon got officially underway with a cocktail hour and barbecue. Everyone changed into bathing suits and *Sugar Cane* set off into the Atlantic Ocean. The day stretched out with happy chatter, laughter and music. At sunset, everyone showered and dressed for dinner and a party. Griffin joined Jarrett at the ship's stern. The golden sun had touched the ocean, causing it to sparkle like millions of diamonds.

"You okay?"

"Better than okay," Jarrett said. Both were a little tipsy.

"Everyone likes you, you know."

"I'm glad to hear that. I like them. They're a great group of people."

Griffin gazed up to the sky, then over the white water trailing behind the yacht. "I love being out here. It's so peaceful and uncomplicated. Nothing but you and God. The sky is infinite. The water seems infinite. And you, for a little while, seem infinite too."

Jarrett agreed. To him the waves provided a soothing soundtrack, and the misty spray off of the ocean was invigorating. It had been a long time since he'd felt this close to himself, this close to nature or this close to someone else.

"I have a confession to make," he uttered.

"You don't love me," Griffin joked.

"Silly," Jarrett chuckled. He took one of Griffin's large hands in both of his. "I wanted to thank you for bringing me out here, for sharing all of this with me. I was thinking to myself how happy and at ease I feel, and it's because of you. One of the best things you can give another person is the very thing that is the hardest to give." Jarrett looked deeply into Griffin's eyes. "You gave me yourself.

You opened up your life to me, gave me your love, gave me room to be myself. I want you to know how much I appreciate that. I was worried I wouldn't make you happy because you're well off, educated, well-traveled. I'm just a townie, and still you love me."

"I do love you," said Griffin. He followed Jarrett to a bench, and sat on the floor before him.

"And I love you," Jarrett said.

"So why do I get the impression there is something you're not telling me?"

Jarrett sat back on the bench. Stars decorated the sky, bit by bit. The moon made a sudden appearance, although the sky was not yet fully dark.

"The whole town loved my mother, Laura, and she used to have parties at Cedar House. The party here on this boat this afternoon reminded me of those days when good friends and neighbors dropped by with any excuse to celebrate, to laugh and be together. Those days were golden and I thought they'd last forever. When my mother died, all of that stopped. My father hardly ever mentions her name, rarely speaks of her, and never reminisces about their life together. It's like he couldn't wait to bury and forget her and all those memories, all those simple, beautiful, wonderful days we shared. Now he's a stranger."

Griffin asked, "Is there someone else?"

"Even if there was, he never talks about *her*. All the good times, everything that made up my life, seems a forbidden topic because they include her."

"And you think you owe your mother…"

"Loyalty," Jarrett snapped. "Honor and respect. She could have left us a very bitter woman, a gay husband *and* a gay son. But she didn't. She stayed, kept us together; there was no divorce, no scandal. And I'm furious! Furious we have given her nothing in return! That we've sullied the memory of everything she's given us. All her good intentions meant nothing. Like *she* meant nothing, like this family meant nothing. It's disrespectful and it's wrong. Because of him, I feel disconnected from her. And because of her death, I feel disconnected from him. She died and I feel like I've lost both my parents."

At that same time back in Rehoboth, the night turned deadly for Dallas Hemingway.

WHO GOES THERE?

David Youngblood entered his Dewey Beach timeshare sweaty and out of breath. Still, he was filled with a startling sense of accomplishment and power, having just served up the perfect revenge for Griffin and Jarrett.

"Where you been?" Pat asked, catching him before he bolted upstairs. David poked his head into the living room to find Blake, Thom, Edgar and Ken glued to the television, drinking beer, and watching a pre-season football game.

"Busy," Youngblood answered. *That fucking nigger and his white bitch got exactly what was coming to them!*

"Hey, keep it down over there! Money's at stake here!" Thom said.

"You guys going out later?" David whispered to Pat.

"Yeah, Blake's seeing some girl who's having a party in Rehoboth. We're invited."

There was a big play, screaming.

"What time's it start?" David asked.

"Late. Near midnight. You going?"

David nodded, then headed for the stairs. Pat called to him.

"Yo, what's that shit you got on your hands?"

David's palms were slick and black. "I was checking the tires on the jeep," he lied. "It's just oil or something."

Uppity nigger. White faggot bitch.

CONDUCT UNBECOMING

"*Man!* I'm gonna bust me some box *tonight!*"

The party was going to start in less than an hour, and David's roommates, already drunk and rowdy, were in various stages of preparation. David had been combing his hair in one of the upstairs bathrooms, studying himself in the mirror meticulously, left then right, for the past twenty minutes. The result, even after much teasing and restyling, was unsatisfactory to him. *He* was unsatisfactory to him. This self-loathing so embedded in him that he hardly remembered a time without it. He was disgusted with his face, his hair, his nose, with *everything.* He looked so *white,* so plain, so ordinary. With him, nothing ever seemed to change, and he hated that about himself. He took another swig of his beer, his third. He would need a fourth before long.

You my boo?

You my jigga-boo?

You my nigga, boo?

David closed his eyes, attempting to lid this can of worms. To stop the shame of being inadequate, white, Jewish, nothing. He felt as if he had no color, no depth. That he lacked definition and dimension. *Something!* Something it seemed he would never have. A sour chuckle escaped his lips and he wanted to cry. Clouds threatened to cover him completely, and he knew if that happened he would never escape the storm of this depression.

You my boo?

"Stop it!" he whispered harshly under his breath. He squeezed his eyes tightly, damming tears, forcing back thoughts of Griffin and Jarrett, despite his revenge, of Lincoln and their history. He guzzled the remains of his beer. He needed another *now*.

There was a knock at the door. It was Pat. "*Man!* I'm gonna bust me some box *tonight!*"

"Well, just make sure you don't bust *my* groove," David said pushing past Pat.

Pat, clad only in his underwear, hugged him around his neck. "Dude, I'm gonna bust something tonight, but it ain't gonna be *your* groove!" He cackled. David only smiled.

They headed downstairs, where Ken and Edgar were talking.

"I got a problem," Edgar said. He was dressed only in a towel. Edgar opened the towel and revealed his flaccid penis, a large tattoo hovering above it that read BLOOD PAIN GLORY. The words were flanked on either side by two large hunting knives that pointed down to his scrotum. "It's not healed and it burns like fucking hell." Ken, Pat and David gathered to get a closer look. Edgar turned his penis gingerly back and forth, the skin around it red and angry. They all winced. Thom and Blake walked in.

"What's going on?" Thom asked.

Pat looked up. "Edgar is showing us his dick."

"It's not healed," Edgar said.

"You all call that a dick?" Thom said with a sly, wide grin on his face. They turned to him, and Thom yanked down his shorts. "*This* is a dick."

"Awww, man, put that shit away!" Ken said, covering his eyes.

David, Edgar and Blake burst out into laughter, their faces reddened.

"Anybody want to go up against this?" Thom bragged. The soldiers continued to laugh, but no one took the bait. Thom challenged Ken. "What's the matter, Red? Ain't got no game?"

"I got game, dawg! I'm just not a faggot!"

There was more laughter.

"Put up or shut up!" Thom threatened, putting Ken on the spot. "Whatcha got for me?"

Ken flushed. "I'm not pulling out my dick! Fuck you!"

"Shit or get off the pot!" Thom barked.

Heads turned back and forth between the two. Thom stared.

"Fine!" Ken protested, his face red with intimidation. The room was blanketed in silence. Ken dropped his boxers to his ankles and laced his fingers atop his head. Thick hair trailed from his navel to his pubic area. He said to Thom, "You happy?"

Thom smiled devilishly and turned to the room. "Anybody else want to lay their cards on the table? Our civilian friend David?"

David smiled, and without a word, yanked open his jeans. He wore no underwear.

Pat whirled on David. "What is you, fucking gay all of a sudden?"

"Patrick," Thom called sweetly, "do you wish to share with the class?"

Pat looked around the room as if cornered. He revealed himself. "I ain't gay!"

"You aren't hung either," Thom cracked. He turned to Blake.

"A bunch of perverts, all of you," Blake said laughing, understanding that Thom had intimidated half of them into doing this. He stepped out of his boxers. "I don't think any of you ladies can hang with this..."

There were whistles and grunts. David turned red.

Edgar said, "He walks around the locker room naked just to show off."

They all laughed, except for Pat, who pulled up his underwear and stormed up the stairs. In silence, their eyes followed him, and then returned to the circle. No one said anything at first, but then seeing each other naked all together, they quickly covered themselves and dispersed without a word.

CIAO, BABY!

It was very late and Warren had waited until it seemed everyone had left Cedar House. He entered quietly from the rear, moved up the stairs, taking a last look at the rooms, the walls, the photographs of Laura Hemingway. He counted his blessings that neither Dallas nor Jarrett were around, and that the always lurking Jarvis Watson was nowhere to be found. He noticed the stillness of the house— that *it* seemed to be watching *him*.

Warren entered the room he shared with Stephanie. He wanted one last look at it. He had come to leave her a note. Startling him was a huge amplified *Boom!,* then another and another. Warren ran to the window and looked out. Multi-colored fireworks streamed against Rehoboth's black starry sky. Another night his life was changing, another night of fireworks. He had come full circle. Before he shut the door on his life with Stephanie, he took one of her head scarves draped over the arm of a chair, sprayed it with perfume, and then was gone as quietly as he had come.

*****

Stephanie and Ethan had ventured out earlier that evening to one of Rehoboth's Italian restaurants. They sat at the bar drinking wine, laughing with the bartender before they were seated for dinner. They'd decided to settle up with Dallas or Jarrett in the morning, escape town before the usual mass exodus on Sunday afternoon. The two drove back to Cedar House in her car, parking on the street so that they could leave as early as possible. They climbed the stairs, and he pulled her into his room. He had secretly been watching the attractive waiters all night and was now so horny that he had to have her. They had no idea Frank and Mario Costello were watching them.

VENDETTA

It had not taken the Costello brothers long to locate Cedar House, only Rehoboth Beach. They drove up north through unfamiliar territory and blinding black night, finally arriving after many wrong turns and an equal number of bad directions. The two seethed with the possibilities of catching Leo, of discovering the details behind their brother's death, of administering a long and severe punishment as retribution. They were, however, split on one thing: Luna. Mario believed she should be killed outright, that she was of no use to them. Frank wanted just the opposite. He wanted her for himself.

"Why?" Mario demanded. They sat in the shadows across from Cedar House, Mario in the driver's seat, Frank sitting pensively beside him. The property appeared deserted, with lights off in many of the windows. They waited for any sign of a gold BMW, for a redheaded beauty. "You only want this fucking bitch because Nicky had her! You *always* want what Nicky's had! For Christ's sake, get a fucking life of your own!"

Frank could not refute this simple truth, so he turned his gaze to the passenger's side window. There was his reflection, handsome but with a deep insecurity in his eyes. This had been the dynamic of the Costellos from birth. Frank the front man because of his good looks. Mario the brains, because he was smart and Nick the muscle, because of his brawn. But the evolution of these personalities brought about a different line-up later on in life. Nick was the most respected, because he was so forceful and everyone feared his temper, while Mario was next even though he was a bit more laid back and watchful, content to be the brains of this trio. Frank, with only his good looks, was always having to earn respect despite the fact that he was the eldest.

"There's no point to you having her," Mario continued.

"Why do you even care?" Frank snapped.

"If you keep this bitch alive and you kill her brother, and she *knows* you've killed her brother, she's going to feel like she has nothing to lose by running to the police. You can't keep her around, Frank. She's a liability. They're running from the law, they're running from us. If we off both of them, no one will miss them. If we leave one of them alive, it can only mean bad news. We came here to get revenge for Nicky. Let's just do it and move on to Luna."

Right then, a gold BMW passed Cedar House and pulled into a parking spot down the street. Mario and Frank sat bolt upright, watching a male and female emerge from the car and go into the house through the back door. It was too dark to make out their faces, but they figured it was Leo and the redhead. Frank reached for his gun, started to exit the car. Mario yanked him back.

"First, I've got a much better idea," he said. "For insurance."

They went to Stephanie's car and picked the lock to get inside.

DESPERADOS

Warren stood in the center of his room at The Voice's apartment, showered, costumed and ready for work. On the bed was his duffel bag. He had already counted three thousand dollars in cash and was eager to get out of town. All that remained was one last performance and this nightmare would come to its end. All his struggles to win, to be free would be over. Come what may tomorrow, today he had survived. Regardless, he felt something remained to be done. This is why he stood in his room alone, afraid to open the door, to get this night underway. There lingered something in the air, overwhelmingly dark despite the stars. It was something he could not ignore, like a cry for help in a burning building.

"*What?*" Warren said aloud. "What is it?"

He shivered, suddenly chilled, despite the warm summer night. He could not get out of his mind a gnawing sense that he was not to leave Rehoboth Beach just yet. Was it Stephanie? Was she in trouble? Should he risk seeing her a final time? *No, it's something else*, he thought. He had paced around madly for the past hour and now it was near midnight. Time for him to go to work. He laid out his street clothes beside his bag, took one last deep breath, and then headed down into the basement.

The club was crowded, and he stood knowing he would remember all this in vivid detail all his life. The cigarette smoke drifting on the air, the combination of alcohol and cologne and mint gum. The bartenders dressed in black, the stage and music and lights, the catcalls, the whistling, the hands; all the things that happened in the shadows. The groping, the sweat, the mouths and tongues that had tasted his skin, the lips his lips had kissed, the requests he had been made to honor. He would never tell anyone what had happened here, ever. He slipped into the dressing room with the other dancers. Their eyes avoided his. He did not belong here they sensed, and their resentment was sharp. Warren asked the DJ to play his regular music, then requested from the bartender a shot of something to numb out his last night.

It's over! He thought to himself. *You've won!*

Just before he was to go on and perform, The Voice grabbed his arm, pulled him from the brink. "Put on your clothes," he said. "Your time here is up."

*****

The trip back to Warren's room was intense and foreboding. They entered the apartment swiftly. The Voice ordered him to get dressed.

"What are you doing? I need to work!"

"No!" The Voice said tightly. He blocked Warren's path as tears welled up in his eyes. "You've proven yourself," The Voice said.

He held out a large manila envelope to Warren, who took it from him and cautiously opened it. Warren gasped and when he looked up The Voice was dangling car keys in front of him. Bewildered, Warren took them, then the cell phone The Voice took out of his jacket pocket. He said, "Get out of here." At first Warren thought this might be a dream or a joke, but then The Voice took him in his arms, held him for a moment and then said, "Go."

Warren looked again into the envelope. There must have been thousands of dollars. He heard The Voice say to him, "That should get you to wherever you need to go. However, if you decide not to run, to turn yourself in, take your chances, I will support you. I will try to protect your family the way you did. The choice is yours."

Warren looked at The Voice, his heart pounding in his chest. He was overwhelmed. He thought for a moment and then said, "Maybe someday…but not today."

The Voice asked, "Can you forgive me?"

Warren was silent.

"It was selfish of me to ask you to do this. I see all these boys, and they come through here with their dramas and their stories and after a while I realized you were different. You remind me of myself before I became what I am today. And if there is anything you take with you, Warren, take this. You have a good heart. Hold on to it, because when the world sinks its teeth into you, and it often does, you're going to have to remember that you have a good heart. That you're a good man. I don't have children, you know my history. A part of me wanted you to be my son. I wanted you in this world with me and I was wrong. You're too good for this. A father should want more for his son, more than he is possibly able to give him. This is not your world, it's mine. I'm holding you back, and you need to go."

Warren went to The Voice. They embraced tightly, and were silent for a very long time. "Let me know if you change your mind about turning yourself in," The Voice whispered in Warren's ear. "I will stand beside you. And call me if you need anything. Anything at all."

Warren nodded. They hugged tighter, and in that moment neither wanted to let go.

Warren whispered in The Voice's ear, *"Adios, papa. Te quiero mucho."*

The Voice replied, *"Adios, hijo. Te quiero mucho, tambien."*

Warren then dressed and walked toward the fate that awaited him.

CINDERELLA, NEAR MIDNIGHT

It was strange that he should walk into a room and crowds would part, that all eyes should be on him. That this night of all nights the world would turn its spotlight in his direction. When Jarvis Watson entered The Velvet Lounge to meet Drescher for their night on the town, Drescher pointed out the looks he received, the nods, the smiles, and he wondered why he garnered so much attention now. Was it really the haircut, the new clothes, his new fragrance? Why did he still feel the same inside? Terrified of this world despite his brave face. Was he ready to live more outside of himself than in?

Jarvis blushed, felt shy. How could they not see beneath this makeover that he was the same Jarvis Watson? He took in a deep breath, relaxed a little, had a drink, laughed with people Drescher introduced him to. He saw in their faces acceptance, curiosity, and in some, their own insecurities. They too had some part of themselves on the line. Overall, Jarvis enjoyed himself as he and Drescher moved from club to club, from circle to circle. For him, this was a dream come true. He felt confident and alive, like a brand new toy on Christmas day, like Cinderella with the stroke of midnight only moments away.

*****

When Drescher and Jarvis finally arrived at The Zodiac Party a little after midnight, Jarvis was already drunk. The martinis, the cosmopolitans, the shots, seemed to have become all one liquid blur, and Jarvis, who had been on his feet all day touring Rehoboth, could not remember the last time he had experienced such an exhausting day, had lost count of the number of cocktails consumed. He was ready to go home very soon after they arrived.

"Let's go," he mumbled to Drescher. He did not want to seem ungrateful, but he could barely walk straight; he wobbled on his feet unable to keep his balance. Drescher didn't hear him; he was preoccupied with surveying the crowd, chatting with friends. The room was dark, the lamps all filled with blue bulbs.

When Drescher finally turned to Jarvis he said, "I know the girl giving this party. Her brother starts med school in a couple of weeks."

Jarvis tapped Drescher, signaled him closer. "I want to go home," he said.

Drescher frowned. "What's the matter? I thought you were having fun."

"I am, but I'm tired."

"Let's just stay a little bit, then we can go." Drescher looked around the room, saw a couple of friends. "I just want to say hello to some people."

Jarvis groaned, feeling queasy. "I'm going to go home."

"No, no, no! Stay!" Drescher pleaded. "Tell you what, let me find Ellie, say hello to her and her brother, we'll have one drink and then we can go."

Jarvis groaned again. He hardly had the strength to stand.

Drescher disappeared into the crowd, leaving Jarvis leaning on a wall by the entrance. The room spun at a nauseating rate, and the booming bass was giving him a skull-splitting headache. He bumped into partygoers as he made his way through the crowd, apologizing, earning sour looks.

Jesus, Jarvis, don't make a fool out of yourself! You're drunk. Just go.

So Jarvis left. He exited the party through the patio, toward the beach, where he was certain the cool midnight air would do him good. Where he'd eventually find his way home, and to sleep. Instead, the black night with all its cruel surprises awaited him.

AS FATE WOULD HAVE IT

David, Thom, Pat, Ken and Edgar showed up at The Zodiac Party moments *before* Drescher and Jarvis. To their surprise, the party was not at all what they thought it would be.

"This shit is whack!" Thom said livid.

Ken agreed, his face red with embarrassment. "Where's Blake? I'm gonna to wring his fucking neck!"

They stood, the five of them banded tightly together at the center of the party. It had become obvious to them that they were outnumbered. The ratio of gays to straights here was vastly uneven. They were immensely uncomfortable,

faggots!

and their repulsion,

ass-eaters!

their shock at being lumped into this arena of gays, was consuming and frightening.

Within the dark-blue hued, bass-thumping rooms, these people crowded up next to them, bodies against bodies, flesh against flesh, them with their tight clothes and their feminine voices, kissing each other and holding each other from behind, checking *them* out with their dog tags and military haircuts. These gays stood grouped like women, chatting like girls, existing confidently within their own world. It struck the soldiers hard that they were in the minority.

"Fuck this shit!" Thom spat venomously, and began shoving his way through the crowd. He pushed past anyone in his path, knocking over drinks. When one partygoer protested, Thom raised an angry fist and threatened to beat him. *"Pussy!"* he yelled.

People nervously backed away as they all filed past. David Youngblood, nervous and watchful, hoped no one here recognized him. "Let's just go," he said, but Thom wasn't listening. He was headed straight for Blake, and to a melee that sent this evening spiraling out of control.

*****

"Why didn't you tell me?" Blake yelled at Ellie, the hostess.

"What's there to tell?" she snapped back.

Blake was furious with Ellie, and her tone indicated that she did not appreciate his interrogation. While they had been seeing each other intermittently since Memorial Day weekend, nothing serious had developed of this summer romance. Her body language was defiant and independent, and reminded him how little power his words, his body, his sex, had over her.

"What do you want me to say? He's my brother and these are his friends. Get over it."

While they had driven here to Henlopen Acres together, Blake had ventured ahead of the others while they located a spot to park blocks away. He, like them, immediately noticed the type of crowd, in his opinion as loathsome as maggots in summer heat. He had no idea what Thom and the rest of them would think once they arrived, but he was certain it would not be good.

"Look," Ellie yelled through the music, "why don't you just leave? This is my brother's party, and I don't need any shit tonight."

Blake fixed his gaze upon her, hating the type of woman she was. Too outspoken. He had an urge to strike her, to shut her up. But then there was Thom standing at his side yelling at him.

"What the fuck, man!"

"Whoa, dude, back up! I didn't know!" Blake said, raising his hands.

Thom looked at Ellie, silently condemning her.

"Why don't you two just grow the fuck up!" she said loudly, the condescension in her tone giving the impression she was talking to little boys. Eyes turned to them, then to David, Ken, Pat and Edgar, who joined them.

Thom reddened, his hatred of these people growing by the second. He tipped her beer into her face and over her breasts. "Why don't you grow the fuck up, bitch?"

When she slapped him, Thom raised his hand to her, to teach her that she was just a woman.

"Yo!" yelled Ellie's brother Bill. Just as tall as Thom, he shoved the soldier away from his sister. He was good-looking with the same thick brown hair.

"Who the fuck are you, bitch?" Thom shoved back. A circle formed around the three.

"I'm her fucking brother, dickweed," Bill yelled, surprising Thom, who had expected him to back down.

Blake grabbed at Thom's arm. "Thom, man, let's just go!"

Thom snatched away, furious. He turned to Bill, assessing him. *"Faggot!"*

Bill rocketed toward Thom, and they tore into each other, falling against a wall and to the floor in a violent ball of flailing arms. Furniture was toppled and sent crashing in the darkness. The crowd around them screamed. Ken, Edgar, Pat, and Blake tried to pull them apart. Other members of the party joined the brawl, attacking the soldiers. Clothes were torn, more furniture overturned, glass shattered. In the confusion, Thom landed a solid fist to Bill's stomach, and he tripped backward, his head meeting with the hard edge of a table. Guests cleared a path as Ellie ran to her brother and helped sit him up. A familiar face pushed past Thom to help and he saw it was one of the two guys who were holding hands at the beach a month ago; the guys they'd gotten into a brawl with. Another guy helping Ellie was his partner.

"Shit!" Blake hissed. He turned away. "We gotta get out of

here."

He tugged at Thom as Ellie pulled Bill to his feet. His forehead was bruised, and his teeth were smeared with blood.

Thom screamed on his way out, "Don't ask, don't tell *that*, bitch! Don't ask, don't tell *that*!"

Ellie hugged her brother when they were gone. "I'm so sorry, Billy. I'm so, so sorry."

A hush descended on the party as everyone helped to clean up and straighten the furniture. Someone said they'd called the police. On the beach, David, Blake, Edgar, Ken, Thom, and Pat headed home angry and riled. On the beach, a drunken Jarvis Watson was not too far ahead.

DARKNESS FALLS

They were beside themselves as they stomped through the darkness in anger. The beach was nearly pitch black where the sand met the water. Here in this area of Henlopen Acres and North Shores, street lamps existed few and far between. The boardwalk did not extend this far, stopping at Grenoble Street a half-mile further. They trudged through the sand, complaining with Thom egging them on. Blake was ahead of the pack, wanting to get as far away as possible from the party. Thom followed close behind, ranting about how this was a fucking nightmare, how if he saw one more faggot in his life it would be one too many.

"How did you *not* know?" Thom shouted at Blake.

"I didn't know!" Blake yelled over his shoulder, feeling humiliated.

"Well, you should've known!" Thom yelled. He turned to David and the rest of the group. "I knew the minute I walked in!" Then he said, catching up to Blake, "You aren't gay, are ya, soldier? Did you like any of that?"

Blake spun. "Fuck you! You know I didn't!"

Thom turned around and yelled, "Any of you soldiers a faggot, speak up *now*!"

They all shook their heads, even David.

"It made me sick to see them kissing," Edgar said.

Pat joined in, "They looked like they wanted to fuck us!"

"I'm just making sure!" Thom said, facing Blake. "I wouldn't want to be surprised again."

"You know what, Thom, lay the fuck off!"

"I'm not going to be surprised in the middle of the night am I, Blake? Or in the shower?" Thom persisted. "You're not going to want a piece of this ass?"

"Where's the fucking *car*?" Blake screamed. "I just want to go home!"

"I think it's still a few blocks away," Ken said.

"It's that way, princess," Thom pointed, but then froze. With a frown on his face he pounded over to someone hunched in the sand, who in this darkness was closer than any of them had realized. He was black, his arms belted around his stomach, and Thom knew immediately that he was gay. It was some vibe they gave off that he could always detect.

Jarvis looked up to Thom, his face slack with inebriation.

Thom offered a malevolent grin, and went over to him. "You need some help?" he flirted.

"Yes, please," Jarvis managed. His stomach turned unmercifully. His eyes were heavy, his thoughts foggy, and his legs were like rubber.

"Where ya coming from?" Thom asked. Evil tinged his tone.

Jarvis lifted his head with great effort. "I...I was at a party."

Thom ran his tongue across his bottom lip. He thumbed. "Back at the house?"

Jarvis nodded slowly. His eyes pleaded for help, embarrassed at his predicament.

Thom said, "So you're a faggot?"

There was a hint of seduction and cruelty in his voice. A cloud passed over Jarvis's face. Cold fright, colder than the night air, caged him, and suddenly he was afraid to move, to breathe. It bit into him that it was after midnight, that he was alone, drunk, and sick on a darkened beach, the elements of this equation reducing him in his helplessness. "Please..."

Thom stared a moment, his eyes like twin furnaces. He closed in on Jarvis's face. "Answer my question, boy. You a faggot?"

Jarvis said nothing, too terrified to speak, using every ounce of will to stay centered. Thom rapped him twice on the back of his head with his knuckles.

"Answer me!"

Jarvis still did not speak, and Thom grasped the collar of his shirt, yanking Jarvis up to face him. Thom was panting heavily, his mind racing, filling his heart with hate, as his own fears turned themselves over in his mind. He tossed Jarvis forward, at the limits of his patience. Bitter tears came to his eyes, and he spat, "I know what you want!" He was pointing now, shaking. "I know what you all want, fucking perverts!" He clenched his fists and looked up to the black sky. Unable to contain himself, he ran to Jarvis and kicked him over onto his back so that he could see the fear and powerlessness in his eyes.

"You see this!" Thom screamed, grabbing at his erection. "This, you and me are going to know each other *real* well tonight! In and out, bitch! In and out!" He turned and demanded, "Isn't that right, soldiers?"

Jarvis's eyes widened, his mind reeling. He pedaled backward as fast as he could, but these men came upon him with nothing but evil in their eyes.

THE RAPE OF JARVIS WATSON

They fell on him like hungry wolves, and there was no escape. All six men pounced on Jarvis, beat him, slapped him, kicked him, spat on him, choked him, and worst of all, they raped him repeatedly.

At first there had been some confusion as to what Thom intended for Jarvis. Pat, David, Blake, Edgar and Ken, all stood frozen as Thom pointed to the shrubbery. "Move him!"

"What the hell are you going to do?" Blake asked, his eyes shifting to Jarvis.

"I'm going to give him exactly what he wants!" Thom retorted. "I'm sick of this shit!"

"Sick of what?" Blake protested. "You don't even know him!"

Thom got in his face. "He was at the party, asshole! The one with the fucking faggots, remember?"

Blake started to back away, his fear of Thom more apparent than ever. He turned to leave. "I'm not getting into this shit. I'm going home."

"Oh, what, you going pussy on me, Blake? You a fucking fag now, soldier? You walk away and I swear to God I'll break your fucking jaw!"

Blake froze, his eyes full of fear. Thom saw Blake's surrender and reveled in it, then spun on his heels and marched back to Jarvis. Removing his belt, he wrapped it once tightly around his hand. Jarvis, who had been attempting to edge away quietly to the main road, knew that of this confrontation he would not come out the victor. *What had possessed him to leave the party as drunk as he was? What made him believe he could make it home in this condition?* He scrambled frantically to his feet, nausea cascading over him, his inebriation dulling his reflexes. Before him was the grueling, sandy corridor that was the beach. To his left was the rolling, beating ocean. Above him the cover of black sky. To his right was shrubbery, and the road to the boardwalk seemed miles away. Jarvis's head swam as he stood suddenly and he thought he would vomit. Tripping sloppily over his feet, he made a dash for safety, but his effort was short-lived. Thom whipped Jarvis's back with his belt, sending him hurling face first into the ground.

Jarvis hit the sand, blood spurting violently from his nose. Sharp grains of sand scratched his eyes, and he had no idea what hit him from behind when someone slammed a fist into the back of his head. Enveloped into an immediate unconsciousness, Jarvis fell over limp and nearly lifeless. Later, he swam up into a hellish reality, and it was then that the ordeal truly started.

It was then that the cigarette burning began.

*****

Thom moved Jarvis himself, dragging him to the dense cover of nearby shrubbery. The soldier straddled him, pinning Jarvis's arms down against his side, yanking Jarvis by his collar. "Wake up!" he shouted. "Wake up!" When Jarvis did not respond, Thom raised him up by his collar and slapped him hard. "Wake up, you fucking coward, wake up!" He slapped him again and again.

When the others rushed over, Thom turned on them, his eyes crazed. "Give me a cigarette!" he ordered.

"What?" Blake asked, frowning.

"Give me a fucking cigarette!" Thom screamed, and Blake produced a half used box. Thom stuck one in his mouth, removed the matches from the plastic surrounding the case and struck a match. He dragged on the cigarette until its tip lit up an autumn orange, hot and glowing. He looked down on Jarvis, his contempt empowering him now.

Thom lifted Jarvis's shirt, and in a bold, angry move, crushed the tip of the cigarette into his chest, into one of his nipples. Jarvis immediately convulsed, his eyes flying open, his back arched in anguish. He screamed in desperation. Thom slapped his hand over Jarvis's mouth, pressing his head into the sand.

"Jesus, Thom!" Blake yelled, feeling sick to his stomach.

"Get down here and help me!" Thom screamed. And when Blake did not move he yelled, "I SAID GET DOWN HERE AND HELP

ME!"

Blake dropped to his knees, his heart pounding in his ears, he at a loss. Jarvis struggled to get free. Thom wrapped his hands around his throat, choking him, "How do you like that, you little faggot? How do you like that?"

Jarvis thrashed around, struggled with whatever energy he had left, screaming as loud as his lungs would allow. Someone yelled "Cover his mouth!" Edgar dropped to his knees frantically, and Jarvis bit into the meat of his palm and would not let go. Edgar screamed out high-pitched, knocking Thom over, snatching at Jarvis's face to pry his hand loose. He fell back, his hand bloodied and flesh loose. Freed, Jarvis scrambled and threw sand everywhere. He clawed his way up a little and tried to run, Ken and Pat taking after him, seizing Jarvis from behind. They fell to the sand once again, and all five soldiers pounced on him and held down a fighting, kicking Jarvis under Thom's instruction. He screamed, "Calm this faggot down, NOW!"

They clawed at him as beasts, snatching off his jeans. Thom ripped off his underwear. Pat frantically removed his shirt and covered Jarvis's mouth. Edgar, now infuriated, took one of Jarvis's wrists and pinned it beneath his knee. Blake did likewise. Jarvis felt his hands deaden, he panicking as his legs were raised and bent back so that his knees were splayed apart. In a frenzy, Thom yanked down his own jeans so that they rested at his ankles, and he smiled and placed his face next to Jarvis's, which was caked with sand, streaked with blood, dripping with saliva. Thom saw housed a fear in Jarvis's eyes, a helplessness that sparked in him an urgent sexual arousal.

"I'm gonna crack you open like a safe!"

Then it started, the taking of Jarvis Watson. One after the other, all six men at their most violent and angry, held him down, jeered him, beat him with their fists, and raped him. When the last was finished, the first began again.

*****

The pain was unbearable.

But for Jarvis it was beyond unbearable. It was like being aboard a plane that had exploded midair and being conscious every minute as he plunged to his death, knowing something awful was happening and that he was powerless to stop it. He watched it all, as if in a dream, outside of himself,

(Is this how it's going to end? Is this how I'm going to die?)

as they wrestled him to the ground and furiously tore off his clothes and called him names *(Enjoying yourself, Black Boy?)*. As they demeaned him *(Moan, you fucking faggot, moan!)*, and gleefully burned him with cigarettes. And he felt that it was happening to him, but that it wasn't. It seemed unreal, surreal, and all he wanted

(God, make them stop! Please, make them stop! It hurts, it hurts!)

was to scream. Scream for God Almighty to come down and just make them stop. But nothing like that happened as they pushed his knees so far back that they touched his face, as they pressed all their weight against him, as they covered his mouth and nose, making it almost impossible to breathe. There was no relief as they viciously bit him, choked him, and laughed at his pain. There was no relief as they hatefully stomped him and tightened a belt around his neck and placed a knife to his throat and warned him not to yell. No relief as they urinated and spat on him.

(Oh God, please make it stop!)

There was no relief, because just before Jarvis's body began to shut down and succumb to the ultimate darkness that awaited—his ordeal masked from the world by a roaring ocean—he began to feel every transgression, every nick, every cut, every punch, every wound. He felt beyond low, more than dirty, like the lowest form of anything that had ever been created.

(Oh, God, just kill me! Please kill me! I can't take anymore!)

Then blackness swept over him, silent and engulfing.

"Shh," his father once said, abandoning him, handing him to his mother, who handed him to her mother, Ethel Watson. A finger over his lips, his father said, "Shh."

He heard no more, felt no more. The last thing he remembered was the faraway moon peeking from behind a thin veil of clouds, candid and remote. That there was no one there to help. And that the pain was unbearable.

HELL TO PAY

Warren Cassie was finally finished with his double life in Rehoboth Beach, and yet he was almost paralyzed with fear, afraid of what awaited him on the outside of this city. For years he had glided along, never daring to stretch the boundaries of his existence. Yet, here he was, all of his capabilities to be tested at once. He did not know if he stood qualified to carry off this feat. To escape Rehoboth, to reach his sister and her son, and to keep them safe. He cursed his fear, was afraid that without The Voice he would crash and burn. What would happen, then, if he managed their freedom? Would he be able to sustain a reinvented life? He came to realize what he feared more than failure was success and the responsibility of maintaining it.

There was a black car outside of The Voice's building waiting for him, and when Warren got in, there was hot food in a bag on the passenger's seat. Warren closed his eyes, grasped the steering wheel, and forced back tears. He could not describe how grateful he was for everything The Voice had done for him, how eager he was to depart this town, this nightmare, how sorry he was to leave the only man who ever believed in him, whom he considered a sort of father. Instead of driving away, Warren exited the car, descending down into the darkness of the beach. For one brief moment he needed to simply breathe a sigh of relief. The ocean wind toyed with his hair. The sound of the rolling waves calmed him. The night in its cloaked stillness served as a confessional. He prayed to his mother, to Jesus Christ and the Holy Father for good fortune and protection. Then he froze as he heard in the distance a shrill scream, the voice oddly familiar. He attempted to place its location in this shrouded night, but for a long while only the roaring ocean was to be heard. Then it came again, like a banshee.

"HELP ME…HELP ME…HELP ME, PLEASE!"

And then it was silenced.

Warren turned and raced to it, but by the time he arrived Jarvis Watson was only moments away from death. All six of his attackers would be waiting.

*****

Dallas Hemingway was also on the beach and had heard the screams.

He had been unable to sleep or concentrate since his fight with Jarrett. There was no doubt his son was angry. Jarrett had not returned any of his calls, had not responded to any of his messages. None of his son's friends had seen a trace of him all day. Dallas snuck onto the beach after-hours to clear his head. It was the only place he could ever go to think. Standing on a dune, he prayed that when he finally saw Jarrett again his son would forgive him. That they could somehow move forward without Jarrett discovering his secret, without him having to sacrifice his love for—

"HELP ME...HELP ME...HELP ME, PLEASE!"

The scream was close. Dallas searched frantically, hearing shouting beneath the recurring roar of the ocean. A storm of angry voices led him to the scene. Six men were gathered around a battered, bleeding Jarvis Watson. His face was swollen and bruised. He was covered with blood and excrement, the sand around him burgundy with it. His back was bruised with welts as he lay nearly lifeless on his stomach, and he was naked, his backside and inner thighs slick and shiny with blood and semen. The palms of his hands faced the sky, his legs were parted wide, and his eyes were open and blank.

Dallas had never been so revolted in his life. *"STOP IT, ALL OF YOU! JUST STOP IT!"*

The soldiers spun to face the senior Hemingway. Thom had a switchblade in his hand. Nearly all the rest looked possessed with murder and destruction.

THE SACRIFICE

"Hey, what do you tell a fag with two black eyes?" Thom asked looking down on Jarvis's lifeless body. "Nothing, you done told him twice already!"

They all burst into loud laughter, some nervous, some crazed.

"You satisfied now, you punk bitch?" Warren heard Thom yell before kicking Jarvis over onto his stomach. Warren had run here wildly, and peering from behind shrubs he saw six men gathered around Jarvis, brutalized worse than he'd ever seen any human being.

"We've got to get out of here!" David warned, fidgety.

"Are we gonna just leave him?" Edgar yelled over the ocean.

Engrossed in Jarvis, Thom did not respond. He studied him as if he were someone he'd known from a long time ago, a memory revisited. He felt empowered by his destruction.

"STOP IT, ALL OF YOU! JUST STOP IT!"

All eyes fell on Dallas Hemingway, enraged and pointing, and totally oblivious that he was outnumbered. Warren was just as stunned as the rest to see him here on the beach at this hour.

"RUN!" David yelled, and they all rushed Dallas, pushing him to the sand, stampeding him as they bolted from the beach. Thom ran over to Dallas. Placing one foot on Dallas's throat, Thom drew the switchblade across the bottom of Dallas's face, from his jaw to his chin, leaving a wide gash and the sting of rushing blood. Dallas cried out in terrible pain. "Next time you'll mind your own fucking business!"

Thom heard over his shoulder, *"Don't you fucking move!"*

The soldier whirled to Warren, who aimed Nick Costello's gun straight at his chest. Warren was fearless, his aim unwavering. *"No jodas conmigo!* You blink and you're fucking dead!"

Thom stared maniacally. He lifted his leg, allowing Dallas to roll away. Hemingway scrambled to his feet and fled to Jarvis, blood running down his chin and his neck. Thom raised his hands and did not take his eyes off Warren. He had to get off of this beach, could not be caught here. And as if in answer to his prayers, Dallas yelled, "Oh, my God, Warren. I think he's still alive. Jarvis is still alive!"

Warren looked over to Dallas, then back to Thom. Thom looked to Dallas, then to Warren.

"We need help!" Dallas called out urgently. "I think we can save him!"

A sly smile snaked across Thom's lips.

"Let him go, Warren! Jarvis isn't going to hang on much longer!"

"*What?*" Warren screamed back, furious. "I'm not letting him go!"

"Let him go or we're going to lose him! HURRY! GET HELP NOW!"

Thom smiled fully. Over Warren's shoulder, he could see the far off approach of headlights.

"Warren, let him go!"

Warren had no other choice. Shooting Thom would only compound his own problems. He should have been gone by now, out of Rehoboth. He lowered his gun. "Get outta here, *pendejo*!"

Thom blew Warren a kiss, and was out of sight in less than a minute. Warren bolted to Dallas, his heart feeling like it would break. Dallas was cradling Jarvis, rocking him, and Warren saw that he was covered with blood and saliva and semen and sand. He smelled of urine and feces, and he shook violently from shock.

"Warren," Dallas urged. "Go get help fast! Go, Warren, go!"

But Warren could not move.

Was this why he was in Rehoboth? To save this man's life?

"Warren!" Dallas screamed. "Go get help, son! Fast!"

Warren climbed numbly to his feet. He looked Dallas in his face, his eyes full of sorrow. Then he ran for help as fast as he could.

Dallas looked down on Jarvis. "You hang in there. Help's on the way."

Jarvis, barely conscious, tried to speak through his own blood, his swollen throat. He could hardly get the words out.

"Hush," Dallas soothed, holding him tightly. "Just hush."

Jarvis tried again, wanted to speak with his last bit of strength. He croaked, "Let me die. Please, let me die. I don't want to live."

THE HUNT FOR WARREN CASSIE

"Warren, you must do me a favor," Dallas begged, standing in front of Beach-County Hospital twenty minutes later. "I can't get Jarrett on his cell, and no one's picking up at Cedar House. Go find Jarrett, see if he's at Cedar House, and tell him he must come right away. And if you can't find him, try to locate Jarvis's friend, Ethan."

Warren had sought out a police officer on the main road, had dragged him to the scene. Within moments, the area was swarmed with officers and EMTs, and he was swept up in getting Jarvis to the hospital, of giving an account of the attack. Keeping his face turned away from anyone that passed, Warren nodded his head that he understood Dallas, and although he did not want to do this, did not wish to become further involved, he did it. Dallas watched him head off toward Cedar House, and in the madness of the night's events, had forgotten that Warren had saved his life, had shoved to the back of his mind that Warren used a gun to stop Thom from possibly killing him. He was only concerned now with finding Jarvis's attackers, catching all of them before they fled town. When Warren was out of sight, he went back inside the hospital.

"Dallas!" Bradley Thomas called. Dallas went to him. "Where is the young man you were talking to just now? One of my men tells me he was reluctant to give his name at the scene."

Dallas blinked. "His name is Warren Cassie. He's staying at Cedar House this summer."

Something passed over Bradley's face. "I need you to look at something, *now*!" An officer behind the police chief handed Dallas three sheets of paper. "Do you recognize any of these men?"

Dallas shook his head to the first faxed photograph. It was Mario Costello. "No."

Dallas shook his head to the second faxed photograph. It was Frank Costello. "No."

Dallas's eyes widened at the third sheet. It was Warren. Above his head was the word WANTED. Beneath it read FOR MURDER. Dallas nodded.

Bradley was handed his cell phone. "It's him, he's here!"

The person on the other end was Adriana Esteban.

*****

Warren knew he should not still be here in this town, and yet here he was, pounding down Rehoboth's darkened side streets, his car left standing at the beach. His heart beating erratically in his ears, his breathing labored, his thoughts fragmented. Which road to take? How to get to Cedar House quickest? How to get out of this town?

He had not intended to still be in the confines of this city, had not ever imagined he would come face to face with so many policemen and *not* be arrested. He cursed himself. He was taking too great a risk staying here. His entire life, everything he had worked and suffered for, could be lost if he were found out. Luna and Buddy were depending on him. If he fucked this up, was caught, he would have only himself to blame, and they would suffer. But the memory of Jarvis lying bloodied and beaten on the sand came back to Warren. Warren knew that Jarvis should be dead. That no man could survive what they'd done to him. And for the briefest of moments, Warren allowed himself to consider the stripping away of one's power to be reduced to such a level that it was no longer worth living, of Luna and how Nick Costello had caused her humiliation in front of her own son.

Warren came upon Cedar House by way of Olive, a smaller street one block over from Maryland. Police cars were everywhere on the main roads, and he skulked beneath the shadows to the rear entrance, finding it locked. Initially he panicked, but then suddenly remembered he still had a house key, one that worked for both the front and back doors. He entered the darkened house quietly. The kitchen light was on, dimly, but lights to the living room and library were off. Warren climbed the stairs, and halfway up he decided it was time to leave. Jarrett was not here and Warren had no idea why he even entertained Dallas's request to find his son. He was about to turn when he heard something above. Shuffling movement.

Warren climbed to the third floor landing, the sound was coming out of Ethan's room. Climbing closer, he heard Stephanie, her distinctive moaning like a knife to his heart. He heard the headboard rhythmically pounding like his own heartbeat. He heard Ethan asking her if she wanted to be fucked harder. Warren shut his eyes when she answered yes, his mind racing with images of them together. Was this to be his final memory before leaving Rehoboth? To hear Stephanie being fucked by another man? He realized he must leave *now*, that Stephanie had made her choice. Their affair was over. She needed a different sort of man, and he must let her go.

He turned from the door and heard on the night air police sirens screaming through the darkness, on their way to Cedar House. He fled to the end of the hall, to a window there, and before he even peeled back the curtain, he saw flashing police lights everywhere, heard screeching cars.

They know! They know!

Before he could even turn and run, he heard the downstairs door burst open and policemen storm Cedar House.

THE NASTY SURPRISE BEHIND THE DOOR

Jarrett and Griffin knew nothing of the night before, not of Jarvis's rape, not of Warren's attempted escape, not of the raid on Cedar House and certainly not that Dallas Hemingway had been urgently trying to locate his son. There was a slight chill in the early evening air when Jarrett and Griffin arrived back in Rehoboth, which seemed less like the encroaching approach of autumn and more like an omen. They had driven from New York, and pulled up to Griffin's place just as the sun began to set. They sat and watched the sky, painted a lilac blue, the clouds colored a dusty rose.

Jarrett turned to Griffin. "Let's get out of here."

Griffin offered Jarrett a wide encouraging smile.

"I'm serious," Jarrett said. "I'll drive anywhere you want to go. Miami, Virginia Beach, you name it. Anywhere but here."

Griffin closed his eyes, unable to recall a time when he felt this close to a lover. Jarrett had slid easily into his life, and their natural compatibility allowed Griffin to see a future with Jarrett. He had opened up to Hemingway in ways he had never done with any lover.

After he and Jarrett had talked and watched the sunset on the boat the night before, they joined Griffin's friends for a wild cocktail party with music and dancing. They docked in Manhattan and were ushered over in a waiting car to Griffin's apartment, the lights, noise and energy of the city surrounding them, intoxicating them. Griffin watched a bewitched Jarrett drink it all in. Jarrett confessed he had never been in a horse-drawn carriage, and Griffin, who had drank a great many cocktails, gleefully suggested they all ride through Central Park. Afterwards, they were joined by more friends at various clubs, among them were celebrities and New York's young elite. The morning found them on a whirlwind tour of Brooklyn, Harlem, the Village, Chelsea, and SoHo, then back to midtown for a late afternoon birthday bash for Griffin.

"You know we can't go anywhere," Griffin said. "I have to head back to New York tomorrow, and you have to return to work to fix things with your dad."

Jarrett sighed his disappointment, he was still very angry with Dallas.

"Hey," Griffin said to Jarrett as he stepped out of the car looking at the house. "Why are the windows all shuttered? Did you do that before we left?"

Jarrett who had been unloading bags, stopped and looked up to the house. Every window was shuttered, the curtains all drawn. "That's strange; no. Did your housekeeper do that?"

Griffin shrugged. "I guess, although I don't see why."

Griffin went to the front door and opened it. Jarrett heard the air catch in his throat. Griffin covered his mouth, went into the house, then came out quickly and slammed the door shut. "…oh, dear God…"

"What's *wrong*?" Jarrett said to Griffin. Griffin jolted with a chill, then lurched forward suddenly. He ran to the bushes and vomited. Jarrett couldn't believe that what lay behind the door was as awful as all that.

It was worse.

DEMONIZED

The keys dangled from the lock, daring Jarrett to enter at his own risk.

Jarrett went to the door, touched the knob. Before he entered, he looked over at Griffin, who was still crouched over the rose garden, retching as if he were attempting to expel something toxic. What Jarrett saw first was blackness, everywhere. Jarrett's hands flew to his mouth, the stench almost unbearable. In black spray paint, on floors, on walls, on tables, on carpeting, on curtains, on stairs, on the ceiling were the words: *UPPITY NIGGER! WHITE FAGGOT BITCH!*

At first it wasn't rage that arrested Jarrett, but wonder. How could anyone think of something so sick? Jarrett wished that by some cartoonish magic he could close and open his eyes and all this would be gone. Anger finally did settle in as he read what was written on every square inch of available space in the house. He began to digest the meaning of the accusations, feel the humiliation he and Griffin would suffer in their home and community. They could never open the doors, the shades, the curtains. The walls would need to be painted, the carpet taken up, the furniture replaced, all of it. This embarrassment would not be confined to just the two of them.

There was black spray-paint everywhere:

DINGE QUEEN! DINGE QUEEN! DINGE QUEEN!

on the sofa, on the lamps, on the paintings, on the carpet, on the chairs,

SNOW QUEEN! SNOW QUEEN!

in the study, in the living room, in the kitchen, in the pantry, in the dining room,

THE DINGE QUEEN SERVES BREAKFAST TO HER SNOW QUEEN IN HERE!

on the cabinets, on the refrigerator, on the dishwasher,

WHERE ARE THE BEAN QUEENS?

on the stove and oven, on the countertops, on doorknobs, on closets,

WHAT NO RICE QUEENS?

down the hall, up the stairs, on the banisters, in the laundry, in the bathrooms,

THE SNOW QUEEN TAKES A DUMP HERE!

on the windows, on the mirrors, and on the bed were two large, reeking piles of shit.

THIS IS WHERE THE SNOW QUEEN SLEEPS WITH HER FAVORITE DINGE QUEEN!

Jarrett descended the staircase as if in a nightmare, apprehensive about touching anything, even the floors. He opened the front door and found Griffin sitting on the stairs, drawn up with his arms wrapped around his legs, he in a sort of shock. Jarrett sat next to him, knowing Griffin must be full of regret about ever coming here.

"I called the police," Griffin said, but it really wasn't to Jarrett, and it really wasn't to himself. Griffin seemed to be in a trance. "How bad is it?"

"It's everywhere," Jarrett said. "All upstairs and down."

They sat in silence until the police came, neither of them knowing what more to say. The two officers who arrived immediately recognized Jarrett as a Hemingway and a close friend of Bradley Thomas. Jarrett was grateful. He could not imagine having to explain this to a stranger.

"What does it all mean?" one officer asked after Jarrett escorted them around the property. For a number of years the law enforcement of this area received sensitivity training regarding diversity within their community, and Jarrett was never happier to know that than now.

"Do you want me to tell them what it means?" Griffin asked from the threshold of the house. His face had hardened, betraying any former character Jarrett had come to know. "It means someone doesn't fucking like me!"

"Griffin," Jarrett said softly, "they're only trying to understand."

Walsh scowled and swept by the three, entering into the living room.

Jarrett said, "A dinge queen is a man who likes black men, exclusively. A snow queen is a man who likes white men, exclusively. Gay men use it disparagingly toward other gay men."

"And a bean queen?" asked one officer.

"Latinos."

"A rice queen?" said the other.

"Asians."

The first officer scratched under his hat trying to take it all in. "And you believe the house was vandalized because the two of you are..."

"...a couple..." Jarrett answered.

"Well, I gotta tell you it's the damnedest thing I've ever seen in my life. You two have any idea who would have done this?"

"No!" Griffin said turning on them. He was shiny with perspiration, his skin flushed as if by fever. "I mean, where do you people fucking *live*?"

"That's not fair," Jarrett said, giving Griffin a look.

"Not *fair*?" Griffin's tone implied Jarrett was out of his mind. "I will tell you what is not fair! *This* is not fair, every *inch* of it! Excuse me for being angry for both of us!"

"What are you talking about, I *am* angry! I'm just trying to be rational here."

"*Rational?* What the fuck is that when I'm looking at shit on my walls, on EVERYTHING?" He slapped a vase, sending it crashing to the floor. "There is nothing rational about this!"

"Sir, calm down," the officer said. "This is a crime scene, we need to preserve it."

"*You need to preserve the crime scene*," Griffin repeated disbelievingly, then he turned to Jarrett. "How funny is that, huh?" He faced the officers and yelled, "NEWS FLASH, FELLAS, THE CRIME SCENE ISN'T GOING ANYWHERE!

"You want to hear another funny one? This isn't even my house! I don't even *live* in this fucking town!" He laughed hysterically. "You gotta see this place, Harlan said! You'll absolutely love it. A good, wholesome, American town!" Griffin spread his arms and whispered almost inaudibly, "What the fuck happened?"

Outside, the officers placed a radio call to Bradley Thomas; this was bigger than both of them, they agreed. Inside, Griffin stood in a corner with his hands over his face. It appeared he was doing everything in his power to keep it together. "People hate, Griffin, and people suffer. That's just the way the world turns. We will get beyond this. We cannot get stuck here. I won't allow it," Jarrett said.

Griffin said nothing, and Jarrett felt that in some way he blamed him. That Griffin would always think of this incident every time he looked at him. Jarrett fled outside into the evening air. A moment later, he heard someone calling his name. It was Bradley Thomas.

The look on his face caused Jarrett's heart to sink. "What's wrong?"

"Your father has been looking all over for you!"

Jarrett shrugged. "I went away."

Bradley took him firmly by the arms, his fingers digging hard into his flesh. "You don't know what's happened then. Something terrible."

Bradley could hardly find the words.

THE DARKEST HOUR

The walk to the critical care unit became one of the longest, darkest moments in Jarrett's life. It called to mind the day he visited the morgue to see his mother, a day in his life when the entire world seemed pushed away. For Jarrett, it was an organic moment: Maker, creation, the thin line between life and death. Jarvis was alive, but barely. His face was unrecognizable and swollen. It was also nicked, cut, scratched, purpled. His eyes, closed, were bulging. His lips were puffy and split. His nose remained strangely untouched, as if the intention were to blind him, to make him mute. His head was bandaged; his arms and hands were bruised.

"Dear Jesus, God…"

Jarrett grasped the railing of the bed, lowered his head to it. He could only imagine the rest of Jarvis's body, what lay beneath these sheets, horrors beyond comprehension. *How could anyone do this to another person? How could anyone survive this?* His own words came back to him. *People hate and people suffer. That's just the way the world turns.* He hated himself for saying them. They sounded so flippant now, so callous.

Jarrett wanted to hug Jarvis, to give him some of his strength, but

Jarvis looked so frail that Jarrett dared not touch him. Instead, he shut his eyes and prayed to God. *Don't let him hang on like this,* Jarrett begged. *God, please, don't let him hang on like this.*

*****

"He was raped," Dallas whispered to Jarrett in the hall outside of the critical care unit. He had taken a seat next to his son. Jarrett didn't respond or look up. "Six men beat him and raped him. I think they were going to leave him for dead. I was on the beach, walking, thinking about you. It was very late and I saw them. We scuffled, and they cut my face."

Jarrett suddenly looked at his father. His right jaw was stitched. "Jesus!"

"Warren was on the beach, too. He saved me, but they got away." Dallas paused, trying to find the right words. "After we got here, I asked Warren to go search for you, and…"

Jarrett winced. "What is it?"

"Warren killed a man in Miami. He's been hiding here in Rehoboth, at Cedar House."

Jarrett slumped back in his chair.

Dallas licked his lips, struggled with what he really meant to say. "I'm sorry. I feel like this summer was a mess. That I made a mess with you, and I'm so very, very sorry. This is not at all what your mother would have wanted. This would never have happened if she were alive."

Dallas wiped his face, and they sat in silence awhile. There was a call over the intercom, the opening and closing of elevator doors, shuffling at the nurses' station. The green and white linoleum pattern on the floor, meant to be soothing, irritated Jarrett just as much as the fluorescent lighting.

Jarrett said angrily, "Dad, where's Drescher? I need to see him now."

*****

"I'm sorry," Drescher said when he saw Jarrett enter the waiting area.

"You should leave," Hemingway ordered. He found it easier to operate like this, colored black, no longer transferring between agreeable and angry. His face reflected that, and Drescher took a step back, afraid of what he might do.

"You're mad."

"Leave."

"Just listen to me," Drescher spoke carefully. "Just let me explain. When we arrived at the party, I went to get us some drinks and say hello to a few friends—that's all. After that we were going home. I had to use the bathroom, so I went upstairs. By the time I got back downstairs there had been a fight. I looked for Jarvis and I couldn't find him. I searched that whole house *twice* and I couldn't find him anywhere!"

Jarrett slapped him across the face, his outburst like a sudden, rapid discharge. He pushed Drescher into a wall, grabbing at his collar. "Have you seen the way he fucking *looks*, the condition he's in? I send him out with you for one night and he gets *gang raped*?" Jarrett tossed Drescher aside dismissively.

"You can't blame me for this!"

"Don't go anywhere *near* Jarvis Watson ever again!"

"Will you just *listen* to me?" Drescher yelled. "This is not my fault!"

Dallas entered the room. "What the hell is going on with you two?"

Jarrett did not look at him, or even over his shoulder, did not notice the group of nurses or the security guard gathered in the hallway. "I don't want him in this hospital! Get him out! He doesn't deserve to be here!"

Dallas looked at Drescher, then his son. "Jarrett, he's not responsible for this."

"The fuck he isn't!"

The head nurse warned, "Sir, if you don't calm down, I'm going to ask that you leave."

Jarrett turned to Dallas. "How are you *not* angry at this? How are you so calm?"

"Sir!"

"Because we need to be calm and rational," Dallas said.

"What is rational about *this*?" His words came to him again. *People hate and people suffer. That's just the way the world works.*

"Sir!"

"SHUT UP!" Jarrett screamed over his shoulder. It came on him then, Griffin, Jarvis, the day. *This is not fair! Every inch of it is not fair! Excuse me for being angry for both of us!* Jarrett shut his eyes, shook his head and bit at his lips. *I understand now, Griffin. I understand, completely.*

DAVID'S DIRTY LITTLE SECRET

"Hello?" she called out, and then stopped, her eyes opened wide.

Spray-paint was everywhere, the inside of the house nearly charcoal. Words on top of words formed a dark, cavernous heart, and the accusations she did not understand made themselves understood by the rage of the script. The smell was indescribable.

"Ma'am?"

She looked over to see an officer, short with buzzed hair and baby faced. She did not answer him, only stared. She crossed her hands over her chest. She was terrified; afraid this evil would jump off the walls and attack her.

"Ma'am, your name please?"

She composed herself. "I am Anna, the housekeeper."

Short and attractive, her hair was tied in a ponytail, her skin fair. Bradley Thomas who had been standing in the center of the living room, approached her. "Ma'am, I'm Bradley Thomas, the police captain here in Rehoboth. We've been expecting you. If you would kindly step this way."

But then she saw Griffin behind him, and the sight of him seething petrified her. He confronted her, grasping her arm and dragged her to the center of the living room.

"Slow down there, friend," Bradley warned. "Ma'am, do you know anything about what's happened here? Any of this?"

She was stunned by the look on Griffin's face and did not answer.

"Ma'am, when were you here last?"

She lowered her eyes then, slowly, afraid Griffin would strike her when he heard what she had to say. "Yesterday morning," she muttered. Her chest quivered, as did her lips.

"Was Mr. Walsh still here in town?"

Anna turned from Griffin slightly and shook her head for Bradley. "He was gone on his trip with Mr. Hemingway."

"Was anyone else here in this house with you?"

Her erosion came sharply and she faced Griffin, wringing her hands, the blood drained from her face. "I'm sorry," she mouthed. She turned to Bradley. "There was a guy I met last week at the market."

"Was he here with you?" Bradley asked.

She licked her lips. Nodded.

"Were you intimate with him here?"

She shut her eyes, her brave face deteriorated. She nodded again. "In the guest bedroom."

"Was he good-looking?"

"Yes," Anna said. Bradley snapped twice. His young officer took notes. "He was tall…brown hair and eyes…football player type of guy. I thought he liked me."

"How many times have you seen him?"

"Four, five times."

"How many times had he been in this house?"

"Only yesterday."

"Have you seen him today?"

"No."

"He give you a name?"

"Robert."

"Last name?"

Anna was silent. She began sniffling, and Bradley went to her.

"He probably left a window unlocked," the young officer said.

Anna shook her head, "…alarm system…"

Bradley said to himself, "Probably saw the passcode, walked right in off the street." He said to Anna, "I want you to go with this officer here. He's going to ask you some more questions about this Robert fella. It'll be okay."

Anna stepped outside with the officer. Bradley went to Griffin.

"Can you stand it?"

Bradley sighed. "You got *me* on your side, whatever it's worth."

"What I mean is: how many Roberts are in Rehoboth Beach?" Griffin asked.

"Well, your perp is lot more crafty than that, Mr. Walsh. I suggest you put on your thinking cap, because he certainly has."

Griffin faced Bradley. "What do you mean?"

The police chief huddled close to the publisher, and in a very low voice said, "I have a son who is gay." He pointed to the room. "I know what all this means. Your perp is gay, too, I assure you. And if he is desperate enough to sleep with a woman to get revenge like this for whatever may have happened between you two, he is not only crafty but also dangerous. He will go far to prove a point. I suggest you not only check the house for anything missing, but you wrack your brain real good. Whose path have you crossed recently since you've been here in Rehoboth?"

Griffin concentrated hard, coming up with nothing. He went to the stairs, to search the house, and stiffened midway, remembering the party, the scuffle, the hatred in David Youngblood's face. *That's right, nigger! Fight for your white piece of ass! Fight for it!*

Griffin spun around, horrified. *No, it couldn't be!*

"I know who did this…" he said to Bradley, to Anna and the young officer standing in the doorway. He looked over the graffiti, surprised to see a small swastika among the evil words that destroyed this house. "I know who did this…"

PARTING SHOTS

As soon as Stephanie laid eyes on Adriana Esteban she knew she was a lesbian, and somehow this annoyed her, because with Ethan in her life she had become secretly sensitive to the issue of homosexuality. Ethan had done nothing wrong and had been very attentive and supportive since the police burst into his room the night before in their search for Warren. Yet, there was a voice lurking within her subconscious, seeding doubt about a happy ending for her and Ethan. This raised in her a level of suspicion about nearly everyone, and for a good deal of the day she walked about Cedar House holding Ethan's hand, believing her proximity to him would somehow change things.

She was under a form of house arrest. After being dragged half naked out of Ethan's room for an inquisition by police officers, she was instructed by Bradley Thomas not to leave town, that the detective handling this matter in Miami was on her way to Rehoboth. At daylight, Stephanie had been picked up by police and taken to the station for further questioning, then photographed but not fingerprinted. She was released back to Cedar House, where she remained under surveillance by a plainclothes female officer.

Stephanie had not phoned her parents about this, did not wish to explain her involvement. The truth of the matter was already too stunning to digest. They would surely believe it within her to have picked up a fugitive murderer, to have brought him to Rehoboth Beach, to have entered into a sexual relationship after knowing this felon less than an hour. Again her pointless, aimless life was an embarrassment. Once again, *she* was an embarrassment.

Then there was the matter with Jarvis. While she did not know him well, Ethan did and was devastated by the brutal attack on him. Stephanie begged him to go to the hospital, but he declined. He wished to remain with Stephanie at Cedar House for support. Regardless, he had also been questioned by police. Did Jarvis have relatives they could contact? Did he have any run-ins while in Rehoboth? There had been talk at the station that Jarvis's attack could be linked to a disturbance at a party earlier in the evening and to another attack by the beach a month back.

"Are you hungry?" Ethan asked Stephanie, as she peered out of the library window.

Stephanie did not answer at first, her eyes on the transition occurring in Rehoboth. It was Sunday at dusk. The mostly gay weekenders were returning home, and the weekday vacationers who were mostly families flooded the town. Her mind was on Warren and every mistake and wrong turn she'd ever made. Was Ethan to be one of them? She felt there was an answer, some common denominator that bound all this together. If only she had time to think, to concentrate, on why there was no stability in her life.

"No," she answered. It was unconvincing.

"You need to eat," Ethan said coming up behind her. He held her by her shoulders, kissed her neck. "You haven't eaten all day."

"Do you love me?" she asked without preamble. How many times had she asked him that question? How many times was she suspicious of his answer? She turned to him, wanting to tell him what was really in her heart.

He wrapped his arms about her tightly and squeezed. "Yes. Now I'm going to get something for us to eat," Ethan said. He knew what she was about to say and wanted to thwart her rejection by doing something as simple as going to fetch food. She would feel better after a hot meal. They would be back on track afterward. "Let me borrow your keys, my car's blocked in."

She held his eyes for a moment, not believing this opportunity was going to pass her by. "Sure," she said, and her gaze fell. She went to her purse and handed him her keys without looking at him. He took them silently.

He said, "Chinese or Indian?"

She found it hard to speak. She answered quietly, "Chinese is fine by me."

There was a lull. He whispered, "I'll be back."

She looked at him then, as if he wouldn't.

On his way out, he greeted Bradley Thomas and Detective Esteban.

"Where are you going?" Bradley asked. He had just left Griffin's house to pick up Esteban at the police station.

"Food. She's hungry, I'm hungry, and there's nothing here."

"You could order in," Bradley suggested.

Ethan grimaced. "Am *I* under house arrest?"

Bradley looked at Adriana Esteban, then back to Ethan. "No."

"I didn't think so," Ethan said. "Excuse me."

Stephanie was waiting for them in the library. Esteban held out her hand, but Stephanie was not quick to take it. "What can I do for you, detective?"

Adriana turned to Bradley. He said, "There's more privacy in the back."

"Would you like to sit down?" the detective asked Stephanie once in the kitchen.

"No," Stephanie responded curtly. She paced the room with her arms folded.

"You seem agitated," Esteban noted.

"I've just found out the person I've been living with is a murderer."

Esteban sighed. "Ms. Newcomer, I understand your distress, but this investigation is much bigger than you could ever imagine and anything you can do to help us along will be greatly appreciated. A number of people have been hurt and have lost their lives already from all of this. I was just hoping you could tell me a little bit about Leo Suarez. How you two met, had he mentioned a guy by the name of Nick Costello."

"No, never."

"Where and how did you meet?"

"A diner in Miami. He fixed my car. It was leaking oil."

"And you offered him a ride out of town?"

Stephanie was quiet a moment. "Among other things."

"Your relationship was primarily sexual?"

"If you must know."

Esteban tried to be delicate. "You're now seeing the young man that just left."

Stephanie crossed the room. "What does he have to with—?" She stopped abruptly, looking down on one of the countertops, at an envelope stuck behind the toaster. It had her name on it.

"What's that?" Esteban asked, as Stephanie tore it open.

Stephanie didn't answer, recognized the writing. She unfolded the letter, five pages, and read. She flipped to the last page where Warren's name was at the end. She flipped back a couple of pages, read more.

"What is it? Is that from Suarez?" Bradley asked.

Stephanie looked up, wide-eyed. "Oh, my God," she said as if in a dream. "Ethan...*Ethan!*" Dropping the letter, Stephanie pushed past the two and ran toward the front of Cedar House.

She heard the explosion as soon as her hand touched the doorknob.

*****

He knew something was wrong when the key snapped off in the ignition.

There was a brief silence, foreboding, and then the car exploded, deafening Ethan, and riddling his body with shards of glass. For a moment he was raised up out of his seat, his head slamming mercilessly against the roof. Blinded and streaked with blood, he clawed wildly at his face and throat. He fell into the seat beside him, frantically pulling glass from his neck, coughing blood, hardly aware the car was on fire, that clouds of black and gray smoke began to pour in. He spat and gagged, struggling with his last bit of consciousness to sit up, to locate an escape. He peeled at the ceiling, hoping to activate the convertible roof, but to no avail. He reached through the smoke, attempting to locate the door handle, and when he did, it was searing hot. He tried to climb through the windshield, but it was filled with unbearable heat and smoke.

Then horror settled in. He was on fire. He could smell his own skin burning, melting, could feel the fabric of his shirt and pants burn away from his flesh. *"Help me!"* he screamed with his last bit of strength, but no sound came out. His throat bled, and with the overpowering smoke and rising temperature, he was driven into unconsciousness.

The car exploded fully then, becoming a ball of yellow-orange flames. It rose completely off the ground, and then slammed back down. Just before Ethan Safra died he thought he heard Stephanie Newcomer screaming. He thought he heard the screams of tourists and racing police sirens. He thought he heard his own screams loudest of all.

<u>EPILOGUE</u>
exit wounds

Sow a thought and you reap an act;
Sow an act and you reap a habit;
Sow a habit and you reap a character;
Sow a character and you reap a destiny.

Ralph Waldo Emerson

THE FATE OF DAVID YOUNGBLOOD

First there was the questioning, then the photographing and fingerprinting. There was a full line-up of all of them together, then the interrogations. Dallas Hemingway identified them. Ellie and Bill from the house party identified them. The two lovers from the beach identified them. Cathy Mason identified them. It was not until later, with the swapping of stories back and forth, that Jarrett, Griffin, and Drescher, each gave a similar description of one of The Rehoboth Six, as the press had labeled them. A likeness corroborated by Griffin's housekeeper, Anna. It was David Youngblood.

David was not allowed to speak to anyone, was jailed separately from the soldiers, and was handcuffed at all times. He was permitted one phone call, one that he dreaded placing, and when the phone rang at Inn View Opticals he asked not for his parents but for his grandmother.

"*Bubby*," he whispered, shaking. He couldn't bring himself to explain why he was in police custody. Instead, he began to cry. "I'm in trouble. I...I did something really bad. Please, come get me."

The phone was snatched away by Bradley Thomas.

"Ma'am? Are you Mr. Youngblood's mother?" *No. I'm his grandmother.* "Well, then you or this boy's parents need to come here to Rehoboth Beach right away." *What's happened?* "Ma'am, the charges against Mr. Youngblood are very serious."

David zoned out as he heard the words "bail," "flight risk," "judge," "hearing." Bradley pulled the phone from his ear. "Hey, quiet!" he roared, pushing David back in his seat. Red-faced, David just cried and cried and cried.

*****

They had fled from the scene of Jarvis's rape, David remembered, had gotten as far as his jeep. It seemed they would escape town in the darkness, but there was a blockade at Silver Lake. Police were all over the city searching for them, and they were asked to step from the vehicle with guns trained on them. They were told to lay face down on the ground, with their fingers knotted behind their heads.

You my boo?

Now here he was again in his circle of hell, all his mistakes, his miserable days, crowded here within his cell. No one would ever understand that he only wanted to be loved. It would only get further complicated from here. His sexuality would come into question, his relationship with African Americans. The image everyone had of him, the perception he had of himself, would only grow worse. He would never be loved.

David balled himself into the corner of his consciousness, tight in the corner of his cell, and faced the reality that there would be a trial, jail time, other prisoners, confinement, and more pain. Things would be worse than ever. He decided that when he got the chance, he would hang himself and end this hideous nightmare he called his life.

THE BROTHERS, GRIM

Frank and Mario Costello were seated together in a jail cell down the hall from David Youngblood. To see the victory on Detective Esteban's face burned them. Outside of this cell, they would have seen her as a stupid dyke who didn't know her fucking ass from a hole in the wall. Yet she had outsmarted them, had bested them. She had requested a blockade all around Rehoboth Beach to trap them, and Bradley Thomas, who already had every cop on the force out patrolling for what would be known as The Rehoboth Six, cast an even wider net to capture these two. If they had not stopped to wire the bomb and did what they came to town to do, they might have escaped town. But the police were suddenly everywhere and they had to cut out early. It turns out the brothers had not cut out early enough. Still, if only Esteban had gotten to Rehoboth Beach sooner, perhaps she could have saved Ethan Safra and spared his parents the most difficult news that their son, their only child, was dead at the hands of the Costellos. That he had died painfully, and that there was no way authorities could have known this danger existed for him.

Esteban recalled racing back to the garage after losing the brothers on the highway, of having to wait until morning to go to a warehouse to find a record of payments made during the same period of time reflected on the sheet the brothers had confiscated from the Baker's Garage job ledger. It was her only lead, the only thing she believed that would help bring this case to an end. She searched desperately through endless boxes of receipts, and many hours later found one for a week in late April with names that stuck out. One had New York plates with the number to a bed and breakfast. She made calls all across Miami, Cedar Manor's among them, and by late afternoon, she found her lead in one Stephanie Newcomer who had gone to another of the Cedar properties in Rehoboth Beach, Delaware. When Esteban had called Cedar House, no one answered.

"Costello brothers still not talking?" Bradley asked her in his office.

"They're waiting for their attorney," Esteban answered. "Can you beat that? Criminals who actually want to sit quietly and wait for counsel?"

"No better than the guilty ones who cry after you put them in a cell."

"I would have been here much sooner," Esteban said, "but Baker has no sense of record keeping. Just piles and piles of receipts in unmarked boxes."

"At least you faxed me the photographs. We had that to work from."

"And thank God I was able to fly into Dover. How lucky was that?"

"*Still,*" said Bradley.

"Still," said Esteban.

They were thinking of Ethan and of the car bomb the Costello brothers had rigged.

"Thank you for putting up roadblocks around the city. It seems you had enough going on without me, the Costello brothers and Leo Suarez."

"What's going to happen when you get back to Miami?"

The detective thought for a moment. "Lots of heat, I'd say. I flew solo on this."

"There was no one to trust. Even that, I understand."

"We'll see…"

"Well, I can't quite guarantee you anything, but if things don't work out there, I guess we can find something for you to do up here. Nice town in the summer."

Adriana Esteban smiled a little. She was tired. "*Gracias, Senor Thomas.*"

"*De nada,*" Bradley Thomas answered, beaming. "My son taught me that."

SPREADING THE BLAME

Drescher Thomas was depressed, and there was nothing Bradley could do about it. Talking was useless, and quiet time did no good. Even a long supportive, fatherly hug seemed inadequate. Jarvis Watson would probably die any moment now. Drescher did not leave the house or take calls or even eat. The shame he felt at Jarvis's attack was only propounded by the blame Jarrett heaped upon him in good measure all around town. He blamed him for the whole incident, and would blame him much more harshly if Jarvis died. As a result, Drescher pushed on alone and busied himself with his photography, printing his pictures of Jarvis, posting them on his wall. He pored over them for hours, studying Jarvis's smile, his intelligent eyes. Drescher Thomas bowed his head and for a long while prayed for him, although he truly believed that prayer would do none of them any good at this point.

*****

Griffin had no idea how long he had been sitting with Jarvis, only that during his visit he dozed off and had awakened to find himself covered with a blanket. He was stiff, and stretched before a window that looked out over Rehoboth Beach. It had rained, and now the sky was clearing just before dusk. He looked over his shoulder to Jarvis and felt an unspeakable sorrow sweep over him. After all it was he who said to Jarvis, *Please tell me you're not hanging out in this house because you're afraid of something. Don't do that. You keep living. Don't let anyone ever stop you from doing that. It's foolish. And pointless.*

Even if Jarvis survived, he'd suffer for the rest of his life. None of his family was here or cared. His grandmother who'd raised him was dead, and the cousins left behind when he went off to university and law school were not close enough to him to feel a trip was warranted. Even Ethan was dead, and the only people to stand beside him now were the ones he had come to know while in Rehoboth Beach. Only these few cared about this poor soul. Griffin looked down on Jarvis, wanting to cry after having cried so much already. *I should have paid more attention to you*, Griffin thought. *You needed a friend and I kept going. I could have lent you a hand, my brother, but I didn't.* "I'm sorry," he said. "I let you down."

Griffin sat and held Jarvis's hand and whispered in his ear. "Jarvis, if you want to leave, to go where there is no more pain, then you go. But if you want to live, then you keep living. Don't let anyone ever stop you from doing that. It's foolish and it's pointless. And if you make it out of this crisis, you have a friend in me. You will definitely have a brother for life."

EL TORMENTO DE AMOR

Warren Cassie suffered panic attacks nowadays, and they came at him repeatedly, gripping him with the belief that he would wake up and find himself in the same cell as the Costello brothers. That everything that had happened over the past seventy-two hours had not really happened at all, and had turned out differently. He stood, unable to get enough sleep, jolting awake every few minutes, leaving his body to demand rest his brain would not allow. He went to a window, large and rectangular, and drew back the curtain, and there was the sun bright and full. Vancouver was below, mountainous, wide and picturesque. Spread out before him was Granville Island, False Creek, Gastown, English Bay Beach, and the snowcapped mountains that watched as custodians of this city.

The Voice had asked him this question, *Do you trust me?* And he had said, *yes.*

He had jumped out the window from the rear of Cedar House, landing in the back hedges scratched and disoriented. The police were all around, the property doused in red and white flashing lights. He ran as hard and as fast as he could, hiding in shadows and under cars. He called The Voice in a panic, whispering frantically, "Help me, please!"

He told The Voice what had happened, where he was, and suddenly The Voice was there like a father, taking him back to the apartment. Warren had to be smuggled out just before dawn, The Voice making arrangements to get him to an abandoned airfield in the neighboring town of Millsboro. The Voice asked him one question.

"Do you trust me?"

"Yes."

"Then let me help you this one last time."

He was brought to Vancouver, and so was Luna and her son Buddy. They all agreed this was safer than Mexico. Flown in by friends of The Voice who had private planes in New York and California, no questions had been asked. Yet, while they were safe in one of The Voice's properties, Warren still found it difficult to relax. So much had happened with Stephanie, Jarvis, and Dallas. There was still so much to think about, starting with yesterday, the day before, this summer, and the rest of his life.

Luna and Buddy slept soundly in one of the bedrooms. He had opted to stay in the living room in case there was trouble and they were forced to flee again, even though he knew that was unlikely to happen. The Voice, whose full name was Vic Lafferty, had shown his unwavering loyalty. Warren went to the sofa, lay down and pulled a blanket over himself. He looked around the apartment, a wide, clean space with soft white hues, a television, a stereo, beautiful furniture, lots of rooms, lots of food.

Warren thought of Stephanie, and apologized to her in his heart. How he loved her and wished she were here with him. How he wished he could have explained to her so many things, including his love. *Uno dia*, Warren promised himself. One day he'd turn himself in and end this whole ordeal. One day he'd contact her and set things right. Today, however, he would try to rest. He would deal with yesterday tomorrow. He would deal with tomorrow another day. Today would be for him. He closed his eyes and dreamed, if a little, of the Atlantic, and of Stephanie Newcomer, and of their little sea-world called Rehoboth Beach.

*****

Stephanie returned to New York, embarrassed. Her mother came to retrieve her in a hired car. Her father, after hearing all that had happened, including Ethan's death, would have nothing to do with her. She barricaded herself in her old room, too ashamed to face even the housekeeper, the driver, and God knew who else was privy to the gossip of her situation.

She would never forget the fiery wreck that was her car, or Ethan's charred corpse, or his distraught parents. She had nearly been able to do it, to face Ethan and tell him it would not work. That she could not live their lie. She was nearly about to look in the mirror and face the truth that was herself, and it was not that she was a waste, or spoiled, or an idiot, or had problems choosing men. It was that she constantly avoided mess and difficulty, running from plane to plane, town to town, man to man, trading one bad situation for another, newer one, replacing people in her life like characters on a television show, a different view, a different dynamic, hoping all would be changed, forgotten, anew. She had no real measure of herself, and was rigidly afraid to discover her true worth.

It was raining heavily, and New York was grumpy and impersonal when it was gray and cold like this. Stephanie used the bathroom and returned to her perch, staring out over Central Park. She thought of Warren and started to cry, her feelings conflicted. He had been so beautiful, had touched her as no man had, had spoken to her in their secret sea-world, but he had lied and murdered. He was not who he said he was. But he had seen through her and loved her, and she loved him.

What then was she thinking giving herself up to a gay man? Was she that desperate for affection? Had her life left her that much at a loss? How she wished she could turn back the hands of time! How she wished she could just zoom into the future and out of this painful period!

She looked down at the applicator she was holding. It read positive.

She was pregnant.

CLIMBING THE STAIRWAY TO HEAVEN

September was upon them and it was brisk. Gray autumn skies would transition into winter, and soon sweaters, jackets and coats would be needed. For now, in this period called Indian Summer—cool but not cold, warm but not hot—it reminded Jarrett Hemingway of his favorite time of day, of twilight. Griffin was right, he would have paid to be on the ocean right now, reflecting, where it was just him and God, where the sky and the sea seemed infinite. Today, the beach would have to do.

Where had the summer gone? At first endless, then suddenly over. Death was in the chilled air, and the leaves would turn before long, as birds formed V-shaped excursions to the south. One by one, each of the boardwalk businesses would shut down for the season, boarded up for Nor'easters and winter storms. The city would thin out dramatically, a ghost town compared to the summer.

Cedar House had also been closed up, the great house standing darkened once again. Already Jarrett had packed away his mother, had closed her up, and it seemed as if he'd never really unpacked her at all, never got to talk to her, or about her, these past few months. Things seemed back to the way they were before he'd arrived, except they weren't. There was water under the bridge now, things said, damage done, change, nothing would be the same ever again, not with this town, these people, not him, not Dallas, not Cedar House, not for anyone who had stayed there this summer.

What was to be their future? Where did they suppose themselves headed?

Jarrett wished he could go back to a time when he was ignorant and blind to certain ways of the world, safe. Knowing too much had turned him into something else, and he wasn't sure he liked this newer him, although he felt he could not stop *being* this other him, darker. Time marched on minute-by-minute, day-by-day, and his biological clock told him that he too must march on. *Deny evolution at your own risk!* Still, he longed to grasp those golden days of yesterday's summers, with he and Drescher as children running wildly around the lawn, with Bradley Thomas at the barbeque pit *(Kiss the cook!)*, with neighbors passing through, and lemonade and baseball games and picnics on the beach, a marathon of endless sunny days, of crickets and fireflies in the night, of fireworks over the ocean, of songs from the radio that returned a flood of happy memories.

Then there was his mother, so beautiful with her comforting smile, her laugh full and reassuring. *God, would this pain in his heart for her never end?* Jarrett thought of Jarvis, of Stephanie, of Ethan and Warren. In this brief time that he had known them, had he really known them at all? He himself sat changed since the summer's beginning, and they sat changed as well. He knew them less than he had before, and yet, he felt strangely and forever bonded with them.

Jarrett had been marking the sand with a stick, lost in his thoughts, and when he looked up he saw the magnificent sky and all its beauty, the sun like some symbolic point of inspiration. He had spent so much time deep in thought, he realized he had missed the beauty of his own hometown.

"Son…?"

It was Dallas, and Jarrett could not help but to wonder where *they* were headed, what the future held in store for *them*. He sighed heavily.

"It's Jarvis," Dallas said from behind him. He touched his shoulder, and Jarrett closed his eyes, bracing for the worst. *No more bad news, please!* "Jarvis opened his eyes. He's regained consciousness."

Jarrett dropped his stick and covered his face. The tears came ruthlessly.

"I love you, son," Dallas said, feeling the need to connect to him as Laura would.

"I love you, too, Dad," he said out of habit, but he thought again of this summer, of Jarvis, of Laura, of Stephanie and Warren, of Griffin and Ethan. The tears rolled down his cheeks unchecked.

"Let's go visit Jarvis, son. I'm sure he'll want to see us."

Jarrett nodded, and Dallas turned and walked away toward the boardwalk. He did not wait for his son at all. *Same old Dallas,* Jarrett thought with a sour chuckle. He pulled deeply on his inner strength and stood. He eyeballed the world around him, skeptical, loving it and hating it simultaneously. He looked up to his mother in heaven. *Never leave me, mom. I love you and I need you. Until next summer. Until...again.*

Jarrett turned and joined his father up ahead. Behind him, the ocean drummed as loud as pulsating blood, eroding the sand, rushing the beach as if it had a point to prove. And like many things, it receded, was gone, and was replaced anew.

AUTHOR'S NOTE

This is how it began, *Summerville*.

It was 1999 and I had been living for many years in a large Philadelphia penthouse apartment in Olde City, Philadelphia (and yes, I'm spelling old with an e, because that neighborhood sat adjacent to and was part of the most historic sections of Philadelphia). This included Independence Hall (where the Declaration of Independence and the United States Constitution were drafted and signed), Society Hill (where I grew up and named so because it was initially inhabited by the 18th century Free Society of Traders), Elfreth's Alley (considered the oldest residential street in the United States), and Penn's Landing (where William Penn—founder of Pennsylvania—docked in 1682 on his trip from England, after first having docked in Delaware, the first state).

I had a roommate named Mark who had a friend who needed a place to live. Her name was Alimah Walker (but we all called her Lee), and she had a friend named Carol Fezuk who lived in Lewes,

Delaware. Carol asked me for a favor, to watch her sick dog while she traveled to Las Vegas for an awards ceremony. She and her business partner Frank Reynolds were publishers of an LGBT newspaper in Rehoboth, the *Rehoboth Beach Gayzette*, and the paper had been nominated for an award. To return the favor, Carol asked if I would write for the publication. I'm not sure who recommended that I pen a serialized drama, but over dinner and drinks the idea was born. I immediately titled the piece *Summerville*, and a continuing episode would be featured in each issue from Memorial Day to Labor Day for the beach crowd. I had never written a serialized story before, but I brokered to have certain elements included in its structure.

First I needed to create a bible for my tale, which pretty much is as it sounds, a background for the setting. This is considered essential for every serialized drama or "soap" (or *novela*, for you Spanish speakers). This includes characters, the setting, the main theme (or themes) of the overall tale, and the set-up of conflict. I wanted to write something I'd never read before, that would be the greatest challenge for me but also the best story for the reader. The main family had to be named Hemingway, an obvious nod to my literary forefather Ernest Hemingway, author of the classic *The Old Man and the Sea*. That book set the theme for *Summerville*. In it, aged Cuban fisherman Santiago has not caught a fish in more than eighty days and eventually becomes obsessed with catching a large marlin very far out in the Gulf Stream. This contest—man versus man, and man versus himself—sets the stage for a dynamic battle of wills. Juxtaposed against the seasons (spring giving life, winter taking it away), I thought such a contest could take place during summer, often symbolized as the height of life (and what better way to add a fine point than to have it play out at a beach resort during high season).

To act out these conflicts, I needed a very interesting cast of characters, from nearly every walk of life. I absolutely despise homogenized storytelling where everything and everyone is the same, be it race, gender, class, sexuality, or age. To me, the best storytelling has diversity, and in this story I pulled characters from various demographics, unleashed them in a beautiful setting, and let them have at each other in the heat of summer. This included my tent pole characters father and son Dallas and Jarrett Hemingway, who are both gay but have little in common besides the woman that binds them together, Laura (an obvious nod to the 1944 film noir of the same name starring Dana Andrews and Gene Tierney). This gave *Summerville* somewhat of a ghostly feel in spots, underscored the history between Dallas and Jarrett, and shed light at times on the disconnect between older and younger gays. Another character, though not human, is the Hemingway bed and breakfast Cedar House (set up as my version of Manderley from Daphne Du

Maurier's novel *Rebecca*, and is "the main house" for the action of the story).

Other characters were added to lend scope and depth, and to add contrast to Rehoboth Beach and life in a seaside community. Jarvis Watson, a gay and meek African-American law student from an "impoverished background" was created to deliberately draw empathy. Ethan Safra, a closeted Lebanese-American medical student, was created to show the underbelly of beauty (which is not always so beautiful). Police chief Bradley Thomas and his gay son Drescher were created as contrast to the Hemingways and to show a bit of a class difference. Griffin Walsh and David Youngblood were opposite sides of the same coin, and lent themselves to a point I wished to raise about race relations in the LGBT community (which are not always difficult, but certainly not always easy). The lesbian detective Adriana Esteban, the mafia-light Costello brothers, and underworld king Ramon served to paint the world as I see it, a mesh of diverse personalities forced to navigate around and rely on each other.

Perhaps the most striking characters became fan favorites immediately during *Summerville's* initial run. Stephanie Newcomer, a rich, vivacious, and beautiful redhead, was considered a heroine of sorts as the story played out and as she tried to determine where her life was headed despite her fortune. The Voice, whose real name and connection to some primary characters is revealed in the last pages of the book, was my hard voice of reason. He was dubbed The Voice after a song of the same name that I fell in love with at the age of thirteen. You can find it on the album *Long Distance Voyager* (wink, wink) by The Moody Blues. And then there is Warren Cassie, who was at first my throwaway villain. He did not become my anti-hero until I realized that he and Stephanie were actually a super-couple (as is termed in soap operas) and that many female readers saw him as a misunderstood bad boy. It was only then that I gave him a back-story, introduced The Voice as his surrogate father (to contrast with the other father/son relationships in the story), and brought in the Costellos as my chief baddies.

Military servicemen (for whom I have a great deal of respect) unfortunately got the short end of the stick in *Summerville*. They were chiefly used here as the conduit to a point I wished to make about the ugly side of the fraternity of men, bullying and coercion. They were created after I had read a story concerning an alarming number of sex abuse and rape scandals at military cadet academies and on military posts (that included male on female and male on male incidents, in addition to an estimated percentage of incidents that went unreported). Along with Jarvis Watson, my group of delinquent soldiers became my socially conscious storyline (male rape, for which an extensive amount of research was done), and it supplied Jarvis, who did not have much to do throughout the season, with both a weighty storyline and a shocking cliffhanger that sneaks up on the audience.

However, there was another obstacle to overcome before I started writing. I had never been to Rehoboth, nor had I ever heard of the town. This is where Lee, Carol, and Frank became my true saviors. They ensured that I got to Rehoboth nearly on a bi-weekly basis to experience and speak with the kind people of this city. That included lots of driving, many dinners and brunches, endless walking, and plenty of research on the town's history. There were often excursions to neighboring towns Cape May, Lewes, Dewey Beach, Bethany Beach, and Slaughter Beach, and by the end of my first summer in Rehoboth, I felt like an honorary citizen.

The success of *Summerville* was swift, and I was unprepared for it. Readers from Rehoboth Beach and other parts of Delaware, Philadelphia, New York, New Jersey, and Washington, DC became instant diehard fans who would interrogate me on the street about what was to happen next. Some questioned the motives of certain storylines, such as the one with Jarvis Watson. Many asked what was my inspiration for the story, and who was my favorite character. A buddy of mine later suggested that I novelize the serial, and although I had been given free reign with the storyline in the *Gayzette*, I would now have the space to deeply explore my character's lives and dysfunctions.

Summerville ran for four seasons and as you can see by the final pages of the novel, there will definitely be a sequel. There are a great many secrets buried between the lines throughout the book and many twists and turns to explore in the follow-up titled *Return to Summerville*. I hope you've enjoyed the story so far. I look forward to seeing you soon. Until again, my friends…

H.

ACKNOWLEDGEMENTS

I am forever indebted to Frank Reynolds, Carol Fezuk and Alimah Walker for their contributions and support during the original run of *Summerville*. Without them, this book would not be a reality. Many thanks to the city of Rehoboth Beach, Delaware, that opened up its arms to welcome me. I tip my hat to my editors extraordinaire Carol Taylor and Molly Callister, who always ensure that I tell a good story. Particular gratitude is extended to Tara Jones, Robert Dodge, and Greg Phillips for their artistic talent on this project. To my supporters everywhere, thank you very much. You keep me going strong! To my better half Geovanny Mendez, thank you for enduring with grace all the quiet days and nights when I am hard at work.

ABOUT THE AUTHOR

H.L. Sudler was born and educated in Philadelphia, Pennsylvania. He has served as a contributing writer for such publications and anthologies as *Lambda Book Report*, *A&U Magazine*, *Nuance Magazine*, *Spirited: Affirming the Soul and Black Gay and Lesbian Identity*, *Mighty Real: An Anthology of African American Same Gender Loving Writing*, and *Off the Rocks: An Anthology of GLBT Writing*. He is the author of a volume of essays titled *PATRIARCH: My Extraordinary Journey from Man to Gentleman*. His short story *The Way of All Flesh* was selected for the PATHS Humanitarian Writing Award. He presently lives in Washington, D.C.